Murphy wanted her.

And it was separate from sex. This was something much bigger. He wanted *her*. In his life, as the mother of his kids, as his helpmate and partner, in good times and bad. He wanted to see Jordan every morning when he woke up, and he wanted to go to sleep beside her every night.

But there was this roadblock between them, and nothing was going to change until they got past that. And maybe things wouldn't change even then. But he had to take a shot at it....

Dear Reader,

It's summer, the perfect time to sit in the shade (or the air conditioning!) and read the latest from Silhouette Intimate Moments. Start off with Marie Ferrarella's newest CHILDFINDERS, INC. title, *A Forever Kind of Hero*. You'll find yourself turning pages at a furious rate, hoping Garrett Wichita and Megan Andreini will not only find the child they're searching for, but will also figure out how right they are for each other.

We've got more miniseries in store for you this month, too. Doreen Roberts offers the last of her RODEO MEN in *The Maverick's Bride*, a fitting conclusion to a wonderful trilogy. And don't miss the next of THE SISTERS WASKOWITZ, in Kathleen Creighton's fabulous *One Summer's Knight*. Don't forget, there's still one sister to go. Judith Duncan makes a welcome return with *Murphy's Child*, a FAMILIES ARE FOREVER title that will capture your emotions and your heart. Lindsay Longford, one of the most unique voices in romance today, is back with *No Surrender*, an EXPECTANTLY YOURS title. And finally, there's Maggie Price's *Most Wanted*, a MEN IN BLUE title that once again allows her to demonstrate her understanding of romance and relationships.

Six marvelous books to brighten your summer—don't miss a single one. And then come back next month, when six more of the most exciting romance novels around will be waiting for you—only in Silhouette Intimate Moments.

Enjoy!

Yours,

Leslie J. Wainger
Leslie J. Wainger
Executive Senior Editor

Please address questions and book requests to:
Silhouette Reader Service
U.S.: 3010 Walden Ave., P.O. Box 1325, Buffalo, NY 14269
Canadian: P.O. Box 609, Fort Erie, Ont. L2A 5X3

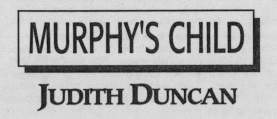

MURPHY'S CHILD

JUDITH DUNCAN

Published by Silhouette Books

America's Publisher of Contemporary Romance

SILHOUETTE BOOKS

ISBN 0-373-07946-X

MURPHY'S CHILD

Copyright © 1999 by Judith Mulholland

This edition published by arrangement with Harlequin Books S.A.

® and TM are trademarks of Harlequin Books S.A., used under license. Trademarks indicated with ® are registered in the United States Patent and Trademark Office, the Canadian Trade Marks Office and in other countries.

Visit us at www.romance.net

Printed in U.S.A.

Books by Judith Duncan

JUDITH DUNCAN

is married and lives, along with two of her five children and her husband, in Calgary, Alberta, Canada. A staunch supporter of anyone wishing to become a published writer, she has lectured at several workshops for Alberta's Department of Culture and participated in conventions in both British Columbia and Oregon. After having served a term as 2nd Vice President for the Canadian Authors' Association, she is currently working with the Alberta Romance Writers' Association, which she helped to found.

Chapter 1

Friday, March 29

A March chinook arch bisected the vast Alberta sky, leaving the bright blue westerly half cloudless and clear, a perfect backdrop for the gray, jagged, snowcapped peaks of the Rocky Mountains. Overhead and to the east, where the blue arc met the furls of cumulus formations, tinges of sunrise cast the underbellies of the fat white clouds in purples and pinks. And beyond that, the upper stratosphere trailed long, thin orange wisps that were slowly dissipated by the warm currents blowing in from the Pacific. It was as if the two mismatched sections had been welded together, creating an artificial dome overhead.

The early-morning air was crisp and crystal clear, the shrill screams of Skil saws splintering the stillness, the *kerthunk, kerthunk* of compression guns adding percussion to the discordant sounds of construction. But there was another, sweeter sound. And it was the sound of spring.

Meltwater gathered in the icy ruts of the unpaved road, the pressure wearing thin channels in the packed snow. Along the gutter the rivulets of spring runoff cut a course to the storm sewer, where they splashed and gurgled on to oblivion, the sound punctuated by the drip, drip, drip of melting icicles.

Straddling the gable of the attached garage, Murphy Munroe straightened, relishing all the signals of winter's end. Yep, no doubt about it, the sound of spring was definitely the sweetest sound of all.

Resting his hand on his hip, Murphy acknowledged the smell of sunshine, damp earth and melting snow, a sense of well-being filling his chest as he surveyed the scene. This new housing development was on the southern outskirts of Calgary, and from his high perch, he could see clear to the foothills and to the mountains peaks beyond. And it was some sight, one that he'd never tired of. There was something about the raw majesty of those mountains, combined with the overwhelming sense of space, that filled him up. This was his place in the bigger scheme of things, and he was rooted here. Just like the big old cottonwoods down by the river.

Rolling his shoulders, Murphy tried to ease a knot of tight muscles as he surveyed the street below. It was one hell of a mess. Mud, piles of dirt-pocked snow, puddles big enough to float a boat and more mud. But he could live with the mud. After the past few months, he'd gladly take the mud. What he did not want to see was another single snowflake or another thermometer that showed minus-thirty-degree weather.

To put it in barroom terms, it had been a royal bitch of

a winter. It was as if the past few months had been engineered to test him. Everything that could possibly go wrong, had, and if he could have had his way, he'd have taken the joker who'd come up with Murphy's Law and stuffed him down a well. He was so damned tired of everything going wrong just when he absolutely needed it to go right. If he didn't know better, he'd swear somebody had put an old Celtic curse on him.

It wasn't as if he was some airheaded adolescent screwup. He was thirty-six years old, for Pete's sake, with a successful construction company and a halfway decent brain in his head. Nor was it as if he was some rotten SOB who deserved a stretch of bad luck. He built good-quality, affordable homes for people, he paid his taxes on time, donated to every charity within a ten-mile radius and he always stopped at crosswalks for dogs, little old ladies and school patrols.

But this year had been enough to test a bloody saint. For every positive thing that had come his way, there had been a string of things that had gone wrong. He was a small operator in the home-construction business, but Calgary had been hit with a housing boom. Everything should have been coming up nothing but roses—he had good, reputable tradespeople contracted, specialized suppliers geared up for business, good interest rates and an even better cash flow.

But here it was, the end of March, and he was four—sneaking up to five—weeks behind schedule. Which was nothing new. In fact, he'd been playing catch-up ever since they'd dug the first basement the previous fall. That was when the weather had gone berserk. First it rained. Then it snowed. Then it rained some more. Then the temperatures plunged to record lows, and from the first lousy raindrop, Murphy's Law had kicked in. It had been one long nightmare. Problems had cropped up like ragweed. Problems with concrete, with bad rafters, with poorly sealed skylights, with the hardwood for the flooring—even problems with the services the land developer had put in. It was one damned thing after another. And to make matters worse, they had suffered through the most bitterly cold winter in recorded history.

But winter was finally on its way out now, and maybe a bit of luck was on its way in. For the past few days, everything had gone like clockwork. And he could thank some on-the-ball, hardworking subcontractors, who happened to be mostly in-laws.

Well, not exactly honest-to-God in-laws. A sister had married into a huge, multigenerational Italian family, and Murphy had discovered that when you got one Rossino as a relative, you got them all. It was such a crazy tangle, he'd given up years ago trying to sort out who was who. Now he saved himself a whole lot of grief and aggravation by accepting it at face value; anyone on the job site who had a name that ended in a vowel was somehow related to Marco, his brother-in-law. Which, through some weird Latin osmosis, also made that person somehow related to the entire Munroe clan.

Given the ethnic makeup of his own family, Murphy figured it almost made sense. Irish father, Swedish mother, a Ukrainian grandmother, Russian and Native American aunts, a Portuguese uncle. So what were a few unrelated Italians? Hell, he had enough trouble keeping track of his two brothers and three sisters.

But all that was beside the point. What counted now was that everything was going as smooth as silk. Touch wood. A chinook had blown in a week ago, raising the temperature by forty degrees in six hours, and maybe, just maybe, it was heralding an early spring. And so far this week, no hiccups. Not even a little one. Suppliers on time. Everybody getting the job done. Now, if things just kept clicking along like they were—and with some extra overtime by his crews—Munroe Construction could conceivably be back on schedule before the first possession date. Barring another disaster.

Experiencing a familiar burning sensation in his gut at just the thought of something else going wrong, Murphy fished a roll of antacid tablets out of his shirt pocket and popped one in his mouth. Maybe now that everything had leveled off a bit, he'd be able to get rid of the lousy things. He had so many rolls of them scattered around, he probably had enough antacid pills to neutralize the whole bloody world.

Rolling his shoulders again, Murphy let go a sigh and picked up a pair of side cutters, then leaned over and snapped the metal binding around the bundle of cedar shakes. He hadn't had a decent night's sleep in months, and he couldn't remember ever being this tired. And there were at least a dozen other things he needed to be doing right now instead of shingling this garage, but his roofing crews were already working on two other houses. If he was willing to take a chance that the spring winds wouldn't rip off the tar paper, he could leave it until a crew got to it. But he wasn't much into taking chances these days.

He fit the compressed-air staple gun onto the pressure hoses, then yelled down for someone to switch on the compressor.

There was the sound of the compressor starting up, then a loud crash and the tinkling of glass, followed by some very colorful cursing. Murphy let his arms hang by his sides and tipped his head back and looked at the sky. As long as it wasn't that custom-made leaded-glass door for the study, he didn't care.

There was more swearing, only this burst was in Italian and far more vehement than the last, and Murphy dropped his head to his chest and let out a weary sigh. Damn. It wasn't the custom-made French door; it was the custom-made sealed unit for the plant window.

And it wasn't even 8:00 a.m. yet. Which meant it was going to be one of those days.

Kicking the red compressor hose out of his way, he shot a staple into the roof to make sure the gun was working, then turned to pick up some of the shakes. And stopped dead in his tracks.

A spotless silver BMW coupe eased through the slush ruts in the nearly impassable street, pulling up behind his mud-spattered pickup, which was parked across the road. Murphy blinked twice to make sure he wasn't seeing things. But this was no hallucination. It was, in fact, his worst nightmare. And the source of all his sleepless nights. His stomach released a killer dose of acid, and wearily he rubbed his eyes. This was absolutely the last thing he needed.

Knowing that there was one chance in a million that someone else in Calgary had that exact same color model, someone who might conceivably have a reason to show up at his building site, someone who could drive through acres of mud and slop and still have a car that looked as if it had just rolled through a car wash, Murphy continued to watch. There was a chance it wasn't her, but he knew he just didn't have that kind of luck.

Not when it came to Ms. Jordan Kennedy.

Locking his jaws together hard enough to shatter bone, he stared down at the car. Maybe, just maybe, it wasn't her. The driver's door swung open and a pair of very long legs appeared, then an elegant blond woman emerged, swathed in an equally elegant long white cashmere coat. Murphy swore, resisting the urge to rear back and pitch the staple gun into the next development. Damn it all to hell— Jordan Kennedy was somebody he could do without.

And if he'd been a whole lot smarter, *would* have done without. He should have seen right from the beginning that she was going to cause him no end of grief. Tall, elegant, aloof, she was one of those cool, contained blondes that made him think of some fabled Nordic ice queen. Completely untouchable. Unreachable. Unattainable. But that hadn't stopped him. Oh, no. Not him. Right from the moment he'd laid eyes on her, he had wanted her like he wanted his next breath. Which didn't say much for his stupidity quotient.

He should have known better. But he'd gone after her anyway. Which was a double disaster. Especially when she was his accountant.

He had changed accounting firms the previous year, and when he went in for a preliminary interview with the senior partner of the new firm, the partner had strongly recommended Ms. Jordan Kennedy as the perfect person to handle his business account. So he'd set up an appointment with her, and that had been his downfall. Because Ms. Jordan Kennedy had knocked his socks off the instant she'd turned those big gray eyes on him.

Watching her pick her way carefully across the chewed-up street, Murphy had to give himself some credit. Even back then, she hadn't completely short-circuited his brain. Right from the beginning, he'd had enough mental capacity left to realize that this woman had more defenses than Fort Knox. And even then he'd known he was going to have to move an inch at a time with her. No overt moves. No flowers. No romantic dinners. She would have spooked on the spot if he'd shown any kind of male-female interest.

So he'd planned a careful, strategic attack, and like some half-witted, hormone-driven adolescent, he'd gone after her with a single-mindedness that would have done his Viking ancestors proud. It had taken him months, but that previous summer, he'd finally got through her defenses. And the memories of her hot and naked beneath him still woke him up in hard, cold sweats. But toward the middle of December, just when he'd thought she might not bolt if he started talking permanence, when he was thinking about giving her a diamond for Christmas, she'd abruptly slammed all the doors.

Just like that. Bam. He'd been dumped out on his ear. He didn't know why. He wasn't even really sure if he knew how. The only explanation she'd given him was that it was a mistake—and that she thought it would be a good idea if he moved his account elsewhere.

That memory still had the power to rankle him. He'd never felt as impotent, as broadsided, as bloody furious as he had then. And he still couldn't think about it without his blood pressure going through the roof. She'd just walked out as if that entire summer and fall had meant nothing at all, and he'd been left standing there like a big dummy who'd just fallen off the turnip truck.

But the one thing he hadn't done was make it easy for her. He hadn't moved his account. Be damned if he was going to accommodate her precious comfort zone.

But that was then. This was now.

His expression hardening even more, Murphy watched her pick her way around a mound of dirt, ice and snow, then tiptoe across the mud-spattered planks that bridged the open service ditch, her off-white coat as meticulous and as immaculate as her car. Resigning himself to a face-to-face confrontation, he wondered where in hell he had parked his common sense. Only a first-class lamebrain would have kept her on as his accountant.

Shifting his gaze, he expelled all his breath and fixed his attention on the old Italian sitting on the doorstep across the street, busy straightening nails on a flat rock. Murphy thought he was Marco's mother's cousin's father-in-law, but he wouldn't want to swear to it. But his name ended in an *o,* and he'd been straightening nails for nearly four years. Which, he supposed wearily, made him somebody's grandfather. It seemed to work that way. He wondered what happened to all those straightened nails. And how much he was paying for them.

Blowing out another heavy breath, Murphy hooked the compression gun on a stack of cedar shakes, then crossed from the garage to the roof of the house. He lowered himself through the gaping hole where one of the replacement skylights was to be installed later that morning, then dropped to the floor below. Shaking his head, he figured he might as well bite the bullet and get this little charade over with. The only reason for Ms. Cold and Heartless Kennedy to be there was that there was some problem with the company's year-end. He had sent his bookkeeper in with the account the previous week, and now he was faced with the consequences. Damn it all to hell anyway. Served him right for trying to pull an end run on her.

Experiencing the familiar rush of bile, Murphy stomped though the newly drywalled master bedroom, his teeth still clenched so hard his jaw ached. This little meeting was going to mean another roll of antacid pills.

His mood grim, Murphy stuffed his work gloves in the pocket of his insulated vest as he strode down the hall, the sound of his steel-toed work boots echoing on the plywood subfloor of the unfinished house. The quicker he got this over with, the happier he'd be.

Absolutely determined not to let her see that she could still push his buttons—or that he hadn't completely recovered from the stunt she'd pulled in December—Murphy clamped his mouth in a hard line, then rounded the corner to the front foyer.

He should have been prepared. He should have known better. He should have realized he couldn't get within five feet of her without all kinds of hell breaking loose.

But there she stood, like something out of a dream, framed in the open doorway. Her white coat swathed her in a kind of royal elegance, the emerald-green, purple and blue multicolored silk scarf draped over one shoulder and fixed with a bold gold pin, adding to her regal look. She had her ash-blond hair pulled back in a perfect French fold, not so much as a single hair out of place, and in her ears, a set of perfectly matched pearl studs. Pearl studs that he had given her for her birthday.

His stomach balled up in his belly as an old reaction kicked in. She was untouchable. She was perfection. And she had broken his heart.

Fixing his face in a flat, unreadable expression, Murphy braced his arm on the raw plaster wall, knowing full well that he was practically hidden in the heavy shadows of the hallway. And damned glad of it. He continued to study her for an instant longer, watching as she pressed her hands tightly together, the pulse in her throat going a mile a minute. Even in the dusky entryway, it was dead apparent that she was so nervous she was inches from climbing right out of her skin.

And so unbelievably beautiful.

Murphy clenched his jaw, a long simmering anger surfacing and percolating through his chest. It had been months, and he still felt as raw as he did when she'd called it off. Knowing he didn't dare go down that road now, not with her standing in the unfinished foyer, he geared up for battle as he hooked his thumb in the front pocket of his jeans. Determined to play this game out to the bitter end, he spoke, his tone flat. "Make a wrong turn, or are you just out slumming?"

She whirled to face him, her coat swinging out, the alarm on her face making her eyes widen. Pressing her hand to her chest, she stared at him, the pulse point in her neck absolutely hectic. A tense silence stretched between them, then Murphy could see her swallow hard and physically collect herself. She moistened her lips, then forced a smile. "I didn't think it would be quite so—thick with mud out here."

His hand still on the wall, he continued to stare at her. And he sure in hell did not return the smile. "I'm sure you didn't."

Her expression wavered and her eyes changed from gray to slate. She held his gaze for a second, then looked down, straightening the tangled threads on the fringed edge of her long scarf. Her long thick lashes concealed her eyes, but Murphy could sense her unease. She continued to fiddle with the fringe, and Murphy felt his blood pressure start to climb. His sisters hadn't worn anything white for years because of grubby little hands, and there was Ms. Jordan Kennedy, standing there in front of him, all wrapped up in off-white perfection. And he'd bet his next house sale that she'd managed to walk across the street without getting a single speck of mud on her pricey shoes. God, he wanted to strangle her.

Clamping down on the flicker of old anger unfurling in him, Murphy clenched and unclenched his jaw, determined to get through this without losing it.

His gaze fixed on her, he spoke, a hard edge to his voice that was decidedly unfriendly. "Let's skip the pleasantries, Jordan. What do you want?"

She looked up, an odd, fleeting expression in her wide gray eyes. She folded her arms and looked down, nudging a little chunk of broken plaster with her toe. Murphy saw her try to swallow, then she met his gaze, her expression somber and uncertain. She hesitated for an instant, making an awkward gesture with her hand. "Is there somewhere we can talk?"

Fixing her with another unwavering stare, Murphy didn't answer, considering his options. If this had something to do with his business, he pretty well had to hear her out. Although he seriously considered showing her the door. But there was something about the anxiety in her eyes, something about the frantic pulse in her neck, that told him this had nothing to do with work at all. Great. Exhaling heavily, he straightened and turned toward the kitchen, knowing, sure as hell, he was going to regret this.

He entered the unfinished room, kicking a long orange extension cord out of the way, then stooped and picked up a piece of counter molding off the floor and tossed it onto the work island. Deliberately keeping his back to her, he went to the window overlooking the backyard. One of his crew was cleaning up the work site and tossing litter into the industrial dumpster, and Murphy caught his eye and signaled him to turn off the compressor. Feeling as if he were wound far too tight, he turned and leaned back against the newly installed cupboards, his face muscles as stiff as boards. Folding his arms across his chest, he fixed his gaze on her and waited. Hell could freeze over before he'd ask a second time what she was doing here.

Her expression tense, she reached out and tested the texture of the molding he'd tossed on the island, then he could almost see her square her shoulders as she lifted her head and looked at him.

She had the most unbelievable eyes. And it had been those eyes that had blasted his common sense to smithereens months before. Gray, steady and intense, with lashes so thick and long, he thought at first they were false. The kind of eyes a man could lose himself in.

Disgusted with how easy she could still sidetrack him, Murphy crossed his ankles, keeping his teeth locked together. No way was he going to ask her, no bloody way.

She stared at him, wide-eyed and motionless, as if she were a deer caught in the headlights of an oncoming car, then she abruptly shifted her gaze, again fingering the molding on the island. A strange feeling began to uncoil in Murphy's gut, and he narrowed his eyes, assessing her. Something was up. Something was definitely up.

Swallowing hard, she crossed her arms and met his gaze again, terrible tension lines etched around her mouth, the pulse in her neck absolutely frantic again. Lifting her chin in a show of sheer grit, she spoke, her voice tight with strain. "I thought I owed you the truth. I'm four months pregnant."

It was as if he got smacked in the back of the head by a two-by-four, and his knees almost buckled. Pregnant? Pregnant? He stared at her, his brain stuck. It was as if someone had dumped a load of concrete into his cranial cavity, and he just could not get his mind around it. She couldn't have said "pregnant."

But the awful, anxious look in her eyes confirmed that that's exactly what she had said.

Feeling as if he was just coming to after a knockout punch, his heart suddenly thundering in his chest, Murphy continued to stare at her. Pregnant? How could that be? He had always, always been exceptionally careful—every single time he had been so damned careful with her. Feeling suddenly light-headed, Murphy did not move a muscle. He didn't dare. *Careful* obviously hadn't cut it, because he didn't doubt for a second that she was telling him the truth, or that the baby was unquestionably his. In spite of what she'd done to him, he had to face one indisputable fact. Ms. Jordan Kennedy had a streak of straitlaced ethics that was a mile wide and six miles deep. She might dodge the truth, and she might be evasive, but Jordan Kennedy would never, never lie. She had far too much stiff-necked pride.

Clearly unnerved by his stunned silence, Jordan went over to the window and stood staring out, and it finally registered that she was trembling. Murphy closed his eyes, the scent of her perfume making every nerve in his body respond. Nothing like kicking a man when he was already down.

Finally getting his reaction under control, he shifted his position slightly so he could watch her. Her arms still folded tightly in front of her, she was absolutely motionless, but he could tell from her taut profile, from the angle of her chin, that she was running on sheer nerves, and no matter what, was determined to finish what she'd started.

Forcing himself to lock down a burst of anger, Murphy watched and waited, his own expression hardening. Four months. Four bloody months, and now she'd finally decided to tell him. For the second time that morning, he wanted to strangle her.

Still staring out the window, she finally spoke. ''Just so you know, I never once considered terminating the pregnancy.'' She paused, tension visible in every line of her body. Then she shot him a quick glance, an odd hint of defiance in her expression, in the lift of her chin. "This was something I'd never anticipated, but I am keeping this baby."

When Murphy made no response, she abruptly looked away. There was a tense silence, then she drew a deep, uneven breath and continued. "I know I've just dropped a bombshell on you," she said, her tone very quiet. "And I know you're going to need time to assimilate all this, but I also want you to know that I'm prepared to accept full responsibility."

The old anger flared, fueling a brand-new anger, and Murphy's tone was cold. "If that's the case, why are you here?"

Shifting her weight, she gave him a quick, nervous glance, then looked back out the window, her whole body stiff with tension. He saw her close her eyes and press her hands together, as if calling on some deep inner strength. Her lips seemed stiff when she finally spoke. "This baby is as much yours as it is mine." Stuffing her hands in her coat pockets, she took another deep breath. "And if you should decide you want to take an active role in its life, I would not oppose that. Our personal fiasco aside, I think you would make an excellent father, and I hope you won't deny your child your participation because of me."

Participation? Murphy felt as if he had his very own compressor start up in his chest. And for one instant, he thought his eyes were going to pop right out of his head. Participation? A few months ago, she'd treated him as if he'd just crawled out of the swamp, and now she decided he would make an excellent father? She was the one that took the hike, not him. Four bloody months, and she finally decided to tell him.

Four months? The mathematical side of his brain finally

kicked into gear, and he abruptly straightened and stared at her. Four months. That meant she very likely suspected she was pregnant when she'd dumped him. Damn her, she'd probably already known.

His anger finally breaking loose, Murphy paced to the end of the room and back, a frenzy of emotions churning through his chest. She'd been sitting on this bit of information for four months.

Forcing himself to stop, to get a grip, he closed his eyes and raked his hand through his hair. He was doing it to himself. He was pushing his own buttons. And as furious as he was with her, his common sense told him that if he didn't put the brakes on, he was apt to blow sky-high.

He closed his eyes again and made himself unclench his fists. He could do this. He definitely could do this.

Straightening his spine, he turned to face her. She, too, had turned and was watching him, her skin so pale it looked translucent, her wide, worried eyes almost overwhelming her face. Sunlight through the window formed a bright aura around her, and she looked so fragile standing there. Anger surged in him again, and he glared at her. "Since the numbers add up, I take it you knew you were pregnant when you called it quits."

She held his gaze for an instant, then turned and looked back out the window. There was a tense pause before she answered. "I thought I might be, but I wasn't absolutely sure."

Murphy stared at her, his face fixed in a hard expression. She was so damned contained, it made his blood boil. He had to give himself a minute before he dared speak. "So how come now? After four bloody months, what made you decide to come forward now?"

She remained motionless for a space, then finally spoke,

a funny tremor in her voice. "There were some problems in the beginning, and my doctor had concerns about a possible miscarriage in the first trimester." She turned and faced him, her expression unreadable. "I wanted to make sure I was past that hurdle before I told you."

"You didn't think I deserved to know as soon as you found out?"

Her chin came up a notch, and she met his gaze dead-on. "No, I didn't. Not until the doctor felt that the risk had passed."

He wanted to challenge her on that—on her I-know-better-than-you attitude—but just then, one of Marco's relatives stuck his head around the door, his dark curly hair poking out from under his hard hat. He gave Jordan an appreciative look, then winked at Murphy and grinned. "Hey, boss, the shipment of new skylights just arrived. Where do you want us to unload 'em?"

Murphy jammed his hands in his back pockets to keep from wiping the smirk off the kid's face. He wanted to tell him exactly what he could do with the damned skylights, but resisted the urge. Instead, he forced himself to be calm. But it was quite a struggle to keep the annoyance out of his tone. "Put them in the garage at 104, and make sure to close the door when you're done. We don't want a rock through this lot."

Jordan's reaction to the interruption was akin to being rescued from a crate of crocodiles. Suddenly she was Ms. Congeniality. Fixing a phony banker's smile on her face, she made a dismissing little gesture with her hand. "This is obviously a bad time for you. So why don't we leave it for now, and if you want to discuss it further, you can give me a call at the office." And as if she were a door-to-door cosmetic sales rep caught on a very bad call, she kept smiling as she edged toward the door. The kid, suddenly trying to look like Valentino, straightened up and pushed out his chest.

Riled at her for acting as if she'd just told him her dog was about to have puppies, and even more riled with Marco's nephew or cousin or whoever he was for his pea-cock display, Murphy felt as if every vein in his body were about to pop.

It took all the self-control he had, but he somehow man-aged to stay right where he was, every muscle in his body stretched to the limit. If she thought that she could drop this on him and then walk away, engineering it into a nice, con-trolled business meeting in her office, she had another think coming.

Playing her game, he gave her a brittle smile back, his gaze riveted on her. His voice taut with ominous warning, he glared at Jordan and set the terms of confrontation. ''I definitely want to discuss this further. But it won't bloody well be in your office.''

Chapter 2

Sunday, August 4

A *stampede of pink bunnies, blue elephants and yellow duckies spilled through the railings of a two-story-high crib, the bodies getting bigger and bigger as they relentlessly flew toward him. Limbs waving, their bodies growing even larger, they started piling in on him, deeper and deeper, their weight suffocating him, burying him alive....*

His own limbs flailing to rid himself of their smothering weight, Murphy came sharply awake, bolting upright in his seat, his heart pounding like a jackhammer. The dream faded, and he realized where he was. He wasn't trapped under some crazy two-story crib. He was seated in the business-class section of a 747, on an evening flight from Toronto to Calgary. And the suffocating weight was nothing more than his jacket and the dinky pillow the flight attendant had given him right after he'd boarded.

His heart still pounding like crazy, Murphy closed his eyes and scrubbed his hand down his face. Just a dream. Just a bloody dream. One that he'd been having regularly the past six weeks—and one that his psychologist sister would have had a ball analyzing. Expelling his breath, Murphy tipped his head back and stared at the call buttons above his head. Lord, but this baby thing was driving him crazy.

In fact, it had been a hell of a few months. One minute, he'd be so damned ticked off with Jordan that he could crush rock with his bare hands; the very next instant, he'd be so pumped up about having a kid that he could hardly find his hand in front of his face. Most of the time, though, he felt as if someone had just run him through a high-voltage regulator.

A kid. A son or daughter. He was still having trouble getting his mind around that. It wasn't that he never wanted kids. It was just that he'd never expected to get one this way. Or with this woman. He'd thought when she walked out that it was game over. And now here they were, about to be parents together. It was enough to twist anybody's brain out of shape.

But there was still part of him that wanted to give her a good shake. And sometimes he wished that he could have doubted his paternity with this kid, but he knew, without a doubt, that the kid was his. Jordan Kennedy was too much of a straight shooter for it not to be.

A flicker of old anger surfaced, and Murphy clamped his jaws together and closed his eyes. It still ticked him off that she'd waited so long to tell him. It was his kid she was carrying, and problems or not, he figured he had a right to know from the very start. But, no, Jordan hadn't seen it that way. It was on her terms. As usual.

Although it still scared the hell out of him, realizing that she could have been in serious trouble and he would never have known. And she could have gone through that kind of loss all by herself. But that aside, even now it made him mad as hell that she didn't trust him enough to tell him as soon as she knew. He had called her on that, but she had stood her ground.

That first meeting had been a doozy, all right. She had openly admitted that she was pretty sure she was pregnant when she pulled the pin, but then she'd clammed up and he hadn't been able to get another word out of her. And to this day, he really didn't know *why* she'd taken a hike. In his calm moments, and when he was feeling judicious toward her, he figured it was because she didn't want him to think he had to marry her. But since he hardly ever felt that judicious, he spent most of his time being ticked off. It had taken him two weeks to wrestle his wounded pride and his male ego to the ground, knowing that if he didn't get a grip on his feelings, he would be the one who'd lose out in the end. Because above all else, he did want to be a big part of this kid's life. He wanted to be a real father, not just someone who showed up at birthdays and every second weekend.

Except it hadn't been that easy. He'd spent a lot of time walking around with acid eating a hole in his gut. But eventually he was able to stuff his personal grudges into cold storage and focus on the baby, and then he could deal with Ms. Kennedy with a kind of guarded neutrality. He had gone with her to every one of her doctor's appointments, and he had attended every single Lamaze class. They'd gone shopping for nursery furniture and baby supplies together. And he had even wallpapered the nursery for her. But every time he left her upscale condominium, he'd wanted to punch somebody's lights out. And then he'd spend two hours in a gym, pumping staggering amounts of iron before he was fit to be around another living soul.

His stomach started churning, and Murphy dragged his hand down his face again. His nerves were shot. And he wasn't sure how he was going to get through the next couple of weeks.

The baby was due in eleven days, and he was on his way home from the big annual trade show in Toronto. And he was so damned tired, he felt as if he were half-dead. He hadn't had a decent night's sleep in months, and it was even worse while he was away. Every time he thought about getting the call that it was time—that she'd gone into labor—he'd go into a cold panic.

Once the baby arrived, he knew he'd be fine. He was the second-oldest of six, he was an uncle several times over and he'd been lugging babies around since he was practically big enough to walk. No, it wasn't the baby that terrified him. It was the actual birth that scared the hell out of him. He just could not visualize the prim, perfect, always-a-lady Ms. Kennedy all hot and sweating and grunting. It was a picture that just refused to compute.

Murphy had actually planned on skipping the National Home Show this year because of Jordan and the baby, but she'd insisted that nothing was going to happen until he got back. And he had to believe her. It was as if she had orchestrated the entire pregnancy on her own terms. She hadn't had morning sickness; she hadn't had swollen feet. She hadn't even had heartburn. All because, he was dead certain, she'd made up her mind she was simply not going to put up with any of it because she didn't have time in her busy schedule for the unpleasant stuff.

The doctor told her she shouldn't gain more than twenty-five pounds. She gained twenty-three. She was so on target that it was downright scary. So if Ms. Kennedy said the baby was not going to be born until the fifteenth of August, he was pretty darned sure he could bet the farm on it. No one would dare defy Ms. Kennedy.

He just wasn't too sure how he was going to make it through the next eleven days. And when the baby finally did arrive, he was really going to have to face the music. Because the only people he'd told were his parents and his big brother, Mitch. He just hadn't been able to face it, trying to make reasonable-sounding explanations to the rest of the family. He didn't dare think about what the clan's reaction was going to be. His insides went berserk every time he even considered it.

It was just after nine in the evening when Murphy picked his truck up at the Park and Ride. The streets were slick from the recent rain, and city lights were reflected in the wet pavement. The overcast sky had broken, and the clouds crowding against the jagged outline of the Rockies were thick with the vivid colors of the setting sun. The clean, damp smell of a recent rain wafted in through his open window, clearing away the last of the jet lag. This was one of his favorite times—a summer evening after a rain. If he were at home, he'd be sitting out on his veranda, enjoying the sunset with a cold beer in his hand.

And as tempting as the idea was, he made a spur-of-the-moment decision and bypassed the off-ramp that would take him to his place. He was going to check on Jordan first.

Resting his elbow in the open window, Murphy grinned to himself. He was very well aware that Jordan hated it when he checked up on her. Maybe that was one reason he'd made a habit of doing it over the past few months— just to get her nose out of joint. The other reason was that he worried himself sick if he didn't. But Jordan didn't know that. And that was okay by him.

Her upscale condo was in a small complex in a trendy part of town, where huge trees formed block-long arches overhead. He found a parking spot right in front, and he killed the engine, turned off the lights, then got out. Fingering through the ring of keys in his hand, he isolated the right one. She had given him a key last summer, when he had fixed her garbage-disposal unit, and he had never given it back. Another twist of amusement surfaced. Something else that got her nose out of joint.

He used the key to unlock the front door, then entered the luxuriously appointed lobby, noticing the fresh-flower arrangement at the front desk. No doubt about it—it was first-class all the way.

The elevator was empty, and Murphy leaned back against the oak paneling, studying the security camera fitted in the corner. He wondered how many people were even aware that it was there. Smiling to himself, he thought back to a couple of times that things could have gotten totally out of hand if it hadn't been for that camera. But that was before. Now when they rode the elevator, they stayed as far apart as possible.

Jordan's apartment was on the fourth floor, and as the elevator door slid open, Murphy thought he heard a baby crying. Giving his head a shake, he stepped into the thickly carpeted vestibule. Lord, this baby thing was driving him stark raving crazy. As if the recurring dream wasn't bad enough, now he was hearing things, as well.

The tastefully decorated vestibule was designed into a large square sitting room, with four apartment doors leading off it. The dark green walls, the winged chairs, the large silk flower arrangements and recessed lighting gave the space a sense of intimacy, as if it were part of the individual units. It definitely added class. But then, Ms. Kennedy was big on class.

He reached Jordan's door and rang the bell—and he heard it again. Only this time, the volume was turned way, way up. The bottom dropped out of his stomach in a sickening rush; this was no figment of his imagination. This was a real live baby.

Alarm shot through him as terrifying images flashed through his mind—visions of Jordan trying to deliver the baby on her own, visions of her unconscious in a pool of blood on the floor. Swearing over his clumsiness with the key and lock, he finally managed to get the door open, his heart trying to clamber right out of his chest.

Fear streaking through him, he charged in and came up short, as if he'd slammed into a glass wall. For a second, he thought he'd broken into the wrong apartment.

Except it was the right decor. And the right furniture. Decorated in subtle shades of cream and taupe—taupe walls, cream suede leather sofas, a lighter taupe-colored carpet— the wrought-iron, green-marble and beveled-glass tables, the mottled ceramic lamps with the ivory silk shades, the lush green plants—that was all Jordan's stuff. Even the subtle watercolors on the walls, the cream-colored lacquered table and chairs in the dining room and the bold Spanish-styled candelabra sitting on the lacquered sideboard—that was right. That stuff belonged. But it was the condition that was all wrong. There was clutter everywhere—in an apartment where there was never so much as a magazine out of place. It looked as if it had been tossed in a drug raid—or vandalized by a gang of thugs.

Another surge of panic shot through him, and he strode through the foyer and into the once elegant living room, his chest so tight he could barely breathe. Maybe it *had* been vandalized. If anything had happened to her...

The crying got louder, and Jordan appeared in the archway, a tiny, howling, dark-haired form clutched protectively against her shoulder.

God, it really was a baby. Struck totally dumb, Murphy stopped dead in his tracks. For one insane instant, he thought again that he was in the wrong apartment. The woman was disheveled and rumpled, her hair a total mess, there wasn't a single trace of perfect grooming—and there was pure panic on her face. On top of all that, it was dead obvious that she'd been crying right along with the baby. Prior to this instant, he would have bet his life that Ms. Kennedy didn't have a single tear in her.

Jordan took one look at him, and pressed a hand over her face and started sobbing. "Oh, Murphy. Thank God you're here." She dropped her hand and held the back of the baby's head, her terror making her overflowing eyes almost black. "There's something terribly wrong with the baby. I was just going to call a cab—we've got to get to the hospital."

Feeling as if he'd just been shoved out of an airplane with no parachute, Murphy stared at her for a split second, unable to take it all in. But one thought surfaced. She'd been wrong. The baby hadn't waited. Realizing he was numb with shock, he made a massive effort and pulled himself together. Knowing, without a single doubt, that he was not going to get a coherent word out of her until the baby quieted, he dredged up a reassuring smile and used his soft-talking tone of voice. "Shh. It's okay, Jordan. It's okay." His heart doing a crazy barrel roll in his chest, he took the incredibly tiny screaming baby from her, his heart doing another wild loop as he held his kid for the very first time.

Feeling as if he'd run through a high-voltage regulator again, he looked down at the howling infant in his arms. This was his kid. His kid!

Wanting to sing and dance—but mostly wanting to grin— and knowing this was definitely *not* the time, he snuggled the baby against his neck. Driven to touch her, he reached out and tucked some of Jordan's wild hair behind her ear. "Hey," he said softly, trying to reassure her. "This sounds more like a Munroe temper tantrum than anything else. I'm sure the baby's fine."

Jordan immediately covered her face with both hands, her shoulders quaking. Her awful distress, her absolute vulnerability, nailed Murphy square in the chest, and a surge of heavy-duty feelings for her made his whole body hurt. More than anything, he wanted to gather her up and comfort her. To hold her and assure her that everything was all right. But that was a line he wouldn't cross.

Holding the back of the howling baby's head, he caught her arm and guided her toward one off-white sofa. Settling himself and the baby, he pulled her down beside him, then drew her to him. As if she didn't have an ounce of fight left in her, she sagged, and he could feel tears soak through his shirt. He couldn't ever remember feeling as topped up with emotion as he did right then.

Closing his eyes, he clenched his jaw and tightened his hold on mother and child, resting his head against hers. It was as though everything he'd ever longed for, everything he wanted, was right there in his arms. As if sensing the circle of completeness, the baby quieted, its tiny face tucked against Murphy's neck.

His throat so tight he couldn't even swallow, Murphy pressed an imperceptible kiss against her hair. He felt as if he'd been totally upended.

Finally able to ease the ache in his throat, he gave her shoulder a little shake. "So," he whispered gruffly, "when are you going to tell me what I've got here?"

Quickly wiping her face with the heel of her hand, Jordan took a deep, shaky breath and sat up. She wiped her face again, then looked at him, even managing a very wobbly smile. "You've got yourself a son. Seven pounds two ounces."

A son. He had himself a son. Another rush of overwhelming feelings surged up in him, and Murphy closed his eyes and tightened his hold on the baby. She had given him a son.

It took several minutes before he could get rid of the big wedge of emotion that was stuck in his throat. And it took another ten minutes to get the whole story. That Baby Munroe had been born seventy-three hours ago. About her waking up with labor pains in the middle of the night. About her trip to the hospital in a cab, and her quick labor and even quicker delivery. And that she and the baby had been discharged the day before. And from the quaver in her voice, he suspected that Little Stuff had been giving her grief ever since.

As if collecting herself, Jordan moved to the other end of the sofa and drew her legs up, clasping her arms around them, strain and fatigue etched into her face. She had on a light blue shirt and wrinkled gray slacks, and there was baby spit-up on one shoulder. She looked like hell. And she looked positively battered. She looked marvelous.

Fishing a tissue out of her pocket, she blew her nose, her eyes immediately filling with tears again. "I'm so afraid something is wrong with him," she whispered brokenly.

Slouching down in the comfortable corner of the sofa, Murphy watched her, lightly rubbing his cheek against his son's downy head. "You should have called me, Jordan," he said, quietly chastising her. "I could have come right home."

She wiped her eyes with the soggy, balled-up tissue, then took a deep, shaky breath and met his gaze. "I did call—this morning." She looked away and swallowed hard, then started fiddling with the tissue. "But they said you'd already checked out."

An odd feeling settled in Murphy's belly. She'd called him. That was almost as big a shocker as coming home to a son. Suddenly wanting to erase the awful anxiety in her eyes, he gave her a small grin. "So," he said, looking right at her, "do you suppose I dare take a look at this kid, or am I going to have to wait until he's old enough to ask for the car keys?"

It was a small smile, and definitely a shaky one, but it was full of maternal pride. Shifting her position, she moved closer to Murphy, caressing the baby's cheek with one finger. "Under the circumstances, we'll just have to risk it."

Supporting the baby's head with one hand, Murphy sat up, then placed his other hand under the tadpole's bum. Feeling suddenly awkward, he carefully lowered the infant, then placed him lengthwise on his legs. The baby made a little whimper, then began to suck noisily on his hand.

Murphy touched his little fist. Lord, he was so little. And so perfect. With a head of black hair. Baby black hair. Awe and wonder and a purely paternal feeling filled up his chest, and he very softly stroked his son's head, so amazed at this tiny, perfect being. His son. His tiny, perfect son.

Not getting what he wanted from his fist and obviously not liking being disturbed from his cozy snuggle, Baby Munroe's face scrunched up and he tuned up again, his tremulous newborn cry fierce and loud. Very loud.

Acute distress immediately reappeared on Jordan's face. "Something has to be wrong for him to be crying like that."

Suddenly very grateful for every ounce of experience he had with his siblings and nieces and nephews, Murphy cradled the baby against him and rose, then began pacing back and forth across the living room, rubbing the baby's back. "Shh, little one. Easy, now. Easy." He looked at Jordan, his expression altering when he saw the terrible anxiety in her eyes. He gave her what he hoped was a reassuring smile. "Hey, don't worry, Kennedy. I'm sure he's fine. I think maybe he's just hungry."

Looking very much like a forlorn waif with her hair held back with some scrunched-up sort of fabric, she stared at him, her anxiety turning to panic. "He can't be hungry. I just fed him before you got here."

Murphy went dead still. She said fed. Which meant breasts. Jordan's breasts. Turning abruptly so she couldn't see his face, he tried to regulate his breathing. That was one picture that definitely did compute. Definitely. And it was something he just didn't dare think about.

Schooling his face into a careful nonexpression, and feeling as if he were about to tread across acres of eggs, he made another fast lap around the room. Trying for both nonchalance and diplomacy, he avoided looking at her. "Well, um... Maybe your, ah, milk hasn't come in yet and, um, maybe we could try him on a bottle of formula and see how that works."

There was a hopeful tone in her voice. "You think so?"

His child's squalling rose to a new crescendo, and Murphy began to understand the source of her desperation. "I think it's worth a try."

She got up from the sofa, absently pushing back the hair that had worked loose from the scrunchie thing. She still looked exhausted but she had definitely brightened. Her expression going all soft, she touched the baby's head. "Poor little man."

Murphy had no idea where it came from, but he got this jolt of intuition. And for some reason, he just knew exactly what she needed to hear. Jiggling the baby in hopes of finding the switch that turned the kid off, he gave her a somewhat amused look. "Poor little man, my ass. He's been giving his mother nothing but a hard time."

She went dead still and shot him a startled look, then she looked away and swallowed hard. "I'll go fix him a bottle," she said, her voice uneven, then fled toward the kitchen. Murphy watched her go, his expression turning very thoughtful. Mother. One word, and it had totally unhinged her.

Suspecting that she was very nearly at the end of her rope, and knowing that the kid's cry could strip paint, let alone fray nerves, he carried his howling son down the hallway to the most distant room from the kitchen. Which just so happened to be the master bedroom. It was a room he was intimately familiar with.

Navy walls with ivory trim and ivory carpet—with a huge antique walnut tester bed dominating the room—it exuded a kind of intimacy that seemed to wrap around a person. The furniture was sparse. Two round bedside tables draped in fabric that held matching brass-and-crystal lamps, two dusty pink wing-back chairs and an antique cherry-wood table that was centered between the two chairs.

Experiencing a funny rush of familiarity, Murphy exhaled slowly. There were two things in this room that he was particularly fond of. One was a beautiful old hand-painted lamp with a tasseled silk shade that sat on the cherry table—it was all elegance and Victorian good taste, but it was the kind of thing that might have come out of a high-class bordello. The other favorite was a handsome old brass-bound trunk that sat at the foot of the bed—it spoke of adventure and mystery. And of all the rooms in her condo, this was the one that revealed the secret, sensual side of Ms. Jordan Kennedy. And it was a side that had nothing to do with a prim, stiff-necked accountant.

Closing the door to dampen the sound reaching the kitchen, Murphy paced the length of the room with his son. He couldn't quite believe his eyes. If he didn't know better, he'd have thought vandals had tossed this room, as well. The bed was unmade. The walk-in closet door was open, and there was a white towel draped over the arm of one of the chairs. Diapers were piled on the steamer trunk, a pair of socks lay on the floor and there was a clutter of baby things on the cherry table. And totally ruining the perfect symmetry of the room was the newly purchased cradle, which was pulled up right alongside the bed. But what really blew his mind was the box of Kleenex sitting on the top of the bordello lamp. This was not the Jordan he knew. For her, this kind of disorder was absolutely unthinkable.

Tired of being stalled and now genuinely ticked off, Junior Munroe wailed even louder. Murphy didn't think a kid that little had that kind of racket in him, but his son definitely did.

Recalling the awful stricken look in Jordan's eyes, and beginning to feel a little bit desperate himself, Murphy cradled the baby in his arm, rocking him back and forth as he tried to figure some way to turn the racket off. Damn, he should have ignored her and bought a pacifier when they'd gone shopping for the baby. The baby was getting so red in the face he looked as if he were going to burst all his tiny blood vessels, and Murphy knew he had to do something.

Knowing that Jordan would have a fit, but desperate for a distraction—any distraction—he stuck his little finger in his son's mouth. The baby stopped crying immediately and latched on like a mini vacuum cleaner.

"Don't you dare tell your mother, Tiger. She'd skin me alive."

With a little jiggling and a whole lot of finger sucking, Murphy managed to quiet his son. At least until Jordan walked in the room, a bottle of formula clutched in her hand, and he had to pull his finger away. Junior was not impressed and started his protest again.

Knowing that she would be nothing if not protective of her child, he shifted his hold, prepared to hand the howling baby to her. But instead of taking the baby, she handed the bottle to him. "Here," she said softly. "You better feed him." She managed a wan smile. "I think he likes you better than me right now anyway."

Murphy suddenly felt as if he were juggling live grenades. Howling baby. Brand-new mom who thought she was a failure after three days. And the look of anguish in her eyes was enough to cut through stone. Feeling as if he was damned if he did and damned if he didn't, he kept his mouth shut and took the bottle from her, then offered it to his son. Silence was immediate. The only sound was that of baby snuffling and hungry suckling. He couldn't help but grin. Happiness right now was a bottle of baby formula.

Careful not to do anything to alter the status quo, Murphy eased his very large frame into one of the chairs. And for the first time since he arrived, everything just sort of leveled out. He had the first really good, uninterrupted look of his brand-new son, feeling as if a big balloon had just gotten inflated in his chest. Until he held his very own son in his arms, he never really considered what an unbelievable miracle a baby was. What an absolute miracle.

Jordan sat on the bed and drew up her legs, then locked her arms around them. Resting her chin on her knees, she just watched. And as if reading Murphy's mind, she smiled a shy mother's smile. "He really is the most perfect little thing, isn't he?"

Knowing the last thing she needed right now was a whole lot of emotion, Murphy gave himself a minute to get rid of the cramp in his throat, then glanced at her. "Now that he has something poked in his mouth, he is."

As worn-out as she obviously was, Jordan chuckled. "And here I thought something was critically wrong with him."

Murphy gave her a wry look. "If someone messes with a Munroe's food chain, we think there is something critically wrong."

She smiled, resting her cheek on her knees. "Too bad you hadn't told me that sooner."

He grinned and changed the angle of the bottle. She lifted her chin toward him. "You're very good at that, you know."

Murphy shrugged. "I've had a lot of practice." Then he shot an amused glance at her. "At our house, a new baby was a shared experience."

Her cheek still against her knees, she continued to watch, a hint of a smile in her eyes. "At least he has one parent with some experience. I'd never held a baby until they gave him to me in the delivery room."

There was something about that comment that set off a red flag in Murphy's brain. But he left it alone. He'd learned a long time ago that there were some questions you just didn't ask around Ms. Jordan Kennedy.

He checked the level of the formula in the bottle, then pulled the nipple out. "Okay, Little Stuff. Burp time." Murphy set the bottle on the table, then lifted his son over his shoulder, making sure his little body wasn't scrunched up. He patted the baby twice and was immediately rewarded with such a resounding burp that it made the baby's head wobble. Steadying his son's head, Murphy grinned. "Sounds like he's been out with the boys, guzzling beer."

Jordan's tone was very wry when she responded. "If I'd thought of it, I would have given it a shot. I was desperate enough to try anything."

Stretching out his legs, Murphy settled the baby in his arm again, then settled more comfortably in the chair. He turned the bottle so he could see the liquid measurements on the side, trying to find the right words to say what needed to be said. He wanted her to know that he was kicking himself for not being there when she needed him. But he was also aware theirs was a very fragile truce. Finally he looked up and met her gaze, his expression solemn. "I'm sorry you had to go through this alone," he said, his tone quiet. "I should have been here."

Jordan gave an embarrassed little shrug, a faint flush creeping up her cheeks. "I was okay on my own. And as I recall, I was the one who told you to go." She hesitated, picking at a nub in the material of her slacks, then she looked up, meeting his gaze with an unwavering directness. "But I am glad you're here now. I was in way over my head."

He held her gaze, experiencing a rush of feelings he didn't want to feel. And one feeling that cut through all the others was anger. The muscles in his jaw hardening, he looked back down at his son, his pulse suddenly running hard. Damn it, he had wanted to be there—permanently. He had wanted to build a life with her—permanently. But all they had now were bits and pieces of jetsam left over from a wreck, held together by one seven-pound, bouncing baby boy.

Needing to get out of there, he used his son as an excuse. "I'd better go change him."

Without looking at her, he got up and grabbed a diaper from the pile on the trunk, then hoisted the baby over his shoulder and headed toward the door. But what he really wanted to do was kick a hole in the wall.

He took the baby into the nursery and carefully placed him on the change table, making himself ignore the anger boiling up, forcing himself to focus on the task at hand. He had no idea if he could still remember how to do this—it had been a very long time, and he was darned sure he'd never changed a baby this small.

Unsnapping the leggings of the sleepers, he couldn't help but smile as he watched his son make guppy movements with his button mouth. By the time he got the old diaper off and the fresh one figured out, Murphy had simmered down a little.

He knew part of his problem was she'd taken a big chunk out of his male ego. Just because he'd been so head over heels in love with her, that didn't automatically mean she felt the same way about him. And maybe that's what bugged him most—that she had blindsided him, and he hadn't even seen it coming. It was as if she'd cut him off at the knees. One day, everything had been just fine, and the next day, she'd told him it was over.

Finally getting the diaper situated at the right angle, he pressed one of the sticky tabs into place, his expression turning very sober. He guessed most of what he was feeling right now was his own problem. Of all the mortal blows she'd dealt him, one of the worst ones was to his pride.

"Murphy?"

Not looking up, he finished with the second tab. "What?"

Her tone had an odd quiet to it, as if she, too, were walking on eggs. "Could I fix you a coffee or something?"

He took a second, trying to let go of the pressure in his chest, then he glanced at her. "No, thanks. I'm fine."

She was standing in the doorway, her arms folded tightly in front of her, her eyes worried and anxious, her face very drawn. She looked exhausted—and scared to death. It was obvious from her expression that she knew she'd made him angry, and that she was terrified he was going to walk out and not come back. Realizing he was adding to the strain she was already under, and knowing that was the last thing the baby needed, he released a sigh and turned back to his son, working his finger-sized leg back into the sleeper.

Keeping his voice devoid of emotion, he spoke. "Why don't you get some sleep, and I'll take care of the tadpole here until his next feeding."

There was a strained pause, then she finally answered, her tone very subdued. "All right."

Doing up the snaps on the baby's sleepers, Murphy didn't look up until he heard her leave. Then he picked up his son and the nearly empty bottle. "Women are a damned pain, kid. And don't you forget it."

He picked up a flannel blanket from the shelf above the change table, then turned down the hallway toward the living room. He heard the master-bedroom door close behind him. "Okay, kid. Now we're going to make a deal. You behave yourself for the next three hours and let your mother sleep, and I'll get you a Porsche when you're nine."

Silently closing the pocket door at the end of the hallway,

he hoped that would set up another sound barrier. He didn't want her to hear so much as a peep for the next three hours if he could help it.

Then Murphy lifted his son over his shoulder and started walking. The baby yawned and Murphy grinned to himself as he patted the baby's back. "And if you're really good, we might even give you your very own name."

Chapter 3

It took Murphy exactly two hours and twenty-three minutes to remember every single thing he'd ever known about colic. And it was a fair amount. One of his nephews had been colicky, and it had taken the entire family to look after that kid.

Murphy wasn't dead sure, and it was eight years ago, but as he recalled, Mark hadn't stopped screaming for three solid months. And the only time the kid was quiet was when he was in a moving car. Murphy clearly remembered being relegated to late-night drives with his father, just to give everyone else a break. He toyed with the idea of phoning his brother-in-law Marco and reminding him of that fact.

Feeling just a little ragged, he made another circle through the living room, dining room and foyer. He'd been around that loop so many times, he was starting to feel that he was running in the Indy 500. The problem was that he was beginning to get motion sick. He'd found a raise-the-perfect-baby book in a stack of baby books on a bookshelf in Jordan's study, and he had spent the past twenty minutes trying to read and walk at the same time.

The book didn't help much. Colic was colic. He understood the theory. The practical information was damned skimpy, though. But now the kid had quit fussing and was sucking on his fist again.

"Is he giving you fits?"

He turned, making sure he kept up the jiggle routine so the baby would think he was still moving. Jordan was standing at the door of the kitchen, hair sticking every which way in the half-off scrunchie, the imprint of her hand on her cheek, still wearing the clothes she'd had on when he arrived. But now they clearly had been slept in. She looked as if she needed a little jiggle of her own. He managed a halfhearted grin. "Well, let's put it this way. He doesn't like to stand still much." He went over to her, turning so she could see the baby sucking on his fist. "But I think maybe he's hungry again."

She opened her eyes wide, as if to make them stay open, then reached up and took the baby. Murphy felt as if a permanent growth had been removed from his chest. Stretching his shoulders back to get rid of the kinks, he observed her with her three-day-old son. Considering he was the first baby she'd ever held, she was remarkably comfortable with him. But then, if Junior had been like this since he was born, she'd already been holding him more than his fair share.

Feeling a little drunk from a lack of sleep, he followed her into the living room. "Do you think we could hang a name on him? He's going to grow up thinking his name is Kid."

He actually got a small smile out of her. "Why don't we

just name him Kid?'' Murphy stared at her. She must be exhausted. She was actually making little jokes.

With her son cradled against her, she settled at one end of the sofa, drawing up her legs to sit cross-legged. Murphy was about to make a smart-mouth retort, but she started undoing the buttons on her shirt, and his entire body went on red alert. Whoa, big fella. That was a whole lot more than he could handle right now. A whole lot more. He turned around and headed back toward the kitchen, his voice sounding slightly strangled when he mumbled over his shoulder. ''I'm going to make myself some coffee.''

''Murphy.''

He probably would have ignored her, but there was something in her tone that made him feel like a total heel. Bracing himself, he turned. The baby was nursing, but it was okay. Everything was covered up. Mostly.

Dragging his gaze higher, he met hers.

''You don't have to stay,'' she said softly, dark smudges of exhaustion under her eyes. ''I can manage.''

The sexual spurt fizzled right out. Gone just like that. Folding his arms, he rested his shoulder against the wall, studying her with new eyes. She was prepared to tough it out on her own—that was clear. But after the past couple of hours, he was convinced that maybe, just maybe she could manage on her own one more day and then she'd collapse from sheer exhaustion. And he'd read all the breast-feeding books. She needed to stay healthy and rested for the baby. So here he was, caught between a rock and a hard place. He tried to joke his way out of it. ''What? And miss all this quality time?''

Jordan attempted a smile, but she just couldn't quite pull it off. ''But you don't have to stay.''

He watched her a moment, assessing her. ''No,'' he finally answered. "You shouldn't even be out of the hospital yet, let alone here on your own."

She tried to smile again. "Lots of women do it. I'm fine. We'll be fine."

His shoulder still anchored against the wall, he continued to assess her. She had said the words, but did she really mean them? He didn't think so; she hadn't been able to quite meet his gaze when she made her declaration. Coming to a decision, he responded. "I'm sure you're right. But I think I'll stick around and see how it goes tonight. Maybe with me here, you can catch up on some sleep."

She held his gaze a minute, relief plainly visible in her eyes, then she bent her head, focusing on the baby. "The coffee is in the pantry," she said, her voice uneven. "Second shelf."

Murphy narrowed his eyes. At least twice tonight, she had capitulated. That had to be some kind of record.

By six the following morning, it was obvious to Murphy that this was definitely a two-man show. Baby Munroe was making up for lost time after a near perfect pregnancy. The kid had slept maybe three hours total, and Murphy had lost track of how many times Jordan had tried to nurse him, or how many loops he'd walked. But one thing he did know for sure—there was no way Jordan could manage on her own. No way.

He considered suggesting hiring a nurse for a week or so, but one glance at that protective, feral look on Jordan's face, and he knew there was no damned way she'd hand that baby over to a stranger. Not that he blamed her.

So there was only one other name on the shortlist, and it was his.

Slouched on the sofa, feeling pretty much like a bag of

old garbage, Murphy stared at the ceiling. He needed a shave, he needed a shower and he needed about twenty hours of uninterrupted sleep. But he was going to have to forgo the last item. He had other things to do.

Rolling his head to one side, he watched as Jordan came into the room, so pale and exhausted that she looked about ready to faint. "I think he's going to sleep," she said, a tone of amazement in her voice.

She still had on the same clothes. "Then go to bed."

Like a zombie, she turned toward the kitchen. "What would you like for breakfast?"

He almost needed a hoist to lever himself off the sofa, but he finally managed it. Catching up to her, he grasped her by the shoulder, then aimed her toward the hallway. "Uh-uh, Kennedy. You're going to bed." He propelled her forward. "And I'm going to the job site to turn the whole show over to my foreman, then I'm coming back here."

She tried to stiffen her legs to stop the forward momentum. "But—"

"No *buts,* Jordan. Go to bed. It says in all the books to sleep when the baby sleeps. I'll be back in an hour, and you can argue all you want then." He pushed her into her bedroom, wanting to laugh when she made it as far as the bed, then crawled across the disheveled blankets and collapsed face first. This was not the Miss Prim and Proper he had known and loved.

Not quite sure he had the energy, he dragged himself downstairs to get his luggage out of his truck, the sunshine so intense that it nearly sucked his eyes right out of his head. Feeling as if he needed a trolley for both himself and his suitcase, he trudged back up to her apartment. He didn't know a day could last this long.

He had a shave, a shower and downed an entire pot of

coffee before heading out. His caffeine level had to be at maximum dosage, or he knew he'd pass out at the first stop sign he came to.

Murphy found Marco at the job site, supervising the installation of eaves troughs and downspouts. Without making any explanations, he walked up to his brother-in-law, told him he was taking a couple of weeks off and that they could contact him on his cell phone if they needed him. Then he turned around and walked away, aware that Marco was watching him as if someone had just dropped a load of bricks on his head. He didn't care. He didn't have the energy to care. He was going to the supermarket to pick up some groceries and some film for his camera, then he was heading back to the condo, and he was going to pass out on the first flat surface he came to.

It was not a good day. Baby slept for two hours and forty minutes. Then he started with the fussing thing again. He slept again for two hours in the afternoon, but he geared up after that, and he was still fussing at nine o'clock that evening. It was Murphy's turn to walk him, and Jordan was on the sofa, looking for answers in the ninth of her seventeen books. "It says here," she said, her head bent over the pages, "that breast-fed babies don't usually get colic."

Murphy spun around and walked the other way. "Tell that to Baby."

She fell over on the sofa, going into fits of hysterical laughter. As exhausted and as useless as he felt, Murphy puffed right up as he kept on walking. He'd never, ever made her laugh like that before, ever. Somewhere along the line, he must have turned into a comedian.

Except her laughter turned to weeping. And he had never felt so helpless. Holding the fussing baby against his shoulder, he crouched down beside her, pulling her tangled hair back off her face. "Hey," he said gruffly. "Hey." Which accomplished nothing, except it gave him a chance to touch her. The baby started sucking on his fist again, and Murphy went dizzy with relief. She always seemed to pull herself together when she fed the baby.

Feeling like a total cop-out, he combed her hair back again. "He's chewing on his fist. And it's been two hours."

She wiped her face on the sofa, then struggled up. Without looking at him, she silently took the baby from him. The breast thing had no effect anymore—well, hardly any effect. And having him as a spectator certainly didn't seem to bother her. So it shouldn't bother him. Well, maybe it wouldn't if he didn't think about it.

Murphy looked straight ahead, out the patio doors to the sunset. He heard the baby start nursing, then a funny, startled sound from Jordan.

She was leaning over the baby as if her chest were about to explode, the most astonished look on her face, and there was milk everywhere. All over the baby's face. On the sofa. Soaking one half of her shirt.

Murphy had heard all about this when he was about nine years old, just at that age when stuff like that embarrassed the hell out of him. About what it was like when a woman's milk "let down." Without saying a word, he went to the bathroom and got a guest towel and a damp facecloth and brought them back, handing them to Jordan. Another mystery of female physiology exposed and solved.

"Thanks," she said a bit breathlessly. There was a slight pause, then she spoke again, a waver of self-chastisement in her voice. "This is really great. First I try to starve him. Then I try to drown him."

Ignoring the naked swell of her breast beneath his son's cheek, he squatted down in front of her. Catching her under the chin, he lifted her head so she had to look at him. Her gray eyes were swimming with tears, and he could tell she was at the point of absolute exhaustion. "Don't, Jordan," he commanded quietly. "You're doing the best you can."

He caught a whiff of the familiar fragrance of her shampoo, and his heartbeat stalled, then went berserk. It took every ounce of control he had to keep from rubbing his thumb along her jaw. Dropping his hand, he rubbed his fingers against the rough fabric of his jeans instead, the heat from her skin still buzzing along his nerve ends like an electrical current. Then he deliberately rested his arm across his thigh, waiting a second for his lungs to start working again. He forced himself to focus on the situation and not her. "If it would make you feel better to have the pediatrician check him—just to make sure everything is okay—we can make an appointment first thing tomorrow."

Tears gathered along her thick lashes, and the look she gave him was a mixture of relief and gratitude. Unable to speak, she simply nodded, the tears spilling over.

Murphy wanted to touch her in the worst way. Instead, he got up and went to the open patio door. Bracing his arm on the wooden frame, he stood staring out, trying to disconnect. It had been bad enough before, but Jordan Kennedy with all her defenses down was almost more than he could handle. And somehow or other, he was going to have to excise this thing he had for her. Or he was going to drive himself stark raving crazy. She was the mother of his son. That was all. Nothing more. And he was not going to think about how she'd got to be the mother of his son.

He continued to stare out. Off in the distance he could hear the chatter of a lawn sprinkler, then the evening song of a robin. He watched the colors fade from the sky, trying to get things back in perspective.

He was going to have to keep reminding himself that this was only temporary—that there was no chance it could be forever. They had established this bizarre kind of truce months ago. And that truce had now altered and changed shape since the birth of their son. Because of the baby, there was a new kind of familiarity between them. And that alone was risky, but what was even more dangerous was that this kind of total exhaustion bred a kind of goofiness—like her falling over laughing on the couch. He had never seen that side of her before—and that side was just a little too disarming.

Murphy stood at the window until all but a few slashes of orange faded from the sky, until his own lack of sleep started catching up on him. Wearily dragging his hand through his hair, he turned.

The scene before him was like a punch in the chest. Jordan had fallen asleep nursing the baby, and the baby had also fallen asleep, a drool of milk running from the corner of his mouth onto her soft, smooth skin. The room was filled with twilight, except for one table lamp at the end of the sofa that cast a soft glow on both their faces. It was a scene that had the impact of a body blow. This was one picture he didn't need the camera to record. And this was going to be a picture that would remain with him until the day he died. His hands in his pockets, he stood watching them for the longest time.

Finally he went around the sofa, experiencing an empty, aching sensation in the middle of his chest. Trying not to wake either one of them, he slipped one hand under the baby's butt, the other under his head. But when he started to lift the feather weight off Jordan, her arm immediately clutched the baby and her eyes flew open. Bending over her, he met her uncomprehending gaze. "It's okay," he said very softly. "I've got him."

She stared up at him for a moment, then she relinquished her hold on the baby, letting him take his son from her, her eyes drifting shut. And Murphy knew she could not have done anything that made his chest fill up more.

The trip to the doctor's was pretty much a waste of time. Baby Munroe was an angel and slept through the whole thing, except when the doctor examined him. The doctor's advice, on a scale from one to ten, rated a zero. Baby Munroe had a simple case of colic. Murphy didn't see anything simple about it.

The doctor reiterated all the advice that was contained in Jordan's seventeen baby books and gave them more literature on colic, as well as a gentle lecture on new-parent anxiety attacks. And how that was bad for the baby, especially when Jordan was nursing. He also gave them a prescription for drops if it got any worse. Suppressing the urge to grab the man by the throat, Murphy wondered if Dr. Jackson had ever, in his whole life, spent even five minutes alone with a colicky baby. He thought not.

Feeling somewhat testy after the appointment, Murphy didn't mess around. He got the prescription filled before they left the building, in the pharmacy located on the ground floor. The only real conclusion the trip to the doctor produced was that Jordan was going to need another vehicle. Getting a baby's car seat in and out of her sports coupe was a pain in the ass. And his truck was just too dirty for a new baby. She needed something big and safe. A big 4×x4 sport utility. One that was built like a tank.

They barely spoke on the way home, except to discuss the number of prints they wanted when he dropped off the rolls of film they'd taken of their progeny. As soon as they got back, Jordan went into her bedroom to change. When she came out, dressed in a pair of leggings and another baggy shirt, her hair yanked back in a practical ponytail, it was as if one person had walked into the bedroom and a totally different one had come out. And it was as if Murphy saw her for the very first time.

On her visit to the doctor, she had been the consummate professional, her hair perfectly groomed into a French fold, her blue power suit perfectly tailored, even her jewelry was elegant and understated—she simply radiated an aura of competency, self-assurance and efficiency. He'd never really thought about it before. Those qualities were what Jordan Kennedy was all about. But when she came back into the living room, dressed to cope with a fussy baby, Murphy saw, for the first time, that all the window dressing was *not* what she was about. It was all camouflage. It was a persona. It was something she slipped on to create and transmit an aura of confidence, competency and self-assurance. It was all one grand cover-up.

The realization shook him up so badly that he had to go out on the terrace to integrate this stunner. It was a role, for Pete's sake. The whole time, she had been playing a role. Lord, but he couldn't believe how thickheaded he'd been. What a damned dunce. And how bloody blind. It was there all along, staring him right in the face—but he'd just been too stupid to see it. But he knew he was right. The real Ms. Jordan Kennedy was always carefully concealed from public view.

No bloody wonder she had walked out on him.

"What would you like for lunch?"

Murphy held his stance. It was a good thing he'd had time to get his reaction under wraps, or the whole realization would have been written all over his face. Making sure there wasn't a trace of expression on his face, he turned and leaned back against the brick retaining wall. She had washed her face, and from the dull look in her eyes, the trip to the doctor had used up whatever reserve of energy she had. He stared at her a minute, then straightened, suddenly, irrationally angry with her. It had all been camouflage. But damn it, she'd never needed to play those kinds of games with him. Never.

"What I would like," he said, his tone a little too curt, "is for you to stretch out in that lounge, get a little fresh air and some sunshine. I'll take care of lunch."

He did a lot of slamming and thumping in the kitchen, burning off steam. Then he did a whole lot of talking to himself. So he'd missed that about her before. So what? It didn't change anything. She'd made it pretty clear their former relationship was over and done with. And he wasn't going to stick his neck out again. But he was playing on a different field now. She could have terminated the pregnancy, but she hadn't. And now she was the mother of his child, and she was doing her level best to be a good one. He owed her for that, if nothing else. It was time he bloody well grew up. But as soon as he came to that conclusion, he promptly backslid and started wondering what else he had missed.

Making sure he had all the food groups covered, Murphy listened for his son, who was still sleeping in his car seat in the living room, then carried the loaded tray out onto the terrace.

Jordan was semireclined on the lounger, one arm covering her eyes. Setting down the tray on the wrought-iron table beside her, he draped a chunk of paper towel across her lap, then dragged over another chair.

Avoiding his gaze, she adjusted the arms of her chair so she was in an upright position. His expression thoughtful, Murphy watched her. It was apparent that she'd read his temper pretty accurately when he stalked into the kitchen, and if he was reading this new Jordan correctly, she was uncertain of him and awash with guilt. She had obviously shed her armor along with her blue power suit.

He passed her plate and she took it, still not meeting his gaze. Knowing the only way he could make it better was to lighten the mood, he grinned and kept his tone casual. "I have a plan."

She looked up at him, a confused look in her eyes. He gave her a warped smile. "I think our Dr. Jackson needs a dose of reality, so how about we take the kid over to his house tonight about midnight, and let him have a go at looking after him. Then we can both get a good night's sleep."

A hint of amusement lightened her eyes, and the tiny dimple at the corner of her mouth appeared. "I don't think your extended medical plan will go for that."

Murphy chuckled, lifting his bottle of beer off the tray. "Damn. I figured he deserved it after his brush-off today."

The expression in her eyes clearly lightened, and Murphy was pretty sure she had just put two and two together and come up with seven; she thought his bad mood was because of the visit to the doctor. And he was quite happy to let her think that.

"Well, at least we know the baby is okay."

After taking a long swig from the bottle, Murphy leaned back in the chair, drilling her with a long, pained look. "We can't just keep calling him Baby, Jordan. Whether we want to or not, we've gotta give the kid a name. They won't let him start school if we don't."

She grinned, taking a forkful of cold chicken. "I was thinking of Ivan."

Murphy stared at her, wondering where that name had come from. Who'd call their kid Ivan? Then a mental light bulb came on. "Ah," he said, his tone knowing. "Ivan the Terrible."

As she mixed the dressing into her salad, the dimple reappeared. "It seems appropriate somehow."

"We could call him Rover and teach him to speak and roll over."

She shot him a quick look, her eyes glinting with amusement. "That's awful."

He grinned at her. "We could call him Tank—he sorta rolls over anything in his way."

She chuckled and plowed through some more food, then glanced at him, her eyes more animated that he could ever recall. "Tank's too—too American. How about something more historically Canadian, like Wilfrid?"

Mesmerized and totally disarmed by this silly side of her, he continued to play the game, not wanting it to stop. "Nah. Too stuffed-shirt. You need a name he can play hockey with and not get creamed. A name with muscle, like Bruce."

They spent a good half hour bantering back and forth, and miracle of miracles, Rover/Wilfrid/Bruce slept through it all, probably hanging in there until they came up with a decent, wearable name for him.

They finally got serious, and by the time Murphy had worked his way through his second beer, they had agreed on James Jeffery Munroe. They even filled out the registration form.

Murphy had known right from the beginning that she wanted the baby to carry Murphy's last name. But now that it was there in black-and-white, it really hit home. Jordan

Kennedy was going to make darned sure her son knew who his father was.

Their lunch break was the one island of tranquillity they had all day. James Jeffery was not a happy camper. The new bunch of literature stated categorically that colicky babies had fussy periods, and those fussy periods were usually isolated to certain times of day. Murphy figured James Jeffery needed to grow up and read all the literature.

Abandoned by science and the medical profession, they drafted their own battle plan. Jordan was to try and get all the sleep she could at night. With the blessing of good old Dr. Jackson, they agreed that Murphy would give James Jeffery a bottle during the night so Jordan could get more than two hours of sleep at a crack. Murphy, who could sleep standing up, would crash during the day.

They got all their ducks in a row. They even ordered a single bed from one of the major department stores, and Murphy agreed to pay an exorbitant delivery fee to get it delivered the same day. That went in the nursery.

It was a great plan, except it didn't work. No one could sleep when His Highness was running wide open. But other than being so damned tired that he fell asleep buttering toast, Murphy figured they were managing as well as could be expected.

And Jordan never ceased to confound, to amaze. It was as if the trip to the doctor's defined her role. As if she realized that they were on their own, and she assumed the role of both protector and guardian.

There were times Murphy felt as if he were some sort of secret voyeur, watching her with his child—times when he swore she'd turned into another person. Every ounce of energy, every ounce of attention, was focused on the baby, and not once had she even come close to losing her patience.

Before, when she was the other Jordan, she had been absolutely fastidious about everything, herself included.

Now the whole apartment looked like a heavily bombed war zone, and for the most part, she looked as if she'd been dragged through a wind tunnel backward. And it was obvious she couldn't care less. She had more important things to attend to. The welfare of their son was her first and only concern.

Murphy caught himself watching her, over and over again, wondering what other surprises she'd hidden under that ice-princess exterior.

But then, he would catch her watching him with the baby, too, and there would be such a wealth of emotion in her eyes, as if his holding their son was something special, something that touched her in a profound way—as if the father-son connection was something very rare and wonderful. And he wondered if he would ever figure out all the pieces that made up the real Jordan Kennedy.

And there were more pieces than he could count. He discovered another one exactly seven days after he'd returned from Toronto—and found himself a father. They had eaten dinner in shifts because James Jeffery was doing the squirmy thing. The baby hadn't been outright fussy, but he kept wriggling around because he was uncomfortable, and they knew from experience that if they kept moving with him, he might settle down.

Murphy had taken a shower in preparation for his evening shift, and he came out into the living room with just his blue jeans on, a towel draped around his neck. He entered the room and stopped short in the archway.

Jordan was in the big old cane-back rocking chair he'd brought over from his place, rocking back and forth, James Jeffery tucked in the crook of her arm. She had on one of

Murphy's Harley-Davidson T-shirts and a pair of leggings, and wads of fair hair had escaped from the ponytail and fell around her face. A book lay open on her thigh. He gave a half smile when he considered his T-shirt on her body. Milk production was in excess, so that was definitely no longer a problem, but getting the laundry done was. Her shape had changed considerably since things had started to happen in the production department. And out of sheer desperation, he had fired that T-shirt at her two hours ago. But maybe that had been a big mistake. There was something about a woman's breasts in a black Harley-Davidson T-shirt.

The only light in the room was from the table lamp, which reflected down one side of her face and onto the pages of the book. Only she wasn't reading for herself. She was reading nursery rhymes to their ten-day-old son. Sitting there like that, in that soft light and in that get-up, looking so intent, she could have easily passed for a teenage baby-sitter. She looked so earnest and so very young—not even close to her thirty years.

Resting his shoulder against the doorway, he folded his arms and watched her, another piece falling into place. It was clear from the way she was reading that she didn't know any of the children's poems by heart. He wondered what kind of home she'd grown up in, that she hadn't learned those old familiar verses. She'd been very close-mouthed about her family when they'd been going out. And he'd never pressed. He figured that if she didn't want to tell him, that was her business. Now he wondered.

He continued to watch her, trying to batten down the empty feeling that kept climbing up his chest. Sometimes he wished he'd never laid eyes on her. But watching her now, he knew that was a lie. Not wanting to let his thoughts sink any deeper than they already were, he spoke, his voice a little gruff. "Have you ever wondered how come kids' nursery rhymes have such gruesome things in them?"

Her head came up like a shot, a startled look in her eyes, and almost immediately a hint of pink started creeping up her cheeks. Which was good. She'd been so pale lately, she could certainly use the color. His arms folded across his chest, Murphy continued to watch her, caught off guard by her reaction. It was as if he'd caught her cheating. No. It was something else. Narrowing his eyes, he contemplated her a second longer. It was almost as if she was embarrassed that he'd caught her reading nursery rhymes.

He never gave her time to go underground on him. "So why do you think that is?"

She closed the book and leaned over, setting it on the end table. That prissy-accountant's look camouflaged her face, as if she had pulled back behind her defenses. "Some were political commentary."

Not liking that she'd reverted to that old form, he went over to the table and picked up the book, then opened it. "Well, whatever it is, it worked on him. I'll have to give it a try later." He gave her a semicross look. "But no way am I reading him that rock-a-bye-baby stuff. It used to scare the hell out of me when I was little."

A sparkle appeared in her eyes, and the prim look disappeared. "Yes," she said, her tone dry. "I can tell it did."

Sprawling on the floor, he rested his back against the sofa and laced his hands behind his head, then crossed his ankles. He nodded toward his bright-eyed son. "Was it my imagination, or was he less fussy today?"

Her expression softening into a tender maternal look, she gently rubbed the crown of her son's head. "He was a very good boy today."

Holding back a smile and, for some reason, needing to

tease her, Murphy lifted his chin toward his son. "He's making those guppy faces again."

She bent over and kissed the top of the baby's head. "Not guppy faces. Baby faces." Leaning back in the chair, she began rocking again. She gave him a small, sheepish smile, something almost conspiratorial in her expression. "But he is pretty cute, isn't he?"

Murphy restrained a twist of amusement. "Right now he is."

Hunching her shoulders forward, she encompassed their baby in an enveloping embrace, a glow on her face that Murphy had never seen before as she kissed their son's crown again. And that expression—the expression that changed her into something almost surreal—was all about unconditional love.

Murphy's expression tightened. At one point in his life, he would have killed to have her look at him that way. Anger building up inside him, he got up and headed toward the nursery. He needed his gym bag and truck keys, then he was going to get the hell out of there. At least until he had a chance to cool off. But maybe anger was a whole lot safer than acknowledging that he wasn't quite as disconnected as he liked to think.

Turning to his own personal release valve, Murphy headed for the gym. But when he pulled up outside, the thought of going in there held about the same appeal as a root canal. He thought about his own house—the one he was renovating in an older, established area. But it was too big, too empty, too quiet. And then he thought of his mother's English country garden, with the fish pond and trickling water, the bird baths and quaint willow lawn chairs under the spreading ornamental cherry tree.

He picked up his cell phone from the top of the gym bag, flipped it open and punched in the familiar number with his thumb. He listened to two rings, then the pickup. Staring out the open window of his vehicle, he moved the mouthpiece closer to his mouth. "Hi. I thought I'd stop by if you weren't busy."

His mother was delighted with the suggestion, and when he arrived, Murphy found his mother sitting under the cherry tree, the heavy twilight from the long days of summer creating dense shadows. On the wicker table there was a pair of garden gloves, a tall glass of iced tea, a bottle of chilled cider with condensation running down it and a pastrami sandwich made with fresh homemade bread.

Her graying blond hair was pulled up in some sort of topknot, she had on shorts and an old blouse and there was dirt on her knees. She was sixty-two, looked fifty-two and seemed a hell of a lot younger than that. She smiled at him as he crossed the yard. "Hello, stranger. We were beginning to think you'd gone intergalactic."

Tossing his cell phone on the table, he sprawled in the chair opposite her. "Yeah. Well, I feel like I've been in outer space." He stretched out his legs and crossed his ankles, then laced his hands behind his head. "Where's Dad?"

"He's off playing poker with his buddies."

Feeling the tranquillity of the huge yard seep into him, Murphy picked up the bottle of cider and raised it to his mouth.

"So," she said, flicking a glob of mud off her shorts, "when are you going to tell us about this new grandchild of ours?"

Choking on the cider, he shot up, coughing and sputtering. Finally able to speak, he gave her an annoyed look. "Good grief, Ma, it's not even due yet."

She gave him a benign smile. "Shame on you, Murphy. Keeping secrets."

Resigned to facing the music, he let go a long sigh. "Just tell me one thing. How did you find out?"

Picking up her own glass, she pursed her lips in a restrained smile. "Murphy. I'm your mother. I know all sorts of things."

He refused to go after that piece of bait. Wedging the bottle between his thighs, he picked up the plate with the sandwich on it, figuring two could play this game. But he'd forgotten that nobody could play like his mother.

Having wolfed down half the sandwich with her sitting there smiling that all-knowing smile, he expelled another long sigh and gave up. "Okay. How did you figure it out?"

She took a long sip, then actually smirked. "Marco."

"What do you mean, Marco?"

"Well," she said, turning the glass in her hand, "I didn't think it was right that the rest of the family didn't know. So I told them you had a baby on the way."

He inhaled a whole chunk of bread with that bombshell, and it took five minutes of coughing to dislodge it. His eyes watering, he stared at her. "What?" he choked out. "You *told* them?"

"Of course, dear."

Knowing he'd been totally outmaneuvered, he rested his head against the chair back and simply stared at her.

"So when Marco phoned to say you'd showed up at work looking like something the cat dragged in—and telling him you were taking some time off—well," she said, grinning at him, "we can all add, Mokey."

He rolled his eyes, mostly because he knew she was using that old nickname, the one that had been hung on him by younger, speech-deficient siblings, just to rattle his chain. His mother wasn't really an ordinary mother.

Resting her arms on the wide arms of the wicker willow chair, she gazed at him, her expression turning serious. Even in the fading light, her concern was visible. "So how are you doing?"

He held her gaze for a second, then took another long swig of cider. Needing to get his thoughts sorted out, he stared at the bottle for a long moment before he answered. "Well, for starters, you have a beautiful grandson, Ma."

She abruptly pressed her hand to her chest, and almost immediately, he could see the glimmer of tears in her eyes. His mother was the softest touch on earth about kids—her own, her kids' kids, any kids. And she was one hell of a grandma. Unfortunately, it had taken him to adulthood before he truly appreciated his parents. A huge surge of emotion nailed him square in the chest. He wondered if his son would ever feel the same way.

"I think maybe you need to do some talking," she said, her tone quiet, kind, full of concern.

Leaning forward, he rested his forearms on his thighs, lacing both hands around the amber bottle. "Hell, Ma. I don't know what to say. She had the baby while I was in Toronto, and I got back, and there he was." He rubbed his thumb against the label on the bottle, his throat tight. "He's beautiful. He weighed seven pounds and two ounces, and he's got this head of thick black hair. And he has colic— there's no way that Jordan can manage on her own. So I've been staying over there." He took another swig, hoping it would make the knot in his throat go away. Finally getting the knot under control, he lowered the bottle. "His name is James Jeffery Munroe—" His throat cramped up again, and he had to stop.

She read him dead-on. "You can only make the best of what you have," she said in the same quiet tone. "Nothing can be gained by playing the 'if only' game, Murphy. She's made her decision, and you're just going to have to live with it. Just be grateful you've got the chance to be involved in his life."

Releasing a long, slow breath, he looked up, his own expression somber. "I know all that, Ma."

She gave his hand a little squeeze. "Then let's concentrate on celebrating this newest little Munroe." She leaned back, a look of pure avarice in her eyes. "So. Did you bring me pictures?"

As lousy as hc was feeling, Murphy couldn't help but grin. "Jeez, Mother. Give me a break, will you?"

"Well, did you?"

He shook his head. "They're in for developing."

Ellen Munroe had the gift for distraction. And after half an hour with her, Murphy felt almost back to normal.

All the light had faded from the sky and it was going on eleven when she stood and picked up the dishes and empty cider bottle. "Come in the house. The mosquitoes are eating me alive, and you look as if you could do with a coffee." She tucked the bottle under her arm and gathered up her garden gloves. "And we have a few things to send home for James Jeffery."

Chapter 4

With the gifts packed in a cardboard box, Murphy drove back to the condo, considering what Jordan's reaction would be. She had never met any of his family—in fact, she had gone out of her way to avoid it. He wasn't sure why, and he wasn't going to start digging around in all that old garbage now. There was no point. They were parents together, and that was it. But he didn't like the hollow feeling that piece of reality left in his gut. Not wanting to get into those emotions right now, he glanced at the box sitting on the passenger's seat, considering the packages his mother had carefully arranged inside.

The gifts were all wrapped in bright baby paper and colorful bows, all addressed to Baby Munroe. The writing on one parcel was his grandmother's, and he had a pretty good idea what Baba's gift was. There were three more packages addressed to Baby Munroe—one in his father's handwriting, two in his mother's. But besides the gifts, he had come away with a kind of mental reinforcement. His mother was right. He could only work with what he had. He wasn't happy about it, but that was the hand he'd been dealt. He either played it, or got out of the game.

Feeling as if he had just excavated a huge hole in the middle of his chest, but oddly awake, Murphy parked the truck on the side street and locked it, then started toward the front entrance. He wondered how much longer he could keep this up without losing his mind. Well, maybe a kid with colic was a good thing. Since J.J. had arrived, he'd been suffering from such a chronic case of sleep deprivation that everything was blurred and out of focus. And maybe that was the trick—to stay out of focus.

The box tucked under one arm, he separated the key for the condo from the others on his key chain, hoping that both parties were asleep upstairs. He felt as if he didn't have a speck of energy left to give to anybody right then.

His wish was half-filled.

When he unlocked the door and opened it, the apartment was absolutely still, not a sound of a baby anywhere. Then Jordan appeared in the foyer, her face so pale that her eyes looked the size of saucers and almost black. Folding her arms tightly in front of her, she managed an uncertain smile. "Hi," she said, her voice as uneven as her smile.

Murphy looked at her, then turned and closed the door, setting the dead bolt. The box still under his arm, he turned to face her, wishing he didn't have to deal with this now. He scolded her. "You should be in bed."

She tried to smile again and made a nervous little gesture with one hand. "I—well. I didn't know if you had your keys or not."

Dropping his keys in the pewter bowl on the vestibule table, Murphy tried to keep his face expressionless. Her being up had nothing to do with keys; it had to do with the fact that she didn't know if he was coming back or not.

Lifting his head, he looked at her, his gaze level. And he called it for what it was. "I'm not going to walk out on you and our son when he's like this," he said, his tone even. "I'm not that big of a louse."

Tightening her arms, she abruptly looked down and straightened the fringe on the hall runner with her toe. Murphy knew he had scored a direct hit, and he immediately felt like the louse he'd just said he wasn't.

Knowing there was really nowhere to go with this conversation, he brushed past her. His tone was softer when he spoke. "Come on. My mother sent some things over for the little monster."

He set the box down in front of the sofa, then went to the fridge and got a beer, knowing he was going to pay big time for having it if the tadpole gave him another run for his money tonight.

When he entered the living room, he caught her poking around in the box. As soon as she heard him, she immediately sat back and clamped her hands between her legs. Catching her doing something so unlike her accountant's persona made his mood lift a little, and he tapped the back of her head as he walked by. "Caughtcha."

Rounding the end of the sofa, he glanced down at her and had to smile when he saw that she was blushing. He settled himself comfortably on the other end of the deep, comfortable couch and raised the bottle to his mouth. So, Ms. Kennedy got all curious and snoopy over presents....

Resting the bottle on his chest, he watched her, amusement surfacing. "You don't have to wait, Jordan. You can open them now."

She shot him a glance, then she gave a guilty little fidget. "Aren't they from your family?"

Slouching down so he could rest his head back against the cushions, he nodded. "From my family."

Jordan looked down at the gifts, then back at him. "What are they?"

He held back a smile. "I guess you're going to have to open them to find out."

Rolling the hem of her T-shirt, she gave an uncertain little shrug. "Shouldn't you open them?"

"Nope. Dads watch. Mothers open."

Jordan stared at him a moment—hesitant, as if uncertain of these parental rules, and for the very first time, Murphy got a glimpse of her as a child. And he experienced a funny clutch around his heart.

Watching her open the first gift was an education all by itself. When he had given her the pearl earrings for her birthday, she had opened the parcel the same way. Slowly, careful not to tear the paper. Back then, he thought it was because she was like that, but now he realized he was wrong. This carefulness was about taking her time, about making the moment last, about savoring every second of the experience. She unstuck all the tape closures, then she lifted off the card and opened it. Murphy watched her, realizing she was simply prolonging the anticipation. She read the card, then flashed him a look of total surprise. "It's from your father."

More intent on watching her than anything else, he answered. "Really?"

Ever so carefully, she unwrapped the gift, fold by fold, not making a single tear in the bright paper. Peeling back the final wrap, she made a delighted sound, then laughed and held the box up for him to see.

Murphy grinned. He should have known—it was a junior fishing rod. Nestling his beer in the crook of his folded arms, he met her gaze. "My father is nuts about fishing, and he likes to drag his grandkids along. When Grandpa goes fishing, it's a very big deal." He indicated the boxed fishing rod. "So that's J.J.'s ticket to the show."

The look on her face was amazing. It was as if someone had just handed her kid the entire world. "That is so wonderful."

Murphy grinned. "We didn't used to think so. We used to whine and carry on, trying to wheedle our way out of it. The grandkids think it's a pretty big deal, though."

The next gift was Murphy's silver baby mug, all freshly polished. A note addressed to the baby said that he was to bring it with him the first time he came to visit, and Grandma would get his birth date and name engraved on it. Jordan lingered over that for several moments, turning it over and over in her hands, caressing the polished surface, tracing the engraving already there, the oddest expression on her face. And for a moment, he thought she was going to cry. But she finally carefully set it aside and picked up the next parcel.

That gift was from Baba, and even for Murphy, this gift was special. It was a handmade baby quilt, and she had sewn one for each of her grandchildren and great-grandchildren. Baba blankets. All done by hand in such tiny, intricate stitches that they were nearly invisible, all trimmed with the traditional Ukrainian cross-stitch. And now his son had been included in the family tradition.

"Oh, Murphy," she whispered, her voice hushed with awe. "This is absolutely beautiful." She stroked it, then ran her hand along the trim. "And it's all done by hand."

"From my grandmother. She's made one for each of us kids. Mine's still around somewhere."

Still caressing the blanket, she looked at him, that same look of awe in her eyes. "But this is truly beautiful."

Propping his feet up on the coffee table, he studied the blanket. "Yeah, it is. Especially when you take into consideration that she's turning seventy-six."

Jordan stroked it again. "It's far too special to use."

Murphy took another swig, then let the bottle rest on his chest. He turned his head, his eyes suddenly not wanting to focus, the beer beginning to interact with his lack of sleep. "Are you kidding? She's going to expect to see the kid eating and sleeping with that quilt." He managed an off-center grin. "It's a Baba Blankie."

A glint of humor in her eyes, she carefully folded the blanket and placed it on top of the fishing rod. "Ah," she said knowingly. "Well, then."

She picked up the next gift with the same carefulness. Unwrapping it to expose a large, thin gift box, she severed the tape with her fingernail, then lifted the lid. Under the protecting tissue was a satin-bound baby book.

Wiping her fingers on her slacks before she touched it, Jordan opened it with great care, and Murphy shoveled closer so he could see. She fanned through the pages, and he saw a flash of writing. He stopped her, turning back several pages.

It was the paternal family tree, and Ellen Munroe had filled it all in, the entries done in beautiful Victorian script.

He lifted a blank onion-skin separator, revealing the opposite page. "And here's the space for your side of the family."

Jordan stared at the entry for a moment, touching the empty box where it said Mother. Then, without saying anything, she replaced the separator page and closed the book, her expression unreadable. "I'll write thank-you notes first thing tomorrow." Her smile was tight and strained as she put the lid back on the box, then she brushed invisible dust off her legs. "It was really thoughtful of your family."

Murphy's eyes narrowed, a flicker of annoyance setting his jaw. It was as if somebody had thrown a switch. One minute, she was clearly excited and moved by the gifts. The next minute, she brushed them off as if they weren't worth the paper they'd been wrapped in. Just like that—in the blink of an eye—she'd reverted to her old, ice-princess self. Renewed anger boiled up in Murphy. Capping his reaction took just about everything he had, and his face felt as if it were about to crack. Deliberately snubbing her comment, he tipped his head and downed the rest of the bottle of beer, angry at himself for letting his guard down, for letting her get to him.

A brittle silence built up around them, and it was so tense, so charged, it would have only taken one small spark to set the whole thing off. Locking his jaw to keep everything contained, Murphy shoved his head back into the soft cushions and closed his eyes. He felt the weight shift as she stood up. She spoke, her voice very quiet. "Just so you know—I fed him just before you came in."

Murphy didn't acknowledge her. He waited until he heard her bedroom door close, then got up and went out on the terrace and stood staring at the darkened horizon. Damn it, why couldn't he just let it all go? And why did he keep crossing lines he knew he had no business crossing? And why in hell did he let her brush-off get to him? It wasn't as if he *liked* feeling the way he did, as if every single emotion were hanging on the end of a yo-yo. And he bloody well didn't like that low-grade anger that was sitting there, simmering just below the surface all the time. One way or another, he was going to have to get on with it. He couldn't keep this up much longer.

He was spared from another round of grim thoughts when Jeffery started his fussing. Murphy brought him from the nursery, and he and his son spent the next few hours doing the colic shuffle. By two in the morning, Murphy had made a decision. No, he couldn't just walk off and leave her with the whole show, at least not until J.J. straightened out a bit and started sleeping better at nights.

If he was going to stay halfway together, he was simply going to have to limit his time here. That was damned obvious. His getting into a snit simply because she'd brushed off the baby-book gift was a good indicator. Somehow or other, he was going to have to find a way to disconnect and stay disconnected. The constant proximity was getting to be too much, and he knew it.

It was a bad night all around. J.J. was fussier than usual. Murphy managed to catch one catnap about 4:00 a.m. when Jordan got up and nursed the baby. Which only made him feel worse. Then at seven he got a phone call from Marco about a major crisis at the site, which he had to go deal with. By the time he got that mess straightened out, he didn't have the energy to drive all the way back to the condo. So he went to his place instead. He turned off his cell phone, flopped on the bed and slept like the dead for six solid hours.

When he woke up, his mind was clear enough that he was actually able to think. And one thing became crystal clear. He had to put some distance between him and Jordan. He knew that as sure as he walked and talked. So he came up with a strategy. He'd maintain the night shift with J.J.

when the baby was his fussiest, and now that Jordan had started stockpiling bottles of breast milk, maybe he could try to work in two bottle feedings instead of one so she'd get a few hours of decent sleep. But as soon as the baby went down after his morning feeding, hc was going to clear out. He'd spend a few hours at the site, and then he'd crash at his own place until it was time to go back to Jordan's. At least that way, maybe he'd regain some emotional equilibrium. And maybe not. But something had to damned well change. Because he was headed for a wreck if it didn't.

That plan worked for four whole days. He told her that things were getting crazy at work and he was going to have to spend more time at the construction site. Which wasn't a total lie. And with a more controlled, limited exposure to Ms. Jordan Kennedy, Murphy didn't feel as if he were hanging from a very high cliff by a very thin thread all the time. But he was still drop-dead tired. Things had piled up at work, and he was getting less sleep than when he'd been at Jordan's full-time—which was maybe a good thing. Chronic exhaustion had him pretty well numbed to the bone. And numb was good. If it hadn't been for his very active guilty conscience, which rose up to haunt him at the most inappropriate times, he could have almost talked himself into thinking he was actually getting a handle on it.

But a weather warning of an approaching storm put an end to all that. Although she'd always tried to hide it, Murphy knew from the previous summer that Jordan was terrified of thunderstorms. And that knowledge would have been bad enough on its own, but his guilty conscience knew it, too. Relentless as ever, it pointed out to him in no uncertain terms, that he had, in fact, pretty much abandoned her. And when push came to shove, the little voice in his head won every time.

So instead of trying to catch a couple of hours of sleep at his place, he grabbed something to eat and had a quick shower, then headed out.

The heavy, ominous clouds, which had collected earlier against the barrier of mountains, were now rolling in, the dark masses billowing and churning, driven by an angry wind. In the distance, he could see lightning fork from cloud to cloud as bad-weather darkness settled in. After a lifetime of experiences with prairie storms, he knew this one was going to be a beaut.

The first fat raindrops splattered against his windshield as he squeezed into a parking spot in front of the building, and a bolt of lightning zigzagged across the turbulent sky just as he ducked into the condo entryway. But it was a good four seconds before the crack of thunder rumbled off in the distance.

There were several people waiting for the elevator, so Murphy took the stairs two at a time, and even the air in the stairwell was dreary with the impending storm.

Her apartment was heavy with gloom—the kind of gloom that enforced a thick silence. Just for an instant, Murphy thought both mother and babe must be asleep, but then he heard familiar fussy sounds from the nursery. Dropping his squall jacket on the back of one of the dining-room chairs, he crossed the living room.

The heavy dusk closed around him as he turned down the hallway, and the fussing increased in intensity.

Murphy paused just outside the nursery door, his heart giving a hard twist when he caught a glimpse of Jordan through the partially open door. She hadn't turned the light on, and the same dusk filled the room. She was in the process of changing their son's diapers, and J.J. was in full

temper, his arms and legs flailing, his shrill cry turned up
to full volume.

But it wasn't the state his son was in that riveted his
attention. It was Jordan's. And she was a mess—her eyes
puffy, her face swollen, and it was obvious, even in the
heavy twilight, that she had been crying for a very long
time. And this was no ordinary distress caused by lack of
sleep. This was more—much more. An odd, taut feeling
settled in his gut. Something was wrong. Very wrong. He
was about to speak, but she tried to comfort their son, new
tears slipping down her face. And there was something in
her tone—something so wrenching, so desolate, something
in the rush of frantic words—that kept him silent in the
heavy dusk.

"Shh, sweetie. Shh. Mommy's trying to hurry. I know
you thought I'd left you all by yourself, but I fell asleep and
didn't hear you. I would never leave you, no matter what.
I'm going to look after you until you're as big as your
daddy. Good moms don't ever leave their babies—not all
by themselves."

Holding J.J. in place with one hand on his belly, Jordan
abruptly covered her face with her other hand, her body
racked with sobs. And in that single instant, something
clicked in Murphy's brain and a cold, awful feeling rose up
in him. And like a surge of high-voltage current, a whole
bunch of pieces slammed together into one awful picture.
And he knew. Without a doubt, he knew. It was as if those
words had opened a book, and it was all there as plain as
day for him to see.

The cold radiated to his brain, and he stared at her, a sick
feeling swimming up through the shock. Abandonment. She
was talking about abandonment. The abandonment of babies. She had been abandoned as a child.

God, he should have put it together a long time ago. But he hadn't. Because he had been so caught up in his own wounded male pride, he hadn't seen beyond his own nose. Closing his eyes in a grimace of self-disgust, he berated himself. Lord, he had been so blind. So bloody blind.

Abruptly another realization pushed through the shock. If his wounded male pride had been a problem, Ms. Jordan Kennedy was armor-plated with pride. She probably had built her whole life on it. If she found out he had witnessed this little scene, it would be the ultimate humiliation for her. And shame was not something he would ever deliberately inflict upon her. Ever.

Propelled by that one thought, he turned, a sick sensation replacing the cold shock. Without making a single sound, he made his way down the corridor, and with the same stealth he collected his squall jacket and let himself out of the apartment.

He walked for miles in the rain. Until he was soaked to the skin. Until night settled in. He walked—head down, hands stuffed in his jacket pockets, so bloody ashamed of himself that he couldn't have lifted his head if wanted to. And sick to the soul. It had all been there, if he had only opened his eyes and seen.

The obsessive neatness. Her compulsion about meeting the rigid standards she set for herself. Yeah. Ms. Jordan Kennedy had sent out all the signals, all right. And abandonment explained everything. Her wariness about getting involved with him. Her walking out on their relationship. Why she never talked about family. It even explained why she wanted this child to know who his father was—that she was so adamant about J.J. carrying the Munroe name. It explained everything, all right. Even right down to the brush-off over the baby book. Only it hadn't been about the baby book. It had been about the blank page of the mother's family tree that had erected all her barriers again. It had been all about family—or lack thereof.

And with every new piece he figured out, a new wave of sickening recrimination would rise up to smack him in the face. He had been such a thick-skulled SOB. No wonder she'd walked out on him.

But—and this *but* came after two hours of walking a dozen miles and being damned cold and wet—but maybe this was his wake-up call. Because one thing was for damned sure: he was not going to give up on this woman. Not now. Not after he'd put the big picture together. Not after he'd seen her fall apart in that nursery. He wanted to comfort her so badly he could taste it, but he was going to have to earn that right. And maybe, just maybe this was their second chance.

It had quit raining by the time he headed back, and he had even dried out a little when he entered her building. But his shoes were still so saturated, he left them outside her door.

Jordan was sitting cross-legged on the sofa feeding the baby when he entered. Murphy experienced a sharp clutch around his heart. She looked like hell—pale, dark circles under her eyes, and he could sense a deep, unsettling despondency in her.

But she managed a wan smile when she saw him. "Hi," she said, trying to make her tone bright. "You look like a drowned rat."

He gave her a wry half smile. "I feel like a drowned rat. It was coming down in buckets out there." He hung his damp jacket on the back of a dining-room chair, then went into the nursery and changed into the dry sweat suit he'd left there. Heading back to the living room, he paused at the archway, his expression turning very sober as he studied her. He couldn't remember her ever looking so fragile. He wondered how she processed her history, especially when, he knew without a doubt, she would have laid down her life for her own child. And he wondered what it would be like, knowing your mother had abandoned you. Or what it was like, growing up knowing you were all alone.

Recognizing that kind of thinking was going to get him in big, big trouble, Murphy eased a deep breath past the sudden tightness in his chest. He told himself he was jumping to conclusions, that he didn't know for sure. But there was something deep in his gut that said he did.

Bracing himself to play out the scene, he entered the room and settled in the opposite sofa. Slouching down and propping his feet on the coffee table, he asked the question he knew she expected. "So how was your day?"

The baby had fallen asleep, and she did up her nursing bra and straightened her clothes. Then she looked up at him, giving him that tight little smile. "Well, it wasn't a hundred percent."

Murphy remembered his sister, the mother of the colicky baby, saying she wished she could just trade the kid in on a new model. Jordan didn't even joke about it. He dragged up a lopsided smile. "Maybe we should quit shooting for the honor roll and just start aiming for a good, solid C-minus."

A tiny glint of amusement appeared in her eyes. "You mean like some sort of remedial program?"

She truly did look like hell. Besides the pallor and dark circles, her hair was sticking out every which way from a disintegrating French braid. She was wearing one of his T-shirts again with damp spots from overproduction, and her slacks looked as if she'd slept in them—which she probably had. And to him, she had never looked more appealing. He wanted to touch her in the worst way.

Unobtrusively clenching both his hands, he managed another wry smile. "Let's face it. This kid has been sent here to test us."

Gazing down at the baby asleep in her arms, she gently stroked his black hair with her thumb. "He's a good boy," she whispered softly. "He just needs a more experienced mom."

It was as if she'd reached over and stabbed Murphy right in the heart, and he got such a sharp pain in his chest he almost winced. It took every ounce of strength he had to keep his hands to himself. His gaze never leaving her, he spoke. "No, he doesn't," he said, his tone quiet and gruff. "He already has the best possible mother he could ever have."

Her head came up and she looked at him, her expression one of sharp surprise. Then all of a sudden, her eyes filled with tears and she quickly looked back down and fussed with the baby's clothing. Murphy couldn't stand it anymore. And he knew it was a good thing he was sitting as far away from her as he was. His gaze was level and steady when he spoke. "I haven't been very easy on you in the past, and there have been times you've royally ticked me off," he said quietly. "But that old history is something else altogether. I want you to know, as far as this parent thing goes," he said, looking straight into her eyes and meaning every word of it, "you are an excellent mother, Jordan. Don't ever doubt that."

More tears appeared, and he made himself smile. "I love this kid to death, and I wouldn't part with him for a million bucks. But let's be frank here. He's a rotten baby, and he's giving us both fits. And if we don't both get a decent night's sleep here pretty soon, I am going to dump him off on Dr. Jackson for a couple of days.''

Jordan tried. She really did. She tried hard to smile. She tried to answer. But the tears just kept coming, and there was such a beseeching look in her eyes that Murphy simply reacted. He got up and went to her. Sitting down beside her, he put his arm around her shoulders and gathered her against him, then pressed her head against the curve of his neck. His voice husky with emotion, he spoke against her hair. ''I'm going to give you ten minutes to have a good cry, then we're going to talk.'' Giving the back of her neck a light squeeze, he rubbed his chin against her temple. ''And you're going to tell me what other nasty little self-doubts have been going through that pretty head of yours, okay?''

From the stifled sobs and the wetness along his neck, it was obvious she was doing exactly what he'd prescribed, but she managed a little nod. Murphy closed his eyes and swallowed hard. Lord, but he wanted to wrap her up in a tight embrace, and he wanted to stroke her hair, and he wanted a whole lot of other things, as well, but he forced his mind to go blank. This was about self-doubt and old, painful baggage. It was a mother thing. He had to deal with it without getting all tangled up in his own feelings—in the male thing.

She finally wiped her face against his sweat top, then took a big, tremulous breath. ''It's just that he's so little, and I don't know what I'm doing.''

For the first time in days, genuine amusement altered Murphy's expression. ''Hey. Look. We get them little *because* we don't know what we're doing. Just think what a hell of a mess we'd be in if we got him at six foot and two hundred pounds.''

He felt her smile, and he also felt some of the tension leave her body. "That might be so...." She hesitated, then she took a deep breath, as if fortifying herself. "But don't you worry if you're doing the right thing or not?"

Some of her hair had sneaked into his mouth, and he used that as an excuse to smooth the rest down. A familiar fullness was expanding in his chest, and he knew that he had to be plumb level with her. "Yeah," he said quietly. "I do. I worry about things like this damned colic, and I'd worry if he got sick. I'll worry about him making the right choices when he's older, and I'll worry about getting through adolescence." Needing to satisfy a deep, aching need inside him, he stroked her hair down one more time. "But do I worry about him growing up well-adjusted and self-confident? No. I don't. Because I know you're going to give him all the emotional security a kid could ever want or need. I know that, Jordan."

She lifted her head and looked at him, a strange assessing expression in her eyes. He didn't let his gaze waver from hers for even a second. And then, just like the baby-book incident, she pulled back into herself. Only this time, whether she realized it or not, she had taken a little part of his reassurance with her. She straightened up, carefully disentangling herself from the baby, leaving him with Murphy. "I think I'll go to bed," she said, her voice uneven. "It's been a long day."

Closing his eyes, Murphy cradled his sleeping son's head to keep from touching her, trying to disengage from the longing racing around inside him. And it was going to be a damned long night.

It was odd, the effect that one tiny encounter had had on him. A whole lot of feelings had gotten geared up again, and he had to make a conscious effort not to think about what it was like before, when they were lovers. The images were just too vivid; consequently, he stayed out of her bedroom at all costs.

But something else had happened, as well; a whole lot of other feelings had geared right down. Like the constant low-grade anger. Like his damned wounded pride.

And the guilt was the worst. Those awful hot rushes would nail him at the most unexpected times. Like early one morning on the way to the job site, when he'd spotted a thin, waiflike, blond-haired young girl waiting alone at a bus stop, her shoes and dress too big, her sweater two sizes too small, her eyes big and solemn. That image was burned into his brain, and it haunted him like a bad dream.

But after a couple of days of mentally beating himself to a pulp, he finally realized he had to give it a rest. Yeah, he'd been a self-centered bastard. And yeah, he shouldn't have to have a load of bricks fall on his head before he figured things out. Or at least *think* he had things figured out. But no matter how much he hated himself, or how much he wished he could go back in time and do it all over again, he couldn't. He couldn't fix the past. He could only deal with the present. As his mother said, he could only work with what he had.

But the image of that thin little girl—probably no more than ten and standing there all alone—drove him crazy, and there were times it would take shape in his mind, only it would be Jordan's features on that drawn little face. Every time he closed his eyes, he saw that kid. And the need to know gnawed at him.

And it was gnawing at him now. His hand braced on the aluminum window frame, Murphy stood looking out the dirty window of his construction trailer, his expression grim.

He kept spinning his wheels—and he tried to rationalize digging into her past. It wasn't that he wanted personal details. He just wanted to know the facts—to know if he was right or not. He'd made nothing but mistakes with her before, but this time his gut told him that he was right on the money.

Bending his head, Murphy wearily massaged his eyes. He was going to have to either fish or cut bait, because he couldn't keep this up much longer. He was slowly driving himself crazy.

Heaving a sigh, he raised his head and stared back out the window. He toyed with the idea of hiring a private investigator, but he just couldn't bring himself to do something that sneaky. He didn't want to dig up a bunch of old dirt; he just needed to know. Because he couldn't afford to screw up again. He'd been so wrong before, and for all he knew he could be dead wrong now. She could have fifty million relatives, six ex-husbands and have murdered her parents in their sleep.

Murphy straightened, a tiny flicker of humor surfacing. If he kept this up, he'd be a babbling idiot by the end of the week. Expelling another heavy sigh, he picked up a sheaf of papers clamped together with a bulldog clip and saw several Post-it notes with messages to call his mother. On top of everything else, his family was driving him crazy. He'd had so many calls from assorted kin that he couldn't count them all. Everybody wanted to know when they were going to get to meet this new baby, and most of them stepped over the bounds of good manners and prodded him about when they were going to get to meet Jordan. As if he could answer that. He riffled through the various work orders and delivery slips, then tossed them back down on top of his battered metal desk. He couldn't have been less interested if he tried.

He glanced at his watch. It was seven minutes after four. Making a split-second decision, he snagged his jacket from the back of his chair. To hell with it. He really didn't want to be here. He was going home.

Murphy stopped at his house, grabbed a shower and got some clean clothes, then headed to the supermarket and loaded up on groceries. It was just after six when he arrived at the condo. The apartment, which now looked as if it had survived a recent earthquake, was dead quiet. Silently closing the door behind him, he went into the kitchen and set the bags of groceries on the counter, trying hard not to make a sound.

With the same carefulness, he went to check on mother and child. He found them both in Jordan's bedroom, which also looked as if a wrecking crew had gone through. But it wasn't the clutter that caught his attention; it was the two curled up on the big bed. Jordan had fallen asleep on her side, her arm encircling the baby, her body curled protectively around their son. In spite of the sudden contraction in his throat, Murphy couldn't help but smile. J.J. looked just like a little old man sprawled out on his back, his arms by his head, his mouth open. And sound asleep for a change. Still smiling, Murphy shifted his gaze to Jordan, and once again, the specter of the girl at the bus stop superimposed itself, and his expression turned somber. He wondered if he would ever know the whole story.

Deciding he had picked at that enough for one day, Murphy closed the door and tiptoed down the hall, also closing the pocket door behind him. What he needed to do was stop thinking and do something productive for a change.

By seven-thirty, he had the living room and kitchen

mucked out and tidied up, and he had started dinner. He was in the kitchen, slicing vegetables for a salad, when he heard a soft sound behind him.

The chef's knife still in his hand, he turned. Jordan was standing at the entrance to the kitchen, her hair snarled into the worst case of bed-head he'd ever seen, the pattern of the quilt imprinted on her cheek. She looked as if she'd just come out of anesthetic. She staggered a little and caught herself, opening her eyes really wide. "You cleaned up," she said, her voice croaky from sleep.

He didn't grin, but he wanted to. "Yes," he said, "I did."

"You didn't have to do that."

He gave her a long pointed look, then went back to slicing mushrooms. "I did have to do. The board of health would have come in here and shut us down if I hadn't."

There was a faint raspy chuckle and the sound of a chair being dragged across the tiled floor, and Murphy turned. She'd already sat down at the kitchen table. But it was as if her spine wouldn't support her, and she flopped across the tabletop, her head on her folded arms. Her eyes closed, she spoke. "They would have never made it through the front door."

Grinning, Murphy scooped up the mushrooms and tossed them on top of the other salad fixings. "Tough talk for a zombie."

"I think somebody drugged the water supply."

He grinned again. "Sleep will do that to you."

She shifted her head and forced her eyes open. "Please tell me you're going to share that. I'm starving."

He dumped the dressing over the salad, set the bowl aside, then glanced back at her. "Well, you're in luck. We're doing it up in style tonight—T-bone steak, baked potatoes, spring squash. I was going to steam some broccoli, but that was on the baby's no-no list.''

She opened her eyes again and gave him a wry smile. ''I think everything is on the baby's no-no list. I think water gives him gas.''

Murphy responded with the required smile, but his gaze was thoughtful. It wasn't that it mattered one way or the other to him, but he knew she'd feel a whole lot better after a shower. But he was afraid if he suggested it, it could be taken as a criticism. He mulled it over in his mind and turned back to the counter, trying to put it as tactfully as he knew how. ''It's going to take a few minutes for the steaks to grill. So if you want to grab a shower while I'm here to watch out for Ivan the Terrible, now's your chance.''

He checked the squash in the built-in oven, then tossed the fork on the counter. Folding his arms, he leaned back against the cupboard. He could tell from the way she was lying there with her eyes closed, as if she didn't have a whole bone in her body, that she barely had the energy to breathe, let alone drag herself into the shower. But he knew she would feel so much better after. Knowing exactly how to get her moving, he watched her. Holding back a smile, he spoke, trying his darnedest to make the offer genuine. ''Would you like me to carry you?''

There was a lapse, just a split second, then her eyes flew open and her head came up like a clumsily activated marionette. Keeping his expression deliberately bland, he raised his eyebrows in query.

It was enough to launch her out of her chair. She was weaving like a drunk, but she made it to the hallway, disappearing around the corner. A smile tugged at his mouth. It was astounding what total exhaustion did to a person.

But what was even more astounding that evening was that

Baby Face cooperated. He woke up just as Jordan got out of the shower, and she nursed him first. Then she put him in his car seat on the floor, and he was content to make guppy faces. He was waving his hands around, that intent look on his face, as if he was trying to get his eyes to focus.

Jordan was a whole new person. Freshly scrubbed, clean clothes that even matched, her wet hair pulled up into some kind of knot on the top of her head. Although she didn't look totally rested, she looked refreshed, and that was the best either of them could hope for.

One hand braced on her thigh, she bent over the baby and softly smoothed down his thick black hair. J.J. made more guppy faces at her. "He's so cute when he does that."

Murphy brought the perfectly grilled steaks to the table and gave his son a dry look. "Are you sure it's him? I don't recognize him without his face all screwed up."

She gave the baby's head another soft caress. "Daddy's making fun of you, J.J. So you be sure and keep him walking the floor all night, okay?"

Thinking she was just a little too cute for words, Murphy slapped a steak on her plate. "Come and get it. We've probably got seven minutes to wolf it down before he tunes up." This was their first sit-down meal together since J.J.'s arrival, except for the lunch on the patio the day they went to the doctor's, and he hoped the tadpole would let them enjoy it.

Straightening, she closed her eyes and inhaled deeply. "Oh, God. This smells so good."

She pulled out the chair and sat down, and Murphy dropped a baked potato on her plate, giving her a scrutinizing look. Maybe someone had pulled a double switch. Or maybe she'd gone blind. He hadn't set the table the way she set the table. And he certainly hadn't come close to her meticulous standards. He'd more or less scattered the dishes and silverware around, the place mats didn't match and the unfolded paper napkins were simply tossed on top of the cutlery. The old Jordan Kennedy would have straightened everything up behind his back. But this new Jordan Kennedy acted as if she hadn't even noticed. She didn't square the place mat or center the plate on it. She didn't line up the silverware like little stainless-steel soldiers, nor did she make one single comment about the paper napkins. She placed the napkin across her lap and tucked in as if she hadn't seen food for a week.

Taking the first bite of steak, she closed her eyes again, clearly savoring every chew. "I don't think I have ever tasted anything this good in my whole life."

His eyes glinting, Murphy lifted a glass of lemonade. "You're a fake, Kennedy. You said that about the stew two nights ago."

She looked at him, a hint of a twinkle in her eyes. "I'm just trying to nudge you toward excellence, Munroe."

Bracing his elbows on the table, he rested his chin on his clasped hands and watched her. He couldn't remember her ever *teasing* him before—yeah, she had a keen and very sharp sense of humor, and she could spar with the best of them, but this was different. This was—just plain old teasing. He continued to stare at her. "I'd watch it, Little Mommy. It could backfire on you."

She grinned and blobbed more butter on her baked potato. "No, it won't. You've got your male ego to uphold."

Abruptly averting his gaze so she couldn't see his eyes, Murphy picked up his knife and fork. She sure in hell had that right. And he found himself back on that old treadmill, wondering about the story of her life.

J.J. started sucking noisily on his fist, and Jordan leaned

over and gave him the soother Murphy had finally bought out of sheer desperation. All the humor was gone, and there was a mother's concern and gentleness in her voice when she spoke. "Do you think he's really going to outgrow this before he goes to school?"

Murphy watched her, his expression thoughtful, then he looked down and carved a piece of steak. The only way he was going to find out anything was to try to pry it out of her. And the comment about school was as good an opening as any. Keeping his expression bland and his tone casual, he looked up at her. "Where did you go to school, Jordan?"

It was like watching shutters close. She became intent on her food again, and the silence was so heavy, he wasn't sure she was going to answer. Without looking at him, she finally gave him a stiff response. "I got my degree from the University of Alberta."

He continued on as if this was normal conversation. "What about high school?"

There was a tenseness in her voice he could almost feel. "Edmonton, as well."

High school in Edmonton. University in Edmonton. Well, it was a start. High school was probably as far he could go without having her run for cover. He took a deliberate detour. "How did you find the program at U of A?"

Murphy heard the relief in her voice. "Okay, for the most part. It's like any educational institution—some good instructors, some bad ones."

He looked up, a glint in his eyes. "And just how high up did you place on the dean's list?"

Giving a discomfited shrug, she looked down at her plate, a definite flush creeping up her face. It was kind of interesting, watching someone blush who was as fair as she was. She didn't look at him. "I did okay."

Right, he just bet she did. He watched her, waiting for her to finish her steak. As soon as she laid her knife and fork on her empty plate, he pushed the limit. "Is your family still in Edmonton?"

Her body went rigid with tension. Her tone was clipped when she answered. "No." Then she abruptly turned to their son, her tone one of brittle brightness. "Oh, Lord, J.J. You definitely need your diapers changed." She scooped him up and was gone in a flash. Pushing his plate aside, Murphy rested his elbows on the table and turned the tall glass around on the tabletop. Well, one thing was clear. He was never going to find out from her. Not in this lifetime.

Angry at himself for his vast stupidity, he picked up the glass and drained it. No wonder she'd walked out on him.

Chapter 5

It was not a good night. The only time the baby didn't fuss was when Murphy walked him. So they walked and walked, and Murphy thought and thought. On top of doing the endless colic shuffle, he had developed a doozy of a headache. And from ten o'clock—when Jordan went to bed—till two in the morning, he had eaten a whole roll of antacid pills. Murphy knew the acid in his gut had nothing to do with indigestion; it had to do with other things. Mostly the haunted look he'd put in Ms. Jordan Kennedy's eyes.

It was just after two when the baby started to squirm and make sucky sounds that indicated real hunger. He'd been so fussy that Murphy had tried feeding him just after midnight, but he only took a little—not enough to last very long. This, though, was the real thing. But he wanted to stall the kid for another half hour if possible.

He had the option of giving J.J. a bottle, but if Jordan went too long between feedings, her breasts would get so engorged that it would get really painful for her. And she was so wiped out, he'd like to give her another half hour if possible. Except he couldn't find the darned soother. Wasn't in the nursery. Wasn't in the car seat. Couldn't find it anywhere. Finally he laid J.J. in the crib and poked around his sleeper. "Hey, kid," he whispered. "We gotta find that yum-yum, or old dad will never keep you quiet."

J.J. gave a little squall and sucked noisily on his fist. He was not pleased about this nothing-in-his-mouth thing.

Murphy's search turned up zero yum-yums, and he knew he was going to have to widen the search zone. He pulled up the safety rail of the crib and locked it. "Just hang on a second, tadpole. I think there's a spare in Mommy's room. I'll have to check it out." Then Murphy did a very bad thing. He separated J.J.'s thumb from his fist and poked the digit into the baby's mouth. "You just suck on your thumb until Dad gets back, okay? We don't want Mommy to hear you fussing."

Closing the nursery door to muffle the sound, he went down the hall to Jordan's room, and being careful to not make any noise, he eased the door open. Only Jordan wasn't in her bed. The drapes covering the French doors to the small balcony were pulled open, and Jordan was outside. Dressed in a blue robe, she was standing with her hip braced against the balcony rail, staring across the street, her arms folded tightly in front of her. And even in the faint, ethereal light filtering up from the street lamps below, he could see the desolate expression on her face. He couldn't be absolutely sure in the dim light, but he also thought he could see the glimmer of tears.

She looked so forlorn and alone, and he remembered the little girl at the bus stop. A heavy, heavy feeling banded his chest, and he wished he could simply reach out and take all that hurt away. But he couldn't. Having a child of her own had probably resurrected a whole lot of old pain from her childhood. Feeling the way she did about J.J., she had to be wondering what had been so wrong, so distasteful about her that she had been abandoned. *If* she had been abandoned.

Knowing he couldn't just leave her like that, and knowing exactly who would chase all those old ghosts away, he made a snap decision. He spoke, his voice just a little gravelly. "Jordan?"

She quickly turned so her back was to him, and he saw her wipe her face.

Not waiting for her to answer, he tried to keep it light. "Our kid is rebelling, and he's made up his mind that he's not going to settle for anything but his mother."

Her voice was soft and uneven. "I'll be right out."

"He's in his crib, okay?"

"Okay."

Murphy studied her a moment longer, then closed the door. He went down the hallway, a determined set to his jaw. Okay. Enough was enough. He was going to have to give her something else to think about.

Entering the nursery, he yanked the light quilt off the bed and collected the pillow, glancing at his son. "You're going to dine outdoors, kid. So just keep your shirt on for a minute, okay?"

J.J. let out an annoyed wail. Murphy figured he could make do with his thumb for another five minutes.

Tucking the quilt and pillow under one arm, he went out onto the terrace. It was a beautiful night—full moon, a few clouds to make the night sky interesting. A little cool with a light breeze coming in from the mountains, but cool he could take care of.

The terrace was large and sheltered, with various sizes of

large urns of blooming flowers and potted plants scattered around, and the mixed scents from the flowers were filling up the night air with an unbelievable fragrance. Just what the doctor ordered. He adjusted the angle on one of the big, comfortable chaise longues, spread the quilt and fixed the pillow in place. Then he got the butane barbecue starter and lit every one of the citronella candles she had scattered around in various jardinieres.

Jordan, dressed in a midnight blue velour robe and with their son cradled in one arm, was just coming into the living room when he went back in. Without giving her a chance to get her bearings, he caught her free arm and piloted her toward the terrace.

He gave her what he hoped was his most disarming grin. "I promised my kid he could have a picnic outside tonight. So you're going to have to help me out on this."

She looked at him as if he'd just lost all his marbles. Her tone was even more incredulous. "What?"

Murphy aimed her toward the lounger he had fixed for her. "It's a gorgeous night, the flowers smell terrific and he put up a real stink that he wanted a picnic. So I said okay."

She looked at the chair, at the candles, then up at him. There was a hint—just a hint—of a smile in her eyes. "I see."

He maneuvered her into the chair, made sure she and their son were comfortably settled, then he pulled the quilt around both of them, making a cozy cocoon. "I'm damned glad you do. Frankly, I think it's bloody insane. But you know what a little tyrant he is."

She rewarded him with a little chuckle as she unzipped her robe, then fixed the nursing bra so J.J. could nurse. She winced as the baby latched on. Snuggling down, she whispered to her son. "I think your dad has finally flipped out, tadpole. He's just up and lost his mind altogether."

Murphy dragged over the other lounger so he was facing her, then straddled the long footrest and sat down. Slouching back into a comfortable position, he propped his feet up and crossed his ankles. "Probably. Chronic sleep deprivation messes up a guy's mind."

Her hair was loose, and there was an unusual wave left from the topknot she'd worn earlier. In the flickering light from the candles, it looked like spun silver. She watched the baby suckle at her breast, her expression intent and filled with such awe and tenderness that it made his chest hurt just to look at her.

Without looking up at him, she spoke. "I want to thank you for being here for him," she said, her voice soft and uneven. "I don't know what I would have done without you."

It was a kicker, that jolt of emotion he got square in his chest. And it took a long time before it eased enough for him to even think about speaking. And he knew it was time for a little honesty of his own. He looked at her, his expression suddenly very solemn. "And I don't know what I would have done without you," he said, his voice quiet. "I could name at least ten women who would have never had that baby, Jordan. So thank you for giving me a son."

She looked up at him, and this time she didn't try to pull back or hide. Tears glimmered in her eyes as she held his gaze. Her smile wasn't quite steady as she softly stroked their small son's head. "You're very welcome."

Murphy didn't get a wink of sleep all night. And he could have. Jordan and J.J. both fell asleep in the lounger, and they looked so cozy and comfortable snuggled up in the quilt, he didn't have the heart to wake them. So he ended up pacing from room to room, feeling as if the devil were chasing him.

He was in a hell of a mess. And he knew it. The lack of sleep and drop-dead exhaustion had pretty well knocked the hell out of any heavy sexual urges. But he was also left vulnerable in other ways. Maybe because he didn't have that low-grade anger to protect him any longer. Maybe because he'd done some growing up in the past few days. He wasn't sure about the whys; all he knew was that her softly spoken admission had knocked him for one hell of a loop, and it had also knocked the lid off a whole set of other feelings. And he was so jammed up inside with this thing for her, he felt as if his rib cage might crack wide open.

He wanted her. And it was separate from sex. This was something much bigger. He wanted *her*. In his life, as the mother of his kids, as his helpmate and partner, in good times and bad. He wanted to see her every morning when he woke up, and he wanted to go to sleep beside her every night.

But there was this roadblock between them, and nothing was going to change until they got past that. And maybe things wouldn't change even then. But he had to take a shot at it.

Once he made the decision, the awful knot in his stomach eased and the panicky feeling left him. Right or wrong, he was going to go for it. Feeling as if a huge load had been lifted off his shoulders, he went back out to the terrace. And he watched them sleep until the first vibrant fingers of summer dawn appeared—and for that space of time, Murphy felt as if all was right with his world.

It was eight o'clock when he arrived at the construction shack. In spite of the fact that he had only caught an hour's sleep from six to seven, he actually didn't feel all that bad. In fact, he felt pretty good. And the reason he felt pretty good was that he'd made the decision to quit living in limbo and take some action. Whether it was the right move or not, he had to make an attempt to get by that roadblock.

The first thing he did was phone a florist and order two dozen white long-stemmed roses to be sent to the condo as soon as possible. The second thing was phone up the Ford dealer he dealt with and place an order for a fully loaded Ford Explorer, with a top-of-the-line infant car seat already installed. And he didn't care what color it was or what they had to do to get it, but he wanted it ASAP.

The third thing. He got butterflies the size of dump trucks every time he thought about the third thing. It was underhanded and it was sneaky, and he knew Jordan would never speak to him again if she ever found out.

But he honestly believed if he was ever going to work his way past Jordan's defenses, he had to be damned sure what he was faced with. And there was only one way he could do it without hiring a PI, and he didn't even know if this way would work. But Jill Richards was his only hope.

Jill had lived across the street from the Munroes, and she and Murphy had started first grade together. They had been buddies all the way through school, and they had remained friends ever since. And Jill was Regional Director of Child Welfare Services.

But there was a catch with Jill. She was a single-parent mom, and she had a fourteen-year-old son that had been giving her all kinds of grief. Murphy had taken the kid under his wing last fall. He'd put him to work, let him know that he was going to come down hard if he screwed up, paid him a fair salary and dragged him to the gym twice a week.

It had turned out even better than he'd expected. The teenager's bad attitude lasted maybe three weeks, and not only did he end up with this big, strapping kid who could move kitchen appliances all by himself, but the kid was also turning into a first-class framer.

The reason he was putting off calling Jill was that he didn't want her thinking she had to do him this favor because she owed him. But Jill was his only chance. And the only person on the whole planet that he would trust with this.

Without weighing the pros and cons, Murphy flipped through the organizer on his desk. Tucking the receiver between his ear and shoulder, he used the end of a pencil to punch in the number for her private line.

Two rings and she answered. "Jill Richards."

"Hey, Jilly. How are you doing?"

He heard her heave a long sigh. "I knew this was too good to last. What's he done now?"

Leaning back in his chair, Murphy grinned and propped his feet on the battered steel desk, flipping the pencil against his thigh. "Lord, woman. Why do mothers always suspect the worst? He's out there working his butt off, hauling concrete paving blocks all over the place, earning an honest dollar."

"How heavy are the paving blocks?"

"About sixty pounds apiece and he's packing two at a time. So cut the kid some slack. He's doing nothing but getting humongous muscles."

There was a tinge of amusement in her voice. "I stand corrected. I apologize."

"So you should."

"So since my kid is the good citizen of the year, why are you bugging me?"

His expression turning dead sober, Murphy rolled the pencil between his fingers.

Her tone had altered when she prompted him. "Murph? What's the matter?"

He exhaled heavily and tossed the pencil on top of the paper clutter on his desk. "I need to ask you a favor, but I don't want you to get involved if it's going to cause problems for you."

"Murphy," she said, her voice dry and chastising. "I wouldn't do *anything* for you that might cause me problems, favor or not. I got into enough trouble because of you when we were kids. I don't need any more grief, thank you very much."

Murphy gave up a small smile, but his mood remained sober. He pinched a crease in his jeans, then let out another sigh and responded. "This is a big one, Jilly," he said, his tone serious.

Her tone was equally serious. "So let's hear it."

"There's this woman I'm involved with. I thought maybe we had something pretty serious going for us, but she walked out on me last fall."

"Is this the mother of your new baby boy, by any chance?"

Murphy slammed his feet down, glaring at the phone. "How in hell did you know that?"

"Hey. I have coffee with your mother at least once a week."

"Well, damn!"

"Now, now, Murphy."

"Do you suppose my mother has ever kept one thing to herself in her whole life?" he snapped.

There was a distinct chuckle from the other end of the phone. "Well, she doesn't tell me *everything*. For example,

I don't know what color underwear you have on this morning.'' There was a change in the level of sound, as if she'd just shifted the receiver. ''Congratulations, Pa. You're going to make an outstanding dad.''

The genuine goodwill in her voice made Murphy's throat close up a little. ''Thanks. He's pretty great.''

''We're going to have a long talk about this kid of yours later. But right now, why don't you tell me what's on your mind?''

He told her what he wanted and why. An old weariness had surfaced in him by the time he finished it all. ''I don't know if you can find out if she was ever a ward of the court. I don't know if those records are even still around.''

''Do you know her full name and birth date?''

He gave her both, then added, ''All I know is that she did her high school in Edmonton, and she went to university there. But that's about it.''

There was a long pause, as if she was making notes, then she spoke. ''I won't guarantee anything, but I'll see what I can do. Records that old, they might be on microfiche, or they might be gone. It's hard to say. But I'll give it my best shot.''

''Jill?''

''Hmm?''

''Just between you and me, okay?''

There was a quiet assurance in her voice. ''Just between you and me, Murph.''

''You can get me at the number here at the trailer or at my cell phone, okay?''

''It'll probably take at least a couple of days.''

Closing his eyes, he rubbed a sudden throbbing in his temple. ''Thanks, Jilly.''

* * *

Murphy couldn't concentrate on anything after that. He was antsy, wired and irritable. So he did his crew a favor and shut himself up in the construction trailer, forcing himself to process paper for a couple of hours. But that only made matters worse. After he snapped at one of the drywall crew for simply being at the wrong place at the wrong time, he decided he'd better give everybody a break and dump it all back on Marco's shoulders. Before he left, he wrote out a work order for his bookkeeper, instructing her to give his brother-in-law a hefty raise. Hell, the way he'd been staying away from work, Murphy should give him half of the business.

Needing to be away from everybody, he went home—to his still and empty house. He'd bought it as an investment a couple of years ago, intending on doing some cosmetic improvements, then putting it back on the market. But that hadn't turned out quite the way he'd planned. Because somewhere along the line, he'd developed a strong attachment for the place. The house was located in an older part of town that had, in its day, been very affluent. Big lot, huge trees in the yard, quiet street with hedges and stonework fences—it had everything he'd been looking for. The house, with its huge wraparound veranda, was basically a Dutch Colonial built in the late thirties. The story-and-a-half structure was sound, but the inside had been badly run-down and allowed to deteriorate. When he started the renovations, it had been about upping the value of his investment, which meant he had to decide what was worth saving time-wise, and what wasn't. But he found himself trying to save everything—the beautiful old lath-and-plaster walls, the water-stained press-molded ceilings, the solid-oak woodwork and trim that had so many coats of varnish and paint that it had taken several months to strip them down. And the floors, which, once stripped and sanded, revealed a very rare find in that they were made of spectacularly grained maple instead of the expected oak.

But as attached as he'd become to what his sisters referred to as the Eternal Work in Progress, it echoed with emptiness now. Pretty much empty of furniture, except in his bedroom and study. Empty of clutter. Empty of baby sounds. Just empty rooms in various states of renovation.

Knowing that kind of thinking was going to get him into more trouble than he could handle, he launched himself into a make-work project outside. He could tell from the state of the large perennial garden along one whole side of the backyard that Baba had been sneaking over, trying to instill some order into flower beds gone wild. And it was obvious that the little kitchen garden in the back corner of the lot had been freshly weeded. As crappy as he felt, Murphy had to smile—his grandmother thought everyone in the family should have a garden whether they wanted one or not. So she had taken it upon herself one weekend in the spring and planted him one. Which he needed like a hole in the head. But Baba loved to garden, and her own small yard didn't have the scope she needed, so if she couldn't garden there, she'd garden wherever it suited her.

But the make-work project had nothing to do with gardening. It had to do with the wobbly honeysuckle-covered trellis and gate leading to the backyard. The entire structure was so rickety, he was surprised it hadn't fallen down long ago.

It was going on two in the afternoon when his cell phone rang, and his heart gave a violent start. He swore at himself. This was nuts. It was going to be a damned long couple of days if he had that kind of reaction every time his phone rang. Forcing himself to get a grip on the wild flutter in his chest, he crossed to the flagstone patio, and to the round table where he'd tossed his shirt and cell phone. Knowing just how slow the wheels of bureaucracy moved, simple common sense told him he'd be lucky if he heard from Jilly by next week.

He flipped the mouthpiece open and pushed the button to make the connection, expecting it to be Marco. But he was dead wrong. It was Jilly on the other end, and he got such a violent hot-and-cold reaction, he had to sit down.

"Well, boyo, you called this one right."

His racing heart jamming up high in his chest, Murphy stared across the yard. "So what did you find out?"

"A fair amount. She was abandoned in the Edmonton bus depot when she was just a couple of months old. The only evidence found with her, besides clothing, was a scrap of paper with some numbers on it. The crisis worker figured it was her date of birth. I think the reason her file was still on record was because there was a rather extensive medical history attached to it."

Feeling suddenly sick to his stomach, Murphy braced his elbow on the table and rubbed his eyes. "What kind of medical history?"

"She was born with a severely clubbed foot, and from the records, it looked like she had other medical problems. She was in and out of the hospital a dozen times by the time she was six, and that doesn't include the surgeries for the foot. So consequently she went through quite a few foster placements. It looks as if it was her first foster mother who named her—her maiden name was Kennedy."

Turning so he squarely faced the table, Murphy picked up a twig that had fallen from the huge willow overhead, his expression drawn as he broke it into tiny little pieces. She didn't even have a name that was her own. Roughly massaging his eyes, he forced himself to speak. "Did the department ever try to track down her mother?"

"Yeah. But the investigation turned up zip. When a baby is abandoned in a place like a bus depot, it's pretty much a given that the mother is a transient." There was a lengthy pause, then Jill spoke again, her voice quiet with concern. "You okay, Murphy?"

He scraped the broken pieces of twig into a little pile. "Yeah."

"Is there anything else you want to know?"

"No."

"Okay. If that's it, then this report goes through the shredder, and I'm never talking about it again."

Murphy got a knot in his throat the size of a baseball. "Thanks, Jill."

There was the weight of understanding in her voice when she answered. "Anytime, Murph. And you take care."

Murphy sat staring at the tabletop for a long time after the call, a hollowness in his belly that seemed to shift from one place to another. So now he knew.

Straightening, he stretched out his legs and stared across the vast expanse of yard, absently watching the sunlight dapple through the leaves on the trees, the light breeze twisting the shadows. Now the sixty-four-thousand-dollar question was what was he going to do about it? He was a damned fine house builder. He wondered how good he was at building bridges.

Picking up his shirt, he got up. It was time he found out. Because if he put it off for even an hour, he'd never be able to face her.

His hair was still damp from his shower when he arrived back at Jordan's condominium, and he had so many knots in his gut that he felt as if a sackful of boulders were rolling around in there. The muscles in his face were so tight he was sure they'd crack if he so much as moved his mouth. And he felt like such a low-down creep for doing what he did—for going behind her back—that he wasn't sure he'd be able to look her square in the eye. He had needed to know; now he did, and he was going to have to carry the ball from here.

But Jordan made it easy for him. She must have been on the terrace and seen him park across the street, because she was waiting in the open door of her apartment when he got off the elevator. J.J., dressed in a weeny little T-shirt and diapers, squirmed and fussed in her arms, but there was a little-girl's excitement in her eyes. "Thank you so much for the flowers, Murphy. They are *so* beautiful—I couldn't believe it when they arrived." Clasping J.J. against her with one arm, she turned inside. "Come. You've just got to see them."

The roses. He'd forgotten all about ordering the damned roses. She led him into the taupe-and-ivory living room, where a huge, fragrant bouquet sat in the middle of the wrought-iron-and-glass table. He had a brother in the greenhouse business, so he knew a rose from a rose. And these were beauties.

The baby started to fuss and squirm some more, and she jiggled him to distract him, unable to take her eyes off the white roses that were tipped with a soft, soft peach. Murphy couldn't take his eyes off her. He'd never seen this Ms. Jordan Kennedy so unguarded, so animated. He wondered if she'd never received flowers before. That thought gave him another sharp jab, and he knew he had to keep it light. He watched her profile as he spoke. "I didn't send you any flowers," he said, his tone blunt.

She turned and looked at him, suppressing a smile. "No, of course you didn't." She reached over and picked the card out of the flowers, then handed it to him.

Dear Mom,
I'm sorry I'm giving you fits, but I promise I'll sleep through the night before I'm twelve.
                                        Love, James Jeffery.

Good. The florist had got it word for word.

He raised his eyebrows in surprise. "So the kid is sending you flowers. How did he get a credit card?"

Her eyes danced as she watched him. "He can't even print yet. So I'm almost positive he couldn't sign a charge slip."

Trying to keep his expression straight, he handed the card back to her. "These kids nowadays. Just charge everything. Now he's going to have to get a job."

She grinned, then set the card back in the flowers. "Maybe you can give him one laying cement or something."

Bam. Just like that, a whole lot of feelings kicked in. And he wanted to hug her so bad for playing along that it took every ounce of strength he had to keep his hands in the back pockets of his jeans. Lord, he had to keep a grip on that sort of thing, or he'd be so far in over his head, he'd never dig himself out.

The baby gave a couple of sharp wails, and the life and sparkle seemed to drain right out of her. Murphy gave Jordan a scrutinizing look. He could tell it had not been a good day. In spite of her burst of animation, she looked totally wiped out, and he wondered, all totaled, just how many hours of sleep she'd actually had over the past five weeks.

Instead of touching her like he wanted to, he reached out and took the baby from her. "Has he been giving you grief all day?"

"I think he's hungry," she said, the animation replaced by a kind of defeat.

"Did you have lunch?"

She nodded, and he got the feeling she was suddenly inches away from tears. He knew what she needed, and he came up with a plan. "I have a lot of running around to do," he said, which was an outright lie. "So why don't you feed him, then I'll take him with me—I can take a bottle just in case. But I'll have to borrow your car because of the car seat."

Her eyes immediately filled with tears, and he could tell she just wanted to lie down right there and never get up. "But you've had just as little sleep as I have."

Jiggling the baby, who was getting dead serious about this crying, Murphy gave her an off-center grin. "Nah. I sleep at work." Holding J.J. against him to keep the kid from smacking his face on his collarbone, he reached out and tucked some of her hair behind her ear. "Let's give this plan a shot," he said softly. "He always sleeps in the car— I'll drive him to Montana and back. You could both do with a nap."

She tried to respond with a smile, but it just didn't happen. The tears of drop-dead exhaustion spilled over instead. "I feel so stupid and incompetent," she whispered, looking down. "I just don't know what to do for him."

Grasping the back of her neck, he gave her head a gentle shake. "I'll make a deal with you. You can feel incompetent today, but it's my turn tomorrow."

He wasn't sure if it was just a sob, or if he did get a little laugh out of her. He thought maybe a bit of both. "Okay?" he asked softly.

She fished a balled-up tissue out of her pocket and wiped her nose. "Okay."

From the miles he covered driving his kid around, Murphy could have gone to Montana and back. Maybe even Wyoming. Just mile after mile up and down country roads. But as long as his son slept, he drove, and he was just thankful Jordan's car had a full tank of gas when they started out. But if he was being honest with himself, the drive was just as much for him as for J.J. And since he'd gotten through that first face-to-face with her after he'd gone snooping around in her past, Murphy needed to do some serious thinking. And he always thought best behind the wheel.

If he was going to get anywhere, he had to do his level best to try to be honest with himself. And he knew he had to own up to some of his own baggage here. He'd never wanted to admit it—in fact, he had gone to inordinate lengths not to admit that her leaving had damned near killed him. So he'd let anger fill up that hole, and he had been hiding behind it ever since, as if it were some sort of heavy armor. But now that anger was gone. And one of the truths he had to admit to was that nothing had changed as far as his feelings for her were concerned.

No, that wasn't exactly accurate. Some things had changed. Finding out the truth about her had explained a whole lot. Now that he had the big picture, he understood why she was the way she was. And he even understood why she had walked out in the first place. That was her defense mechanism. But only now, knowing everything he did about her, did he fully realize the raw courage it had taken for her to face him when she'd come to tell him she was pregnant. But she had done that because she desperately wanted something for her baby. And now. Ah, God—now he desperately wanted something for them all.

Which meant that somehow he was going to have to convince her that he was in it for the long haul. And somehow prove to her that she was—was what?

A thick ache started in Murphy's chest, and he had to rub his eyes to keep them from blurring. He'd always let her know he had wanted her. But he now realized she needed far more than that—she needed to know that he *needed* her. Somehow he was going to have to make her see that she mattered to him. And then maybe she could learn to believe that she had no reason to run. He knew what had happened last time—that he had gotten too close and she had bolted. But things were different now. He was a whole lot wiser. And there was J.J. So all he had to do was get her to understand that they had something worth hanging on to.

It should be so easy, but Murphy didn't kid himself. She was like a wary, terrified animal that would shy away the instant anyone got too close. And he knew that trust wasn't something that blossomed overnight. He had also let her play the game her way last time, and that had gotten him nowhere. But then, he'd been damned stupid in the past. Now that he knew her background, though, he could see he had made one very major mistake. Yeah, she'd walked, all right, but he had let her. That had been the stupidest thing he had ever done. But his wounded male ego had gotten in the way—which probably reinforced her wariness of people in general, and him in particular. With his bloody self-righteous attitude, he'd deserved to have her walk out on him.

But where to go from here? He could see his own accountability for what had gone wrong in the past. But he wasn't sure what to do about it. Last time, he had toed her line and let her call the shots, and that left him out in the cold. Maybe this time he had to change his strategy. Maybe he needed to crowd her a little. Maybe lay down a line of his own.

His cell phone rang, and he answered it.

"Murphy Munroe."

His mother's voice was rich with amusement. "I'm so glad you still know who you are."

Murphy gave a wry grin. "Don't get cute, Ma. I'm a little cranky lately."

She chuckled, then spoke. "Is now a good time to talk, or are you busy?"

"No. Now's fine. What's on your mind?"

There was a brief hesitation, then he heard her take a breath. "Your dad and I are in a Labor Day golf tournament this weekend, so we're planning on having the annual barbecue a week late this year. The whole family is coming over. So your dad and I thought it would be really nice if you brought Jordan and baby along. We're all dying to see that son of yours."

Driving with one hand, Murphy let his gaze sweep over the countryside. He mulled it over for a minute, then answered, his tone quiet. "Let me run it by Jordan first."

"Do try to persuade her to come, Murphy. Both your dad and I think it's important that she get to know the rest of the family."

His own tone was equally serious. "So do I, Mom."

Jordan was still out cold when they returned to the condo. She was on her bed, asleep on her side with her hands tucked under her face, her long, long lashes fanned out against her cheek. She looked so damned vulnerable and defenseless that Murphy's throat cramped shut, a terrible sense of loss swarming up in him. Dragging up some inner reserve, he made himself disconnect from that kind of reaction.

Watching her sleep, he continued to jiggle J.J. He did not want to wake her, but J.J. was sucking on both fists, and Murphy knew if he let her go any longer without a feeding, she was going to be in real agony.

Tucking his son against his shoulder, he sat down in the curve of her legs, then gave her a gentle shake. "Jordan, honey," he said softly. "You're going to have to wake up. We've got a kid here who's trying to eat his elbows."

She stirred and rolled over on her back, her eyes still closed. The front of the navy-blue T-shirt she had on—his navy-blue T-shirt—had two large damp spots on it, and he had to smile to himself. The old Miss Prim and Proper Jordan would have been appalled. A wisp of hair was stuck to her face and he lifted it off, the now-familiar achy feeling rising in his chest. He didn't think he'd ever seen her look more beautiful than she did right then. J.J. let out an I'm-getting-really-ticked-off mewl, and Murphy gave her another light shake. "Sorry, babe, but it's time to open those eyes."

Her eyes still closed, she wet her lips. "I can't," she said, her voice thick with sleep.

The hint of orneriness in her tone made Murphy smile. He tightened his grip on his squirming son. "Do you want me to give him a bottle?"

She sighed and dragged her hair back off her face with both hands. "No, I'll be a mess if I don't feed him." Finally forcing her eyes open, she lay still for a moment, then struggled into a sitting position. Still clearly groggy, she stacked the pillows behind her, then reached for the baby. "Here," she said, her voice still rusty. "Let me have him."

Normally Murphy did not hang around her bedroom—for obvious reasons—and normally he would have left at that point, but two things kept him there. One was his new strategy—to not give her the room he usually did. The second reason was that she was so out of it, he wasn't entirely sure that she wouldn't simply pass out and topple over in a coma.

She didn't even seem to notice that he'd moved into her territory. Her attention was focused on the baby, but once J.J. was nursing, she tipped her head back against the pillows and closed her eyes. "Lord," she murmured thickly, "I feel as if I've been drugged."

Drawing one knee up on the bed, he braced his arm on the other side of her legs. A glimmer of humor tugged at his mouth. "Maybe you have."

She opened her eyes and checked the baby, then looked at Murphy, a woeful look in her eyes. "Do you suppose we're ever going to catch up on our sleep, or are we going to be tired until he leaves home?"

Grinning at her, Murphy met her gaze dead-on. "Well, I think we'd better be wide-awake and on our toes before he turns sixteen. Munroe kids don't have a great record of staying out of trouble at that age."

She gave him a wry look. "I can't tell you how glad I am you told me that."

Murphy studied her face, watching as she slowly caressed J.J.'s head. Then he steeled himself and broached the reason for his mother's call. "Mom called me while we were out driving," he said, trying to keep his tone offhand.

She kept her gaze averted and focused on the baby, but Murphy saw her retreat. "Oh?"

Watching her like a hawk for any telltale signs, he continued. "My parents always have a big end-of-summer family barbecue. And they've planned it for next weekend." He waited for a moment, then dropped it on her, still keeping it very casual. "She wants me to bring you and J.J.—they're all getting pretty anxious to see this phantom kid."

Her sudden tension was so apparent, it was as if Murphy had plugged right into it. She didn't speak for a moment, then finally answered, her tone artificially offhand. "I don't really think it's necessary for me to go. You can take J.J. on your own."

A week ago, her response would have ticked him off, but he could see the anxious flutter in the pulse point in her neck. Reaching out, Murphy hooked his knuckles under her chin and exerted pressure, forcing her to look at him. His gaze was dead serious. "The invitation was to all of us, Jordan," he said. "Mom thinks it's important that you get to meet the rest of the family, and so do I." Smoothing his thumb along her jaw to try to soften his approach, he gave her a lopsided smile. "And besides, I can't leave you at home. You're J.J.'s dinner."

She stared at him, the color gone from her face, her eyes wide with apprehension. And Murphy knew this invitation alarmed her like little else had. He tried to keep his tone even as he met her gaze. "I want you to come, Jordan. I want you to meet my family."

She held his gaze for a moment, then abruptly looked down, fussing with the collar on J.J.'s sleeper. She finally wet her lips and whispered. "I think your mother is just being polite."

He quietly chastised her. "My parents don't play those kinds of games, Jordan. If she invited you, it's because they both want you to come." He caught her free hand and threaded his fingers through hers, giving it a little squeeze as he smiled at her. "And I promise I'll stick to you like glue."

She tried to smile, but anxiety stiffened her face. Trying to win her over, he gave her hand another squeeze. "Just say yes, okay?"

She stared at him a moment longer, then gripped his hand and drew a deep breath. "Okay," she said unevenly.

Murphy wanted to hug her. Now he knew exactly how it felt to win a ten-million-dollar lottery.

Chapter 6

By the following day, Murphy wished he had never mentioned the family barbecue. What he should have done, he realized in retrospect, was catch her unawares. If he'd been smart and had used his head, he would have said nothing, come up with some excuse to get her and the tadpole into the car, then simply kidnapped them both. By lunchtime, she had worried herself into a nervous wreck and changed her mind nine times. But she had finally exhausted herself and gone to bed.

Wanting to keep the apartment as quiet as possible, Murphy was sitting on the terrace in the shade, rocking his son in the canopied garden swing, both of them trying to catnap. J.J., God bless him, had fussed so much during the night that neither Pa nor Ma got much sleep. Murphy was beginning to feel as if he were suffering the aftereffects of a five-day drunk. But—touch wood—Little Stuff had finally worn himself out and had crashed on Murphy's chest, sucking sporadically on his soother. Which was not a good sign. Nope, that meant the kid wasn't sound asleep. And Murphy didn't want to do anything to upset the status quo. He knew, as sure as he breathed, that if he quit rocking for even an instant, James Jeffery's little eyes would pop open, and that would be that. He wondered how the hell single parents could live through a colicky baby—they must finally disintegrate from sheer exhaustion.

His bare feet planted on the terrazzo flooring, Murphy kept the motion going, little bursts of colored shooting stars dancing behind his closed lids, the wooden slats of the swing cutting into the back of his neck. He didn't even care. He was so damned tired, he was sure, given the opportunity, he could sleep for seventy-two hours straight.

"Murphy—about the barbecue—I don't think it's a good idea if I go. Maybe you'd better call your mother back and tell her I can't make it."

Murphy didn't have the strength or energy to open his eyes. "Go to bed, Jordan."

He could almost hear her wringing her hands. "No, I've made up my mind. You take J.J. on his own."

Murphy just kept rocking the swing, aware that baby drool was running down his bare chest and his son's cheek was stuck to his skin. "I've made up *my* mind," he said, sounding just a little cranky. "You're coming to the barbecue if I have to throw you over my shoulder and bodily haul you there."

There was absolute dead silence. Then a very odd sounding "Pardon?"

"Give it up, Jordan. We're not going around that track one more time. You're coming to the barbecue."

He really expected her to flounce off in a huff, but he heard her sit down on one of the chaise longues. Dredging

up every ounce of energy he had, he opened one eye. She
looked frazzled from the top of her head to the tips of her
toes. And she was sitting in such bright sunlight it nearly
blinded him. Letting his eye drift shut, he wiggled his free
hand at her. "Come here. Sit in the shade. "

There was a brief hesitation, and he wiggled his fingers
again. He really didn't expect her to move, so he was surprised when he felt her settle on the swing beside him. Without moving his head or opening his eyes, he caught her
around the neck and pulled her head down on his shoulder.

Lightly caressing her upper arm, he spoke. "Let's face it,
Kennedy. If he keeps this up, we'll both likely be dead from
exhaustion before the weekend, and neither one of us will
have to worry about the barbecue."

He got a strained little laugh. There was a brief silence,
then she spoke, an odd tone in her voice, as if she was trying
to cast her son in a positive light and was afraid he would
disagree. "He's really good when he isn't fussing," she said
softly.

Which was hardly ever. But Murphy gave her what she
needed to hear. "He's an angel when he's not fussing.
Which scares me more. Having been a small boy myself, I
know what's really going on when they're behaving like
little angels."

That got another chuckle out of her, but this one was
genuine. In spite of her response, Murphy could feel her
grow heavy against him, as if she was dozing off. Then she
said ever so softly, with a quiet wistfulness, "It must have
been so nice, having a big family."

Murphy's heart thundered. His eyes flew open and he got
nailed with such a shot of pure adrenaline that he thought
his heart was going to leap right out of his chest. A first.
An absolute, mind-blowing first. Not once, in all the time

he had known her, had she ever made any reference to family—hers, his or otherwise. Sure, she'd asked the polite, requisite questions about his—how many, who did what. But this was different. This was Ms. Jordan Kennedy expressing what was inside of her. This was a tiny glimpse past all the barriers.

The sudden cramp in Murphy's throat was so tight that he couldn't even swallow, and he closed his eyes and locked his jaw, drawing her imperceptibly closer. Someday, damn it, he was going to get the chance to prove to this woman just how much he loved her. Someday.

Willing away the awful ache, he rubbed his hand up her bare arm. "It has its moments."

As if totally separated from the rest of her body, like a leaf falling off a tree, her hand drifted down his chest onto his lap, and she shifted her head on his shoulder and let out a long sigh. "Nice," she murmured.

Oh, yeah, Murphy thought, suddenly wide-awake, the weight of her hand on his groin sending shock waves of raw heat pumping through him. Oh, yeah. He was at the brink—at the absolute brink—of losing himself in the sensation, of letting himself go, of moving his hips up against the weight of her hand. Then common sense and a shred of decency kicked in. Gritting his teeth, he closed his eyes and dug his neck against the slats on the backrest, trying to give himself something else to think about.

It took a while, but he finally willed away the response and opened his eyes to stare at the bright blue sky, concentrating on how good it felt to have her curled up against him with his son asleep on his chest. It filled him up so much inside it was almost enough. Almost.

It seemed as if he'd just fallen asleep when the annoying sound of the intercom buzzer nagged him awake. The arm he had around Jordan had gone to sleep, and the back of his neck felt as if it had been impaled on steel spikes. Stretching his eyes open, he checked his watch behind Jordan's head. He'd been out cold for over an hour.

The buzzer sounded again, and Jordan stirred. "Phone?" she said, her voice mushy with sleep.

He shook his head to clear away the fog, then lifted J.J. off his chest. "No. Intercom."

Without saying anything, she took the baby as Murphy stood up. He crossed the patio, stopped just inside the door and picked up the intercom phone. "Yeah?"

"Mr. Munroe?"

"Speaking."

"Ken Martin. I'm a driver for Johnson Ford. I have a delivery here for you."

Murphy shook his head to wake himself up. His mind was really falling apart. He'd totally forgotten that the new, top-of-the-line sport-utility vehicle was to be delivered today. He scrubbed his face to try to rid himself of the last trailers of sleep. "I'll be right down."

Picking up his shirt off the chair, he wiped baby stickies off his chest with the tail and slipped it on. Jordan was coming through the patio door, the baby still asleep and nestled against her. She looked as if she'd just crawled out of a Dumpster. A flicker of humor surfaced. She also looked as if she could do with a jolt.

Grasping her by the arm, he pulled her along. "Come on," he said. "We need to go downstairs."

Looking as if she didn't even know her own name, let alone comprehend a whole sentence, she mutely let him propel her to the foyer. Picking up a key to get back in, he opened the door and just as if he were the little tugboat, he piloted her out.

It was a kid about nineteen who had delivered the Explorer, and Murphy signed the delivery form, tipped him and took the keys.

Jordan had yawned so hard her eyes watered, and she was so out of it, he was sure if he gave her a poke on the shoulder, she would simply topple over.

The midnight blue truck was parked in front of the condo. And his directions had been followed to a T. A huge cluster of balloons was hooked under the door handle, and the card was stuck under the windshield wipers.

Without saying anything, he took J.J. from her. He grinned to himself. It was going to take a while for everything to click into place. She had this dazed look on her face, as if not one single thing were making any sense. She glanced at the truck, then back at him, still not getting it. Restraining a smile, he handed her the keys.

It was as if he'd dumped her in ice. She went so still, he was sure she even quit breathing. Finally taking a breath, she looked from him to the truck, her face transfixed with confusion, then she looked back down at the keys in her hand. He could actually see all the pieces fall into place, and her eyes widened as she looked up at him, a stunned expression on her face. "Oh, my God."

Murphy wanted to laugh. It had taken her ten minutes, but she'd finally figured it out.

Raking her hand into her hair to hold it back, she again stared at the keys in her hand, her shock as transparent as glass. Finally she looked up at him again, and he could see she was on the verge of losing it.

"I can't accept this, Murphy," she whispered, her voice breaking.

This time he had her. He knew she'd never accept a gift like that from him. And he *knew* that was exactly what she would say, but this time—ah, this time—he had done an end run on her. Holding his son against him, he raised his eyebrows. "You're getting ahead of yourself, Kennedy. You'd better read the card."

She gave him a bewildered look, then went over and took the card off the windshield and opened the envelope. The card had blue bunnies on it. Which seemed appropriate, given the recurring nightmares he'd had before the baby was born. He remembered word for word what he had written.

Dear James Jeffery,
I want you and your mom to have something big and strong and safe to go see Dr. Jackson in. So this is for you. But you have to let Mom drive until your feet reach the pedals.

                                                    Love, Dad.

He'd wondered what her reaction would be—prim and prissy, annoyed, cool and distant—and he was pretty sure he had left her no place to go. But with Jordan, you never really knew for sure. Except in a million years he would have never expected her to do what she did. She just sort of unraveled before his very eyes. Laughing and crying, she came into his free arm, put her arms around his waist and held on for dear life.

Going dead still, Murphy stood there, feeling as if he'd been run through another high-voltage regulator. Then his lungs kicked in and started to work, and he hugged her hard against him, a dozen feelings breaking loose like some crazy logjam. Pressing his cheek against her hair, he clenched and unclenched his jaw, his heart going into overdrive. She had totally bowled him over. It was the first spontaneous response he'd ever had from her except in bed, and he was so staggered by it, he felt as if the world had spun right off its axis. Knowing if he started thinking with the wrong end of his body, he could make a really stupid move here without even trying, he took a deep breath and tightened his arm around her. "Now remember, Jordan. You can't give him the keys, no matter how much he whines."

She was still doing that laughing-crying thing. "I won't."

Murphy would have been content to hold her like that the entire night, but Little Stuff's diaper was very wet and if Murphy stood there like that much longer, it was going to be a damned sight more than his emotions that got out of hand. "Wanna take it for a test drive for him?"

She wiped her face on his unbuttoned shirt. "We need a car seat," she said, her voice very uneven.

His heart so full that it felt as if it might split wide open at any moment, he pulled a fast one and brushed his mouth ever so lightly against her hair. "Taken care of, ma'am. You just need to get in and drive."

She looked up at him, her eyes all red and bleary, but she tried to smile. "This is pretty outrageous, even for you."

He grinned down at her. "Nah. I've got this great accountant who's going to fudge my books."

Seeing her emotions were starting to get away on her again, he gave her a quick hug and hauled her around to the driver's side. "Come on. A quick spin before Mighty Mouse roars."

She tried to put on the brakes. "But I don't have my driver's license."

"To hell with your driver's license. The kid wants to try out his new set of wheels."

The drive lasted maybe ten blocks, then J.J. woke up and let the whole world know he was hungry.

Murphy didn't know whether it was just because she was so bloody tired that her guard had slipped, or if it was because of the goofiness over the truck, but there was a difference that night. For the first time in months, Murphy felt as if he could deliberately touch her without setting off alarm bells. And he wanted to hold her so badly that he felt it right down to the soles of his feet. But he wasn't going to rush his fences. One step at a time.

It was as if the truck had knocked her off her tracks for one whole day, and she drifted around in a weird, detached state. Murphy didn't let optimism override common sense, though. He knew that floaty daze of hers was probably nothing more than sleep deprivation. She had only mentioned the family barbecue once, and that time he pretended he didn't hear her. And surprisingly she let it drop.

He figured he had it made. But his smugness came back at him, and the following four days were straight from hell.

First of all, there were some major problems on the job site. Then Jordan and baby both had their six-week checkups, which required more strategizing, organizing and equipment than the average military campaign. Murphy had no idea you needed so much stuff to take one tiny baby out for one afternoon—thank God he'd bought the Explorer. He probably should have bought a bus. One thing was for sure: they never would have stuffed everything into her car.

Of course, J.J. was an absolute angel at Dr. Jackson's. He was all cute and full of smiles. Murphy was beginning to think the kid was simply giving them grief for the hell of it. The tadpole checked out one hundred percent. Murphy didn't know how Jordan checked out. By the time they got to her appointment, J.J. had started fussing, so Murphy had spent the entire time walking up and down the corridor. And by the time they made it back home, he and Jordan were both wiped right out.

It didn't get any better, at least not as far as J.J. was concerned. James Jeffery had only been teasing them with his good behavior during his trip to Dr. Jackson's. At home, it was a different story altogether. The longest he slept at a crack was two hours, and one night both he and Jordan fell asleep at the dinner table. It would have been funny if it hadn't been so pathetic.

And the closer it got to the weekend, the more fidgety Jordan became. Except it was worse than that. Jordan dithered. He never would have figured her for a ditherer. But she was. She'd paced back and forth when she should have been sleeping. And she couldn't hold two thoughts together to save her soul. She wasn't going to go. Then she was. Then she thought it would be best if Murphy took J.J. by himself. If Murphy had had the energy, he would have tied her to the bed. Up until the baby arrived, he didn't know she was capable of that kind of hand-wringing anxiety. But then, he'd never seen her in tears before, either. And now he was getting a good dose of both. He figured it was hormones. All the books said it was hormones. But what in hell did the books know anyway? They hadn't been one bit of help with the colic.

Every once in a while, though, she would finally wear herself out and crash from sheer exhaustion, and sometimes he would simply sit and watch her sleep. Then guilt would swoop in, and he'd get knots the size of bulldozers, hoping he was doing the right thing by pushing her into going. It got so tense that he was damned near as bad as she was.

By Saturday—the day before the family barbecue—they

were both in such a fog of exhaustion that Murphy's short-term memory had deteriorated into ten-second bits, and he finally crashed himself. He slept for three whole hours. When he got up, Jordan was drifting around like a waif, and every time he said something to her, she'd look at him with those huge gray despairing eyes. It got to the point where he couldn't take it anymore, and he sent her to bed.

He was beginning to feel like such a total heel that he had pretty much decided to let her opt out. But when she got up, she didn't bring it up, so neither did he. He persuaded her to go back to bed just after eight that evening. Once she was lying down, he took J.J. out to the terrace, and they did the swing thing. His kid was turning into a real swinger, and Murphy could usually coax at least two hours of sleep out of J.J.—just as long as he kept the motion going.

They actually made it to three. And it was obvious that J.J. was just plain hungry when he woke up. Peeling away the light blanket he'd covered his son with, he entered the kitchen with the intent of getting a bottle of breast milk out of the fridge. All the lights were off in the apartment, except the night-light under the built-in microwave. But even in the semidarkness, Murphy caught a glimpse of Jordan pacing the well-worn loop that ran through the living room, dining room and foyer, looking so pale and stressed it nearly broke his heart.

He slid the screen shut on the patio door, and she jumped and covered her heart, whirling to face him. For a minute, he thought she was going to pass out cold.

His son squirming against him, he turned on the kitchen light and gave her a pointed look. "You should be in bed, Jordan," he said, his tone quietly censuring. "You're absolutely exhausted."

She made a tense gesture toward the hallway. "I thought you were in the nursery. The door was shut."

He stared at her a minute, then went to the fridge to get the bottle. She intercepted him. "Here," she said, reaching for the baby. "I may as well feed him." Clearly avoiding Murphy's gaze, she left the room, turning down the hallway to her bedroom.

Murphy wearily dragged his hand down his face and exhaled heavily. He didn't know what in hell to do, but right then he was too tired to think. Stripping off his shirt, he headed for the second bathroom. Maybe a shower would wake him up enough to talk to her.

The scalding-hot, then ice-cold shower did wonders, and he felt almost human when he knocked on her bedroom door. Her soft "come in" had that kind of hush that told him J.J. was either asleep or close to it. The light on the table was turned down low, leaving the room in muted shadows. It was clear from her done-up buttons that she had finished feeding the baby, and she was bending over him on her bed, changing his diapers.

She didn't look at him, and he could hear that she was very close to tears when she spoke, her voice breaking. "He's probably going to be so fussy tomorrow, and your family will think he's a terrible baby."

Murphy stared at her, his heart skipping at least three beats as realization rushed from the top of his head to the tips of his rocked-out toes. Well, hell, he'd never even considered it from that angle.

Finally getting his thoughts together, he went over to the bed and slid his hands under his sleeping son, gently moving him to the cradle. Careful not to wake him, Murphy covered J.J. with the Baba Blankie. Without saying a word, he caught Jordan by the wrist and hauled her down on the bed alongside him. Drawing a deep, steadying breath, he lifted her head onto his shoulder, then wrapped her up in a tight embrace.

Inhaling the scent of her, he rested his head against hers, his chest so jam-packed with emotion he could barely draw a breath, let alone speak. "Jordan, honey," he said softly, tightening his hold. "Let me tell you about my family." He smoothed down her hair, then began rubbing her back, trying to reassure her. "There have been so many babies through our house that everybody just takes each one as they come. It wouldn't enter any of their heads to judge him. They're going to make a big fuss over him, then give us enough advice to sink a tanker." Breaking his own rule, he brushed a light kiss against her forehead. "They'll love him, Jordan. Warts, colic and all."

He heard her swallow hard, then she whispered against his neck. "He doesn't have any warts."

Murphy smiled, loving the fact that she was right there to champion their son. Giving in to impulse, he did what he'd been dying to do for days. He hugged her hard. "I was speaking of figurative warts, darlin'. We all have 'em, you know."

He felt her smile, and some of the tension left her and her body softened just a little. His head still resting against hers, Murphy continued to stroke her back as he stared up at the ceiling of her bedroom, trying to find exactly the right words. Giving her another light squeeze, he spoke. "I know that meeting my family is going to be a little daunting for you," he said, his tone very quiet. "But I really want you to come. They're good people, Jordan."

Her hand closed into a fist on his chest, and her voice was still a tight little whisper when she answered. "But maybe it's best if I don't go, if they never get to know who I am.''

Shifting his head so he could see her, he caught her under the chin, prompting her to look at him. His gaze was absolutely sober. "No matter what happens," he said, his voice gruff, "you're always going to be J.J.'s mom, and that makes you a part of the whole Munroe clan. That's just how it is with my family." She stared at him, and he caught glimpses of fear and uncertainty, but he also caught a glimpse of something else—something like wistfulness— something that made his chest plug up. It cost him big time, but he somehow managed to give her a reassuring smile. "And they are all going to have such a good time, telling you about all the rotten things I did."

It was almost as if she were huddling in his warmth. "What things?" she whispered.

Unable to handle the somber look in her eyes, he tucked her head against his neck, smoothing his hand up and down her bare arm. He wanted nothing more than to just hold her, to shield her from her past, but he made himself talk instead. "My father is going to tell you about the time I dropped the garage door on his brand-new car, and my mother is going to tell about the time I cracked both my wrists trying to hang glide off the roof of the garage in this contraption my brother and I built. And my sisters are going to tell how Mitch—my big brother—and I used to make life hell for their boyfriends." He rubbed his jaw against her hair and tightened his hold. "Stuff like that." There was a brief silence, then he gave her another little squeeze to get her attention. "But I gotta level with you, Kennedy. One of the reasons I want you to come is because I'd really rather not face them on my own."

She abruptly shifted her head and stared at him, trying to

determine if he was lying. He wasn't. She held his gaze for an instant longer, then nodded. "All right. I'll go."

He smiled back at her. "Thank you."

Murphy really, truly expected her to make some excuse and get up, but she didn't. Instead she turned her face into his neck and grasped the back of his shirt, hanging on for dear life. It knocked the wind right out of him, and he closed his eyes and tightened his hold on her, his whole body responding and his pulse running totally amok. A hot want sizzled through him, and he clenched his jaw against the rush, his lower body growing hard, his swollen flesh pulsating. He tried not to react, tried not to respond, but it was damned near impossible, especially when some sixth sense told him that if he pressed her just a little, she would give him what he wanted. But a sliver of rationality held him back. If he was ever going to build a lasting bridge with her, next time she was going to have to come to him.

Except his throbbing body had a mind of its own, and he had to block out the ache that was urging him to turn on his side and press her full length against him. If it got too bad, he had the choice to leave, but he knew that wasn't even a remote possibility. He would suffer the agony for the pure relief of having her in his arms. And he'd hold her all night if he got the chance.

Murphy had no idea what brought him sharply awake. But he knew exactly where he was and whose weight was pressing against him. Ever so carefully he tightened his hold on her, then pressed a kiss against her hair.

The table lamp was still on, its light muted and suppressed by the classy bordello shade, and he opened his eyes wide, feeling as if he'd actually gotten some decent sleep. He shifted his head slightly, his attention landing on the split in the drapes covering the balcony doors. A sharp buzz of recognition shot through him. There was no doubt about it; that was the faint gray light of dawn peeking through. Dumbfounded, he swiveled his head to check the clock on the bedside table—5:43 a.m. Hell, it had been after eleven when they put J.J. down. Alarmed, he tightened his hold on Jordan and raised his head, looking at the cradle. His heart clamoring, Murphy braced himself, half expecting to find his son gone. But he was right there, asleep on his side, sucking on his thumb and looking like the absolute little angel he was not.

His pulse still going like gangbusters, he dropped his head back on the pillow and closed his eyes, relief making him dizzy. Man, he hoped it was a long while before he had another scare like that.

As the fizz of alarm settled, two things registered. One was that his chest was wet. And two—his son had slept through the night. The whole entire night! That was so astonishing he wanted to shake Jordan awake and tell her the amazing news. But he smiled at the ceiling instead, thinking that finally here was a kid with a sense of timing. Shifting his head on the pillow, he ran his hand up Jordan's arm, suddenly aware of just how wet his chest was. His grin deepened. She was going to be as embarrassed as hell when she woke up and discovered she'd leaked all over him.

Tightening his arm around her, he pressed another soft kiss against her forehead, a sudden thickness forming in his chest. If he had one wish right then, it would be that he could spend the rest of the day like this. His kid asleep in his cradle by the bed, her asleep in his arms. It couldn't get much better than this.

His lower body sharply reminded him that he was dead wrong—that it could definitely get much, much better than this. Murphy closed his eyes and tried not to think about it. Sex was not part of the big picture. At least not right now. Even setting aside what had happened between them before and the caution required, he had to think of Jordan. She was exhausted, almost dead on her feet from breast-feeding and dealing night and day with a fussy new baby, who—if they were lucky—might sleep two hours at a stretch. The very last thing she needed right now was a big come-on from him. Although it was tempting. Damned tempting.

Gritting his teeth and trying to disengage from the heavy throbbing between his legs, Murphy turned his face into her disheveled hair, a different kind of need welling up inside him. God, but she felt so good, so right in his arms, and he realized just how desperately he wanted her permanently in his life. Except he knew that if he brought it up, she was almost as likely to bolt now as she had last time. That gave him such a knot in his gut that it felt as if his insides were being ripped out.

Jordan stirred and emitted a long sigh, and Murphy tried to disengage from his suddenly sober mood. Rubbing his stubbled jaw against her hair, he smoothed his hand up her arm, knowing he didn't have much longer before he was going to have to let her go.

He felt her come awake, then go suddenly still, as if she was trying to get her bearings. Then like a diver exploding from the water, she bolted upright, her face frozen in alarm as she looked at the cradle. He gave her enough time to assure herself that Little Stuff was okay, then pulled her back down into his arms, folding her up in a tight embrace before she had a chance to get all flustered about their situation.

"It's a miracle, Mama," he said, hoping that she thought his gruff tone was from sleep. "The kid finally took mercy on us. He slept through the night. The whole, entire night. Maybe there is hope after all.''

She was so still that not a single muscle moved. The corner of his mouth lifted in amusement, and he ran his hand up her spine. ''It's okay, Kennedy. Breathe in. Breathe out. That's what you do when you find out you're alive.''

He got a little huff of laughter, then she went still again. ''Oh, God,'' she breathed, a tone of horror in her voice. Ah. She had just figured out why he was very wet.

Murphy chuckled and tightened his hold on her, deciding to give her a hard time. ''You know, if you were a dairy cow, you'd be some farmer's major asset.''

She wasn't kidding around when she jabbed him hard in the ribs. ''That's not funny, Murphy.''

Still grinning, he caught her hand so she couldn't give him another kidney shot. ''Yeah, it is.''

He could feel her heart pounding and she sounded just a little breathless when she whispered, ''I'm sorry I got you all wet.''

Last night's need came swarming back, making his heart pound and his chest thicken, and Murphy knew he was inches away from doing something really stupid. He wanted her so bad. Sooo bad.

''Murphy?''

The quaver of uncertainty in her voice shut him down like nothing else could, and he pulled away slightly so he could see her face. ''What?'' he asked, his voice still thick with emotion.

She looked up at him, her eyes so dark with worry they were the color of slate, and he could feel the frantic beat of her pulse where he gripped her wrist. He let go of her and carefully brushed the hair back from her face. ''What?'' he prompted.

She swallowed hard and looked away, then began fiddling with the button on his damp shirt. "Are you sure it's a good idea that I go with you to meet your family?"

"Look at me, Jordan," he commanded, his tone quiet.

He could almost feel her fortifying herself, but she did as he asked. His gaze was steady and level when he spoke. "Yeah, I do think it's a good idea." He knew he was playing dirty, but he had to say it anyway. "It's about family, and I want J.J. to know that. I want us to parent together whenever we can, Jordan. I don't want to shut you out of the things that I do with him, and I hope you don't shut me out of the things you do with him." Needing to touch her skin, he brushed a loose eyelash off her cheek with his thumb, then managed a lopsided smile. "You can't *not* be part of the family, Kennedy. My grandma is going to take you under her wing, and that's going to be that. And if we don't go over there today, we can sure in hell expect her to show up here tomorrow."

Sharply aware of how intently she was watching him, Murphy caressed her cheek again, his own gaze turning sober. "I really want you to come, Jordan. I want us to show off our son together."

As if caught in some kind of trance, she continued to stare at him. Then her breath caught and she closed her eyes, the pulse in her neck very erratic. His own pulse going a little crazy, Murphy knew, as sure as he was lying there, that she had never been more vulnerable than she was right then. Feeling as if an entire cavalry had just been turned loose in his chest, he tried to ignore the demon in his head urging him to go for it. His breathing was getting hot and labored when his conscience finally got into the battle, telling him it wasn't fair to make a move when her defenses were down, and that if he was a decent man he'd do the honorable thing.

His entire body primed to go, Murphy listened to his conscience. With every nerve in his body on red alert, he tried to quell the ruckus in his chest as he carefully, so very carefully began combing his fingers through her tangled hair. God, he felt as if he were suffocating.

He heard Jordan haul in a jagged breath, then she abruptly turned her face against his neck. Overpowered by raw, driving emotion, Murphy closed his eyes and clasped her head hard against him, his whole body one big pulsing ache. More than anything, he wanted to feel her flush on top of him, and more than anything he wanted to let go. But as much as he wanted to follow through, he knew he'd done the right thing—and maybe, just maybe, he'd gained some critical ground with her. He had to believe that, or he'd go right out of his ever lovin' mind.

It was J.J., starving and soaked, who put a sharp end to any shreds of hope the little demon inside Murphy's head might have had.

From there it deteriorated into a personal war against plain old sexual frustration. Deciding he had to do something to keep from climbing out of his skin, Murphy drove over to his house while Jordan was feeding the kid. He had a shower—a very long, cold shower—then picked a huge bouquet of flowers from his out-of-control garden on the way to the truck. Although Murphy noticed it wasn't as out of control as it had been the last time he'd been there—which meant Baba had been over again. Which probably also meant his fridge and stove were now spotless, and she had refolded all the towels in his linen closet.

Murphy smiled to himself. When he first got his own place years ago, he thought it had come staffed with laundry fairies. His dirty laundry would disappear, only to miraculously reappear—mended, starched, ironed and precisely folded. His married sisters all prayed to the housekeeping gods that he and his two brothers would stay single, because it kept their grandmother so busy looking after them that she didn't have time to do housekeeping inspections on their houses.

It was just going on ten when Murphy returned to the condo. J.J., strapped in his molded chair, was sitting on the kitchen floor in a patch of sunshine, blowing bubbles and watching his fingers with cross-eyed intensity. Murphy set the flowers in the sink, then crouched down in front of his son, pride swelling up in his chest. Grinning at J.J., he reached out and pressed his finger against the tiny palm, and J.J. immediately gripped it. "Well, hi, tiger. You were such a big man last night—sleeping so long." He reached out and straightened the twisted cuff of his son's sleepers, which were assembled to look like a baseball uniform. "And look at you. All ready for a base hit."

J.J. turned his head and gave his dad a sloppy smile, and Murphy felt it go right to his chest—as if somebody had pumped his heart up like a balloon. His kid had been smiling for a while, and he was particularly full of them after he had his bath—which Murphy knew was the case now. J.J. had that unbelievable scent of a freshly bathed baby. He shook his son's hand. "So where's your mother, slugger? Is she having fits this morning?"

He no sooner got the words out than Jordan came whizzing into the kitchen, looking more frazzled than he'd ever seen her. She had on a pair of linen slacks and a cherry-red short-sleeve top that shone like silk. Her hair still wrapped in a towel, she pulled up short when she saw him crouched in front of his son.

He gave her a slow grin. "Looking good, Kennedy."

She made a helpless gesture with her hands. "Nothing fits. My blouses are too small and these pants are too big and I can't find the shoes I want. And—" She spotted the flowers in the sink, and it was as if someone had pulled her plug. "Oh."

Murphy glanced at her, feeling pretty smug that the flowers had stopped her cold. "The flower gardens at the house have kinda gone wild with all this heat. I thought you might like a collection."

It was odd, how she could go so still, so quiet. With that same stillness, she went to the sink and picked up the bouquet and buried her face in it, inhaling deeply. Then she looked at him, her eyes glowing with appreciation. "They are absolutely beautiful. Thank you so much." She touched the petals of one of the lilies, then smelled it before getting a vase out of the cupboard. Jordan didn't just jam a bouquet of flowers in a vase and rearrange them after, like his mother or sisters did. She placed them in, one by one, as if they were very rare and fragile—and extremely precious. It said so much about her that Murphy had to look away.

She came over and set the flowers on the floor by J.J., the camera in her hand. There were bright yellow smears of lily pollen all over her red blouse, but she didn't seem to notice. She crouched down beside Murphy. "We've got to get a picture of you, J.J., with Daddy's pretty flowers." She snapped the photo and J.J. obliged her with another wet smile; she smiled back, using her thumb to wipe the drool away. Then she glanced at the clock. "Oh, God. Look at the time." She was on her feet, dragging the towel off her head and looking all frazzled again as she rushed toward the hallway.

Sitting cross-legged on the floor, Murphy shook his son's

hand again. "Women are very strange creatures, kid. Just remember your old man told you that."

He heard the hair dryer, then about five minutes after it shut off, Jordan reappeared in the kitchen, wearing a totally different outfit. She gave him a frantic, beseeching look. "Is this more appropriate?"

Murphy knew that most of his family would be in either jeans or hacked-off shorts. But he also knew that Jordan didn't own either. Trying to keep his tone noncommittal, he nodded. "That's fine."

But Jordan didn't hear him. She got that startled look on her face—the one he'd come to recognize as the milk alarm—and she leaned over and grabbed her breasts. She swore, using language he had never heard her use the whole time he'd known her. Before he could peel his son's teeny fingers from around his, she rushed out of the room. He tapped his son's nose, then rose. "James Jeffery, I think it's time for a little damage control." He found her in her bedroom, raking hangers across the bar in her closet, openly weeping. For a woman who never, ever cried, she had certainly generated a lot of tears over the past six weeks. He tried to think of something to do to turn off the tap.

Catching her by the shoulder, he turned her around and wrapped her up in a comforting embrace. "Hey, it's not a big deal," he said softly. "One wet top is not the end of the world." Except it was for her, and right then she needed help—which meant he had to come up with a solution. Maybe there really were laundry fairies, because suddenly there was a clear recollection hanging on his mental clothesline. Nearly dizzy with relief, he gave her a little squeeze. "Remember that white gauzy outfit you wore last summer—you know, with the long skirt and the jacket thing that went with it? The top had big gold buttons, and you wore a long gold belt with the skirt.'' Hell, he couldn't remember exactly what the outfit was like, except that she looked like something out of *The Great Gatsby* in it. He glanced around the room. It was obvious by the multicolored piles heaped on the bed that the clothes dilemma had been going on for quite a while. If it was anyone other than Jordan, it would have been funny. He still wanted to smile but he didn't dare. Instead, he gave her another encouraging squeeze. ''You know which one I'm talking about?''

She sniffled and nodded. Bolstered by her response, he continued. ''I really like that outfit, and it would be perfect. Nice and cool, and if you, um, leak, no one will know because of the jacket.'' Loosening his hold, he leaned back so he could see her face. ''Okay? Would that work?''

She nodded again, tears spiking her long lashes, and Murphy wanted to kiss her in the worst way—but he didn't. That would be a little too underhanded when she was barely hanging on by a thread. Taking her face between his hands, he smiled into her eyes. ''Okay?'' She gave her head a little jerk, and he let his hands slide to her shoulders. ''Okay,'' he repeated, confirming her answer.

Except it wasn't okay. The little demon in his mind said it wasn't okay. He didn't want her putting clothes on. He wanted her taking her clothes all off.

Disgusted with himself, he turned and headed out the door. Man, there was something about being in a room with her where there was an unmade bed that just about drove him crazy.

Chapter 7

By the time Murphy finished loading everything into the Explorer, he was sure they had enough baby stuff to go on a six-month trek. If he'd thought the trip to the doctor was bad, it had nothing on this expedition. Just how could a kid who would fit in a large shoe box require so much for a day's outing? He didn't get it.

But the packing was the least of it. Jordan was a mental wreck. At the very last minute, she got in a panic because she hadn't prepared anything to take in the way of food. He told her no one expected them to bring anything to eat— they were bringing the star attraction. That got a tiny smile out of her, except she was so pale, he half expected her to pass out.

But she did look beautiful. She'd pulled her glossy blond hair back from her face and secured it with a white ruffly thing. And the white outfit, with a pale yellow camisole underneath the jacket, was even more gauzy and light than he remembered. She had on gold sandals, the long gold belt and gold loops in her ears. She looked as if she'd just floated off the cover of a fashion magazine, and he told her so. She went from pale to pink, which he thought was darned cute, as well as being a very good sign.

By the time they got to his parents', she'd gone all pale again, and from the pulse in her neck, Murphy figured her heart rate must be running about 150 beats a minute. She hadn't said more than ten words since they left her place, and she looked as if she was ready to either bolt or throw up. He pretended not to notice.

He parked on the street, but when he opened the door to get out, she grasped his wrist, looking at him with panicky eyes. "I don't remember all their names. Or what they do."

Figuring the family chronology might take her mind off it, he settled back in his seat. "Okay. Baba is my paternal grandmother, and everybody calls her Baba. She was a twenty-something war bride, and spoke barely any English when she and my grandfather—and my father—immigrated to Canada right after the war. Grandfather had been married before, but his first wife died when Dad was born. So my dad is one hundred percent Irish. But Baba is the only mother he's ever known—and Dad thinks the sun rises and sets on her—but so did my grandfather.

"My parents are Ellen and Patrick. Dad is semiretired and they spend a lot of time on the golf course these days." He rested his wrist on top of the steering wheel as he watched her. "Got that?"

She nodded, concentrating so hard she had creases in her forehead.

He shifted in his seat and continued. "Kids, from the top. Mitchell, divorced for fifteen years, owns and operates a big garden center with greenhouses and a nursery. He's fifteen months older than me. I'm next. Then there's Jessica. She's exactly nine months younger than I am—which has been the source of some serious ribbing as far as my parents are concerned. So she's thirty-five, a psychologist with the Calgary Public School Board, married to Marco, my crew foreman. They have three kids. Mark is eight, Molly's six and Sarah, two. The next in line is Cameron, thirty-two. He's a civil engineer and is working on a big dam project in Bolivia. The last in line are the twins, Caroline and Cora. They're almost thirty. Caroline is married to Jake, and they have two kids. Cassie, five, and Kevin, three. She was a computer programmer but quit when Kevin was born. And she and Jake have their own business, setting up computer networks. Cora is married to Martin. No kids, both of them lawyers.''

Jordan had her eyes shut, and he could tell by the way her lips were moving that she was reciting names. Figuring that was going to keep her distracted, he got out and unloaded baby stuff, including the Baba Blankie. There was such a pile on the ground that he figured it was going to take a whole mule train to get everything moved to the backyard. He also unloaded the car seat with his son still in it, who was frowning at the world, as if trying to figure out what in heck was going on. Murphy set him in the shade of the truck, then opened the passenger's door. Jordan was sitting there with her head pressed back against the headrest, her eyes shut tight, her hand pressed against her middle as if she was going to be sick.

Because she was so fair, he'd suggested she bring a sun hat, and the white straw confection with a rolled brim was sitting on her knees. He picked it up, laid it on top of the diaper bag, then leaned back in the truck and undid her seat belt. "Come on," he said quietly. "Let's get this over with."

He grasped her hand, which was like ice, and urged her out, then slammed the door. She was looking up at him with those wide gray eyes, anxiety making her whole body rigid.

Murphy knew the anxiety was more about J.J. than about her. And he knew that because of her history, the one thing she wanted more than anything else in the world was for her son to be accepted into the Munroe clan. To have the family she never had.

But somehow he had to get her from here to there. Wanting to erase that awful panicky expression in her eyes, he decided to give her something else to think about.

Grasping her face in his hands, he tipped her head back and covered her mouth with a soft, slow kiss. For an instant, he figured maybe he had blown it big time, but then she made a low sound and grasped his wrists, her mouth going slack beneath his. The moist warmth of that kiss sent a jolt of heat right through him, and he tightened his grip on her face, his heart starting to lumber like crazy in his chest. Getting far more than he bargained for, and a whole hell of a lot less than he wanted, Murphy put everything he had into that kiss—need, want, passion—but mostly it was all his pure, unadulterated feelings for her. He wanted to widen his stance and crush her against him, to feel her heat against his hardness, but he clamped down hard on that fevered urge, and simply held her face as he drank from her mouth.

Knowing he had to put the brakes on before this got entirely out of hand, he clasped her face tighter and slowly withdrew. His breathing was labored and his heart was pounding; his knees were so weak that he was surprised he was still standing. Lord, he was pumped. Right down to his toes. Taking a very deep, uneven breath, he brushed her mouth with one last kiss, aware that her pulse and respiration were just as ragged as his. Lifting his head, he gazed down at her, giving her an intimate smile. "Nice, Kennedy. Very, very nice."

She looked absolutely stunned. Taking a certain amount of male satisfaction from the glazed, staggered expression in her eyes, Murphy wiped her mouth with his thumb, then abruptly let her go. He picked up her hat, jammed it on her head, then grabbed the car seat with J.J. in it in one hand, her wrist in the other and headed to the side gate. Now all he had to do was get her into the yard before she recovered.

The whole family was going to be there, except Cameron. Even Mitch, who weaseled out of family get-togethers if at all possible, said he'd come. But Murphy didn't blame her for being apprehensive. With his brother, his three sisters, along with their spouses, plus nieces and nephews, his parents and of course Baba, it was quite a crowd. Usually, there would have been an additional swarm of aunts and uncles and assorted cousins, but there was no way he wanted to dump all that on Jordan—at least not the very first time. It was his father who had suggested they keep it just immediate family, for Jordan's sake. Which said a whole lot for his old man.

Urging her through the gate ahead of him, Murphy pressed his palm against the small of her back, then once through, grasped her hand and forced his fingers through hers. Her skin was still as cold as ice, and she gripped him, her whole body taut.

Ellen Munroe was the first to spot them, and dropped a beach ball and started toward them. "Well, finally. Here they are."

It was sort of like being attacked by a flock of hungry sea gulls, with everyone flapping around them and squawking over the baby. Murphy made all the introductions and handed over J.J., but he hung on to Jordan. He drew her closer when he realized she was trembling. It was his big brother, Mitch, who came to their rescue. He was as tall as Murphy—six foot two on the nose, and their wide-shouldered builds were identical. They looked enough alike that some people had trouble telling them apart. Except Mitch's hair was a darker shade of blond. But it was in disposition that they differed. Murphy had always been more of a hothead and hell-raiser, at least until he started his own business. Mitch had been more serious, more reserved and, as a kid, more responsible. His mother claimed it was because he was the eldest of six. The rest of the family said it was because he didn't get a drop of Irish blood in him.

Mitch didn't pay a whole lot of attention to the baby. And other than a slap on the shoulder, he pretty much ignored Murphy. Instead, he gave Jordan that slow, lopsided smile of his that made his hazel eyes crease—the exact same smile that he used to make all the girls collapse at his feet. Holding her gaze, he stretched out his hand. "Jordan—welcome. Just so you know—my brothers and sisters are sort of like mosquitoes. You have to keep slapping them away to get them to leave you alone. So until you get the hang of it, I'll give you a hand."

Murphy could actually feel some of the tension leave her, and her smile, although a little strained, was real enough. She took his brother's hand. "I think I can handle mosquitoes."

Mitch continued to hold Jordan's hand, and Murphy cocked an eyebrow at him. Mitch gave her a bad-boy grin and kissed her knuckles. Baba appeared beside him and slapped his hand away. "Mosquitoes with hands. Enough."

She gave him a scolding look, then fixed her gaze on Jordan. Baba was maybe five foot three and a little on the roly-poly side, but she had almond-shaped hazel eyes and the high cheekbones of her Slavic ancestors. She had been beautiful as a young woman, but the beauty had aged and softened into gentle wrinkles.

But in spite of her small stature, Baba was a force to be reckoned with. And every one of her grandkids would have walked over hot coals for her.

She sized up Jordan, unabashedly assessing her, then she smiled that smile that made her eyes twinkle. Taking Jordan's face between her hands, she pulled her down and planted a kiss on either cheek. Then she patted Jordan's face, and announced, "This one we keep." Smacking Murphy's hand so he'd let go of Jordan's, Baba caught her arm and led her away. "Come. We talk."

Jordan shot Murphy a bemused look, as if to say, *What do I do now?* He grinned and winked at her, letting her know she was on her own.

Ellen Munroe had J.J. out of his car seat and was holding him down for his little cousins to see. Jessica, the sister who was married to Marco, had three kids of her own, and she'd always been sappy over babies. Moving in from the side, she tried to snitch J.J. His mother turned away, not about to give up her newest grandson. "Not a chance, Jess. If we start passing him around, this poor little man will be mauled to death inside an hour."

The "poor little man" made baby sounds, blew bubbles and actually chortled, totally charming Grandma by waving his fists at her. Grandma got that mushy look in her eye. Murphy figured Jessica would have to wrestle his mother to the ground if she was ever going to get to hold the baby.

Mitch watched the goings-on between his sister and

mother, then grinned and slapped his brother on the back. "Now you've done it, bro. Thrown the chicken in with the foxes, so to speak."

"Yeah. Well." Murphy could see that Baba had taken Jordan over to sit under the sprawling ornamental cherry tree, where the lawn furniture was arranged—four bent-willow chairs, an old willow rocker and a park bench situated in a vine-covered arbor. They were sitting side by side on the bench, and Baba was holding Jordan's hand, focused completely on whatever Jordan was saying.

Mitch headed toward the huge cooler. "Come on. I'll buy you a beer."

Within an hour, it was clear that Jordan was going to be just fine. And Murphy was damned proud of how his family handled the whole situation. It was if they all sensed Jordan's apprehension, and everyone gave her time to settle in. His sisters didn't all gather around her as they normally would have done, but they sought her out, one at a time. But once it was obvious that Jordan had settled into a comfort zone, they'd gathered around, and now all the women were clustered together under the shade of the cherry tree. Baba was in the rocking chair holding J.J., and Jordan was sitting on the grass beside her, her legs stretched out in front of her, her arms braced, her white hat on the grass by her thigh. Off to the side, in full sunshine, Murphy's dad had set up the huge paddle pool and the sprinkler, and the kids were tearing through them both, shrieking and shouting, their wet bathing suits glistening in the sun.

But Jordan sat framed within the circle of shade from the cherry tree, her white filmy skirt dappled with shadows. Directly behind her, the wide, three-tier flower gardens provided a backdrop of vivid splashes—reds and purples, pinks and yellows, clumps of white. Hundreds of shades of colors and textures, superimposed against the clear blue sky, the lush green grass. With the bright red-and-blue-and-yellow beach balls and wet-skinned children, and with the women sitting in the shade around her, it was as if Jordan had been framed in a Renoir painting. He couldn't take his eyes off her.

His three brothers-in-law and his father had gone inside for a game of pool, but Mitch was stretched out on the grass beside him, a beer resting on his chest. He spoke, interrupting their silence. "So," his brother asked, "are you going to marry her?"

Murphy was sitting with his back braced against the trunk of the willow tree that had once held their tree house. Stalling for time, he took a long swig from his bottle, then wedged it between his thighs. His expression sober, he picked up a leaf from the ground and began stripping out the vein. "I don't know."

Mitch turned his head and gave him a sharp look. "Why not?"

Murphy met his gaze and shrugged. "I would have married her five days after I met her, but she's got some baggage. And she's running scared."

"Divorced?"

Murphy picked up his bottle and raised it to his lips. "Nope."

Mitch let a couple of beats go by, then commented in a good-old-boy tone. "How about them Cannons?"

He may as well have whacked Murphy on the back while he was trying to drink. Coughing and choking, he felt as if he'd inhaled the entire contents of the bottle. Damn, what was it about this place? First his mother nearly strangled him, now Mitch.

Mitch grinned broadly as Murphy tried to cough his lungs

out. As shots went, it was a good one—an old family joke among the kids about their father. Whenever things got a little too uncomfortable around the dinner table, or if the tensions were high and Patrick Munroe didn't know what to do about it, he would do something exactly like that. Something—anything—to change the subject. It became such a joke that Caroline, the eldest twin, would have to leave the table whenever he did it. As for the Cannons, Murphy couldn't remember the last time he'd been to a baseball game, and he didn't have a clue where they were in the standings. Finally clearing his throat, he gave Mitch a dirty look. "I'm going to remember that, Mitchell."

His brother grinned and tucked his hands under his head. "I'm sure you will."

Jess had finally gotten her hands on the baby, and she was holding him under his arms, his feet pedaling on her bare legs as she talked baby talk to him. And J.J. was chuckling at his aunt. Murphy fixed his gaze on Jordan, wondering how she felt about everyone taking over her son. But it only took one glance to figure that out. She was watching the two of them, with an odd, gratified expression on her face, a glow of maternal pride beneath it all. And it hit him. This was what she had wanted so much for her son—family and acceptance.

As he watched, Jessica's two-year-old daughter, Sarah, came running up, barefoot, with a shoe in her hand. Unable to get her mother's attention, she plopped herself on Jordan's lap, handing her the shoe and jabbering something at her. The look on Jordan's face was absolutely amazing to watch—startlement, hesitancy, then a kind of pleasure that lit her up from the inside out. Shifting so she was sitting cross-legged, she encircled the toddler with her arms, her head alongside Sarah's as she undid the laces on the shoe.

Murphy's chest got real tight. It was a picture that was going to stick in his mind for a very long time.

Her shoe back on, Miss Sarah clambered off Jordan's lap and went running off to join the rest of the kids, with one shoe on and one shoe off, just as J.J. started making squawking sounds. Getting up, Jordan reached over and took him from Jessica, and Cora, the second twin, led her toward the house. Murphy finished off his beer, then got up, sticking the bottle in the case with the other empties. All the baby stuff had been taken into the house, but Jordan had left her brightly woven shoulder bag on the picnic table on the deck, and Murphy knew there were things in there she would need—like fresh liners for her nursing bra or maybe a change of tops. Swinging the bag up from the table, he took off his sunglasses, hooked them on the neck of his tank top and followed her into the house.

He met Cora coming out of the living room, and she gave him a big wink and two thumbs up, then headed down the stairs to the family room. The drapes in the living room had been closed to keep the heat out, and he found Jordan sitting cross-legged on one of the sofas, with J.J. already gulping down lunch. He set the bag on the coffee table in front of her just as she looked up at him, and there was something in her eyes—perhaps heartfelt gratitude, maybe a tiny feeling of actually belonging—but whatever it was, it put such an unbelievable softness in her eyes that it made his chest tighten. And there was something in that look that he just could not resist. Resting one hand on the back of the sofa, he caught her along her jawline with the other, then bent down and covered her mouth with a light, soft kiss.

Which was a really stupid thing to do, because all hell broke loose inside him. His heart pounded, his lungs seized up and a crazy weakness pumped through him, clogging up his veins.

Her breath caught and Jordan grasped his arm as if to steady herself, her mouth moist and oh so yielding. Making a low sound, Murphy slipped his hand to the back of her head and deepened the kiss, his whole body straining for more, but J.J. let out an annoyed yell. Murphy closed his eyes and rested his head against hers, trying to get a full breath past the commotion in his chest. She was hanging on to him so hard that her nails were digging into his skin, and her breathing was even more ragged than his. J.J. made another protest, and Murphy released his hold and straightened. Without looking at her, he turned and headed down the hallway to the bathroom. He just couldn't take it any longer. No damned way.

By the time he returned, J.J. was nursing on the other side, and Jordan looked up, a trace of uncertainty in her eyes. He'd gotten a lemonade for her and one for himself. Setting hers on a coaster on the end table, he sat down on the coffee table right in front of her. Cradling his glass in his hands, he rested his forearms on his thighs and glanced up. He met her worried gaze and gave her an off-center smile. "I've gotta quit doing that to myself, Jordan."

His frankness totally discombobulated her, and she looked down at the baby and blushed like he had never seen her blush before. He reached out and tucked a loose wisp of hair behind her ear. "You do pack a punch, lady."

She closed her eyes and abruptly turned her face against the pressure of his hand, and Murphy got nailed with such another rush of emotion that it made his mind swim. He was damned sure he could never want anyone the way he wanted her.

"You," scolded Baba from the doorway. As if they'd

both gotten caught with their hands in the cookie jar, Murphy and Jordan jumped apart. Baba shook her finger at Murphy. "Let the poor thing be." She bustled into the room carrying a glass of beer. "Here," she said, handing the beer to Jordan with one hand, snagging the glass of lemonade with the other. Her tone gentled. "For you. Makes strong, healthy milk, and baby will sleep."

Jordan took the glass, a hint of shyness showing as she smiled at the old woman. "Thank you. But you didn't have to bring that all the way in for me."

Baba sat down on the coffee table beside Murphy. There was a sly twinkle in her eyes when she looked at him. "If we break this table, *hoy,* we will be in big trouble." Murphy grinned at her and draped his arm around her shoulders. Baba reached over and patted Jordan's knees. "Serious. Beer is good. Always in the old country, mothers drink beer." She patted Jordan again. "You drink." Then she patted Murphy's thigh—Baba was a great patter. "Go get the albums, so Jordan sees the whole family."

Murphy rolled his eyes. "Baba, she doesn't want to see the damned family albums."

"Yes," said Jordan, butting in. "I do."

Baba flapped her hands at him. "See? I tell you. Go. Go."

Shaking his head, Murphy got up and did as he was told. She still bossed them around as if they were all five years old. He went into the den and collected a stack of albums and brought them out, setting them on the coffee table by Baba. He gave his grandmother a "gotcha" look and opened the top one, showing Jordan the sepia picture on the first page. "This is Baba when she married my grandfather."

Holding the now sleeping J.J. with one arm, Jordan

looked at the old photograph, then cast a glance at Baba. "Oh, Baba. You were just beautiful."

Baba chuckled and tapped her finger against her temple. "Better than beautiful, I was smart."

Jordan's eyes lit up and she laughed out loud. "I'm sure you were."

Baba's expression clouded over, and she gently touched the face of the groom in the picture. "I married a very good man," she said softly. "A very good man." Then she looked up at Murphy and shook her finger, a twinkle in her eyes. "And you have his bad act, Murphy. The one that gets you into trouble."

Grinning at her "bad act" comment, Murphy leaned down and kissed her wrinkled cheek. "Hey. I know what you're up to. You're trying to stir up some trouble of your own. So I'm clearing out of here."

Her eyes still twinkling, Baba pinched his cheek. "Is good. You go. We will talk woman talk."

Murphy shot Jordan a glance, and her eyes were dancing just about as much as Baba's. He wasn't sure if that was a good thing or a bad thing.

It was going on ten when they finally packed up and left Murphy's parents'. The traffic was light on the drive home, and Jordan was very quiet. As Murphy drove through the darkening streets, he considered the subtle change he'd seen in her. It was as if something very tight in her had let go; he could even see it in her body language and in her posture. As if all her anxiety had turned into a limp elastic band. As if something in her had been satisfied.

And he was pretty sure what had brought the change about.

In all honesty, the day couldn't have gone better. The

family had made a huge fuss over the baby, and it would have been obvious to a blind man that the kid had been accepted as part of the clan. And Murphy was well aware of how important his being accepted was to her. More than anything, she wanted him to have everything she'd missed. There had been one specific incident that stood out among the rest—when she discovered Grandpa Munroe carting J.J. around as Grandpa played ringtoss with the rest of the grandkids, trying to get a six-week-old kid to throw his bright yellow ring. The look of pure delight on Jordan's face had been something to behold.

But there was more to it than that. It was as if she had found something for herself. He could see with his own eyes that a definite bond had developed between Jordan and his grandmother. And he had to admit that it gave him quite a jolt to see how solicitous and attentive she had been toward the old woman, so—hell, he couldn't find exactly the right words—but so full of respect. And it also made him realize just how much he had taken for granted his entire life.

"She's wonderful—your grandmother," Jordan said softly.

Murphy shot her a glance, as if she'd read his mind. She was sitting with her arm braced on the window ledge, her head propped on her hand. "It must have been so terrifying for her, moving here, knowing no one, barely speaking the language. That must have taken such courage." She dropped her arm and looked at Murphy, the city lights casting half of her face in shadow. "You've got a great family, Murphy. Your sisters, your parents, Mitch." She looked down and began fiddling with the strap of her handbag, as if gathering her own courage. Then she looked at him again, her gaze solemn. "Thank you for not letting me back out. It was wonderful."

"I'm glad you enjoyed yourself. They can be a bit over-whelming at times."

Dropping her gaze, she continued to roll the handle of the bag between her fingers, and Murphy wanted to reach across and stop her from worrying the rolled fabric. It was as if her inner tension was feeding his own. He slowed for a car that had pulled out in front of him, his expression growing taut. If he couldn't smell the scent of sunshine on her, maybe it wouldn't be so bad. Maybe if she weren't so close. Or maybe if he were stone-cold dead.

Somehow or other, he had to get through the next couple of hours without doing something stupid. Like getting even closer. Like being driven by another part of his body instead of his brain. Like getting in over his head.

If he was smart, he'd find some excuse to go back to his house for the night, but he was afraid she would misunder-stand, misinterpret. And the last thing he wanted to do was destroy all the positive things that had happened today. But he was afraid if he so much as touched her, he'd bloody well lose it.

Feeling suddenly edgy and strung out right to the limit, he pulled into the ramp for her underground parking, reached through the open window and punched in her security code, then waited for the garage door to open. He had to do something that would drain him absolutely empty, or he really would lose his mind. Just the thought of a brightly lit gym made his skin crawl. What he needed to do was go for a long run. Yeah, a run. Maybe that would do it. Having an escape plan eased the tension chasing around in his belly, and he loosened his grip on the wheel. He would get everything unloaded and make sure she and J.J. were okay, then he'd put on some sweats and he'd run until he burned off all that awful edginess or until he dropped dead—whichever came first.

The garage was well lit, and he squinted against the bright halogen lights as he pulled into her second stall beside her BMW. Experiencing a sensation that could best be described as sexual claustrophobia, he put the vehicle in Park, switched off the engine and took the keys out of the ignition.

Jordan opened her door. He spoke to her, his tone clipped. "You take J.J., and I'll bring the rest of the stuff up."

She hesitated, then slid out of the vehicle. "All right," she said, her voice very quiet.

Murphy clenched his jaw, wanting to bang his head against the steel girder. Damn, damn, damn. He'd sworn he wasn't going to do that. To get cranky with her.

Jordan actually held the elevator for him, but she didn't say a word. She just jiggled J.J. and watched the numbers flash by. When the elevator stopped at her floor, she stepped out ahead of him, immediately exited, and she had her apartment door unlocked and open by the time he got there. That prissy-accountant's look was on her face, which made him even more cranky, and for some reason, it ticked him off all over again.

But that feeling collapsed onto itself when he saw how stiff her spine was and how erect she was holding her head. That had always been Jordan's first line of defense. She turned to hang her handbag on the knob of the closet door, and Murphy caught a glimmer of tears in her eyes. Disgusted with himself, he grimly wondered why he kept doing such stupid things. He hauled the baby stuff into the nursery and dumped it in a big pile in the middle of the floor. Yanking open the closet door, he dug out his gym bag and emptied the contents on the single bed. Swearing to himself, he dug through and located his track shoes and a pair of biker shorts. He should never have kissed her. Then maybe he could have kept a lid on it. But no. He had to go stick his head into a loaded cannon. And now he was going to have to pay for it. He'd have to run all the way to Banff and back to unload all the sexual edginess screaming around inside him. Then he would probably have to turn around and do it all over again.

Her bedroom door was closed when he left the nursery, and he hesitated, a sweatband in his hand. If he was smart, he'd turn the other way. Exhaling heavily, he yanked the band around his forehead, then opened her door without knocking. She hadn't turned the lights on, and she was sitting in the chair feeding J.J. The instant the door swung open, she quickly wiped her face with the heel of her hand, keeping her head bent.

His hand on the doorknob, Murphy studied her, then letting out another sigh, he crossed the room and crouched down in front of her. He stared at the floor for a moment, trying to figure out what to say. Finally he looked up at her. "It's not you, Jordan. It's me. I need to blow off some steam so I'm going for a run, okay?"

She avoided looking at him, and instead wiped a tiny bit of mucus out of the corner of the baby's eye. Her voice had a taut edge to it. "Are you coming back?"

He should be getting used to feeling like a heel, but lately every time was like the first time. He caught her by the back of her neck and gave her head a little shake. "Yeah, I'm coming back. But if you were smart, you wouldn't let me back in."

The corner of her mouth lifted and Murphy knew he could do something really, really dumb right now if he didn't use his head. He could still smell sunshine on her, and now there was the scent of mother's milk, as well. And his whole body kicked into gear. As if he wasn't in a big enough mess as it was.

He gave her neck a light squeeze and stood up. "I won't be long." Yeah, right. After being this close to her, he would have to run from here to Vancouver before he'd be able to put a lid on it.

Chapter 8

Unfortunately, a nice, easy jog didn't cut it. Murphy's brain kept running at that speed, and he kept thinking about her, about the taste of her mouth. He knew he had to do something to shut down all systems, or all his galloping around town in the middle of the night was going to be a total waste of time and energy.

So in the end, he went for speed instead of distance. He wasn't sure how far he ran, but by the time he got back to the condo, he felt as if both his lungs were on fire, and he had the kind of cramps in the calves of his legs that blocked out thought altogether.

Wiping the sweat off his forearm, he entered the stairwell, jogged up two flights, then used the steps and handrail to do some stretching exercises. He used every swear word in his vocabulary when he tried to stretch out the painful muscle spasms in his legs. His teeth gritted, he hung on to the stretch. Lord, he'd forgotten how damned much that could hurt.

But he figured he had a handle on his testosterone, at least he did until he entered the apartment. Maybe it was the fading scent of roses, or maybe it was the fresh scent of lilies, or maybe it was the lingering scent of Jordan. But by the time he got to the guest bathroom, he was in the exact same condition as when he'd left. Ripping off his sweat band and T-shirt, he turned the shower on cold. It was more of a punishment than anything—if a killer run hadn't bled off that feeling of having too much blood pulsing through his body, a dose of cold water wasn't going to touch it, either.

And it didn't. Barely drying off, Murphy pulled on the blue jeans he'd left on the hook behind the door earlier, then he shut off the light and left the bathroom.

They'd gotten in the habit of leaving two lights on so they weren't staggering around in the dark during the night—a small night-light in the hallway and one under the built-in microwave in the kitchen. But there was no light on in Jordan's room, and Murphy entered the nursery, leaving the door open so he'd hear the baby, who had obviously been put to bed in the cradle in his mother's room.

That same old edginess was back as Murphy tossed the contents of his gym bag back in the bag, aware that the pile of baby paraphernalia had been cleared away. He zipped the bag and dropped it on the floor at the end of the bed, thinking he should get as far away from her as possible and bunk out on the terrace for the night.

A movement at the door distracted him, and he turned. His stomach shot to his shoes when he saw Jordan standing there, the soft illumination from the night-light in the hall framing her. Even in that weak light, he could see the nervous tension in her, and he could also see that his son was definitely not with her. Which meant this little visit had nothing to do with putting baby to bed.

She nervously tucked some hair behind her ear, and Murphy felt it in a way he had no business feeling it. It was almost as if she had reached out and intimately touched him, and his insides balled up and his pulse went crazy. Not sure he could physically withstand another surge of that kind of crippling need, he locked his jaw together and rested his hand on his hip.

As if picking up on his tension, Jordan shoved her hands in the pockets of her robe. Murphy could have sworn that the sound of her heartbeat carried clear across the room. She wet her lips and spoke. "I just wanted to thank you for the wonderful day," she said, her voice very unsteady. "Your family is fantastic."

Sensing that they were both standing on the threshold of something very critical—but also very shaky—Murphy stared at her, not sure he could handle this tentative attempt of hers. Every muscle in his body was braced against the onslaught that was happening inside him. He didn't want to be an SOB with her, but right then, it was a matter of self-preservation. Murphy clenched and unclenched his jaw, then took a deep breath. "You thanked me already," he said, his tone blunt. "So what's this really about?"

Folding her arms across her chest, she looked away, the light from the hallway grazing her face. Murphy could see the terrible strain in her eyes, and he realized she was fighting with a very heavy emotional muddle.

The band of anger let go in him, and he knew he was going to be damned if he did and damned if he didn't. Releasing a heavy sigh, he extended his hand. "Come here, Jordan," he said quietly.

Murphy wasn't quite sure what kind of reaction he expected from her—he was too busy trying to gird up his loins, so to speak. So when she crossed the room and stepped into his arms, he felt as if she'd yanked the rug out from underneath him. He gathered her up in a fierce embrace, his face pressed against hers, a crazy kind of energizing weakness pumping through him. She gave a soft sob and twisted her head, her lips seeking his. And right then, Murphy lost it. Widening his stance, he hooked his arm around her hips and hauled her against the juncture of his thighs, covering her mouth in a blistering kiss that set off flares of heat and need.

Jordan whimpered and clutched him closer, twisting her pelvis against his, her mouth moist and hungry. She moved against him again, and Murphy let out a ragged groan, knowing he was inches away from really, truly losing it.

Dragging his mouth away, he jammed her head against his neck, his breathing ragged and raw. Closing his eyes, he crushed her against him, his heart thundering, his whole body throbbing. "We need to slow this down a bit," he whispered hoarsely. Trying to provide some relief for both of them, he tightened his arm around her hip, pressing her hard against him. "It's too soon for you, babe. So we're going to have to look at alternatives."

She clung to him even tighter, and to Murphy, it felt as if she were trying to climb right inside him. Her breath hot against his neck, she choked out unevenly. "The doctor— six weeks—he said it was okay."

Nothing could have hauled Murphy back to the real world as fast as that admission. So, he hadn't been the only one who'd been thinking about something other than diapers and colic. In another life, that little bit of news might have amused him. But not in this life. Not when his body was screaming for release. But he'd deal with the doctor's visit later. Right now. Ah, right now he had her crushed hard against him, and it wasn't nearly enough.

Hugging her even tighter, he slid his hand up the back of her head and pressed a kiss along her jaw. "That may be so," he said, his voice unsteady and gruff. "But we got into a wreck once already when we were being careful. So I'm not going to chance it without using anything."

She twisted her face against his neck and took a deep, uneven breath. "There were…leftovers from before."

Murphy's eyes flew open, a hot surge of anticipation making his heart pound even harder. "There were?"

"In my pocket."

Easing his hold on her hips, he snaked his hand into the pocket of her robe. His heart did a crazy roll as he closed his fingers around small foil squares.

That feeling of anticipation exploded into something wild and urgent, and he dragged his mouth across hers, the long denied need scalding through him, setting off a frenzied reaction. He jammed the foil packages in his jeans pocket, then caught her robe, dragging it from her shoulders, his heart slamming to a stop when he realized she was stark naked beneath.

His breathing was so ragged and hoarse that the sound filled the whole room, and he stripped the garment off her, letting it fall to the floor. Emitting a ragged sound, he crushed her against him, reality spinning out of control as he experienced skin against skin, flesh against flesh.

Almost as if she were fighting him, Jordan jerked her arms free and slid her hands under the waistband of his jeans, trying to push them down. His need shot to a whole new level, and Murphy groaned a denial against her mouth as he caught her wrists, pulling her hands away. "No, baby. No." He gathered her close, entrapping her hand, trying to keep from hurting her. He kissed her again, whispering raggedly against her mouth. "That's all that's keeping me together."

She made a desperate sound and fought against his hold.

Sweeping her up, he dumped her on the bed, coming down on top of her, and she drew up her knees, cradling his hips, urging him on, urging him in. His body slick with sweat, he eased away and ran his hand between her thighs, and she sobbed out his name, trying to pull his hand away. And Murphy had no resistance left. It had been too long, and now their common need was too frantic, too desperate, and they were both just too close.

He raised himself up on his knees and found a packet, ripping it open with his teeth and stifling another raw groan as she shoved his jeans down. He nearly lost it—so nearly lost it—when she touched him, fumbling to sheathe him. Desperate for relief, he let her pull him down on top of her. He had to grit his teeth, had to fight to hang on as she guided him into her. His whole body taut and quivering, he tried to ease slowly into her, to be careful with her, but she twisted her head and thrust her hips up, driving him in. What little was left of his restraint exploded out of control, and he thrust his arm under her hips and pressed her head against the curve of his neck, letting the need pull him under.

One, two, three driving strokes, and she cried out and arched up against him, and his face contorted into a grimace of raw, agonizing pleasure as her body clenched around him. And on another ragged groan, his own release came, pulsating from him in spasm after spasm. It wrung him out. And it filled him up. And he knew, no matter what, he would love her until the day he died.

It seemed to take forever for the star bursts to settle in his brain, and he felt as if he'd used up every speck of energy he had. His whole body suffusing with heavy, humming weakness, he finally forced himself to move. Taking her face in his hands, he covered her mouth in a soft, slow kiss that was meant to soothe and comfort. She gave him full access and clung to him with a desperate strength, her body trembling, her face wet. Still holding her head, he slowly broke off the kiss, releasing a long sigh as he raised his head. Using the heel of his hand to dry the tears spilling down her temple, he gazed down at her, loving her so much his chest was jam-packed full of it. He smiled at her, smoothing his thumb along her bottom lip. "You okay?"

She nodded and tried to smile, more tears slipping down. Bracing his weight on his arms, he leaned down and kissed them away, continuing to stroke her face with his thumbs. Murphy wanted to tell her exactly what he was feeling, but he knew from past experience that now was not the time.

A funny buzz started deep in his belly when he lifted his head and realized she was still watching him, her heart in her eyes. She had always dropped all her barriers in bed— as she did this time. But before, she'd keep her eyes closed afterward, even when her hands were soft and caressing. It was as if she was afraid he'd see too much, as if she was hiding from him.

Feeling he was quite capable of swinging from rafters, he drew his thumb across her mouth again, another smile starting in his eyes. "I gotta tell you, Kennedy. This was a long time coming."

Suddenly she went all shy on him, shifting her gaze as she traced the line of his collarbone. But she didn't close her eyes. "I don't know what you mean."

He put pressure on her jaw so she'd look at him. "Yeah, you do. I've been practically crawling the walls since that kid of ours arrived. It has not exactly been good for my manhood.''

He thought she blushed, but he couldn't be sure with only the faint light coming from the hallway. She slanted a long look at him, one corner of her mouth lifting in a funny little quirk, then she went back to tracing the line of his collarbone. ''Your manhood does just fine, Murphy.''

He laughed and gave her head a little shake. ''So, you actually got an okay at your six-week checkup, did you?''

This time he knew she blushed, but she didn't give an inch. ''I also got an okay to carry heavy parcels. I don't see you crowing about that.''

Propping his head on his hand, he trailed his finger down her jawline, grinning broadly. ''You know, you're pretty cute, Kennedy.''

She shivered and caught his finger, then gave him a pointed look. ''And you are a very bad boy, Munroe.''

Still grinning, he bent down and planted another kiss on her mouth. The movement intimately shifted both their bodies, and another sizzle of pleasure shot through him. It was all he could do to keep from groaning. Closing his eyes, he rested his forehead against hers and made himself take a couple of deep breaths, sharply aware of her moist heat gloving him.

Establishing some control, he gave her another soft kiss, then raised his head. Staring down at her, he braced himself to withdraw, but the instant he tensed his muscles, her eyes darkened and she hooked her legs across his hips. Gazing up at him, she whispered, ''Not yet.''

Not ever, he mentally retorted, but he stroked her cheek with the backs of two fingers. ''Honey,'' he said, his voice much huskier than usual. ''I think maybe that's how we got in trouble last time.'' He gave a slow smile, and was dead honest with her. "And as much as I would love to make you pregnant again, this is just a little too soon."

Her eyes got wide and she stopped breathing altogether, and he *knew* he'd gotten her that time. But he wasn't going to give her too much time to think about it. Sliding his hand under her head, he kissed her again, only this time there was no comfort or solace. This kiss was all about intent.

He felt her pulse falter, and she opened her mouth beneath his, giving him full access.

His breathing suddenly labored, he eased away and trailed a row of soft kisses along her jaw and down her neck. "Or I could go change, and we could pick up where we left off."

Her arms came around him and she drew her knees up around his hips, moving ever so slightly beneath him. "Change? Like a diaper?"

He laughed against her mouth and hugged her hard. "Exactly."

Murphy woke up in Jordan's big bed just after five the next morning, his sleep interrupted by little snuffling sounds coming from the cradle, sounds that said *hungry baby.* Being careful not to disturb Jordan, he collected his son and took him to the nursery, where Pa pulled on his jeans and changed Junior. Then Murphy picked up his son and headed for the living area, closing the pocket door behind him. He fastened J.J. in his molded chair, and left him trying to catch sunbeams in front of the patio doors as he took the chill off the bottle and put the coffee on.

By rights, he should have felt like roadkill, but instead he felt as if he'd just arm wrestled Atlas and won. He had no idea how many times they'd made love the night before. But the last one had been the best. Because it was initiated by a blond angel with no good on her mind. They had ended up in her bed after J.J.'s two-o'clock feeding, and Murphy had been asleep maybe two hours when he'd surfaced from a hot, erotic dream of her. He'd come sharply awake, so hard and so ready he had to grit his teeth—aware of her with every damned cell in his body, aware with every breath that her hand was cupping him. He'd figured that he had the dream because his damned hormones were so clearly in overdrive again. But then he realized she was rigid in his arms, her own breathing strained. And the real explanation came when she slowly, ever so slowly stroked him. She had nearly put him through the roof.

That time had been like a trip to the moon and back, but maybe it was all so unbelievable for one reason. And that reason was that Murphy had seen it in her eyes—that she wanted him with the same driving need that he'd wanted her. And right then, he could have moved mountains.

But in the light of day, he was a bit more realistic. It didn't really change anything. Yeah, knowing that he had that effect on her made him feel pretty damned good—and it was going to make him a whole lot more determined. But the truth was, this had always been about Jordan. Jordan had to learn to believe.

He poured himself a cup of coffee. Then, after testing the bottle, he took both the mug of coffee and the bottle to the kitchen table and set them down. Lifting the baby seat with his son in it onto the table, Murphy sat down and faced his kid. He offered J.J. the bottle, and the baby latched on as if he hadn't seen food for a week. Murphy watched him, amusement surfacing. "So, kid, what did you think of the relatives?"

Still working on the bottle, J.J. gave him half a smile.

Murphy grinned at him. "Good. Glad you approved."

Resting his arms on the table, Murphy supported the bottle of breast milk for his son. "And your Mom was a big hit—bowled them over. They'll likely toss us out and just keep her."

J.J. gave him another runny smile, and Murphy plucked a napkin from the holder and mopped up the trickle of milk.

He'd stuffed it down beside J.J. when Jordan came flying into the room, her robe tied haphazardly around the waist, her hands pressed against her breasts. "Aaah, I should have known you were feeding him." She gave Murphy a desperate look. "I've got to feed him."

Murphy pulled the bottle out of J.J.'s mouth, set it down and began unbuckling him, trying not to grin. Nothing like a little overproduction to override the morning-after jitters. He handed his son to his mother, then got up. "Would you like some juice?"

Sitting down at the table, she shook her head. "No. I want a cup of coffee. Surely one won't kill him."

Murphy went to the counter and poured her a mug, added some cream out of the fridge. Turning back to the table, he got such a jolt of male awareness, he nearly dropped the mug. Just like last night, she had nothing on under her robe—no nursing bra, no nightie. The sane, in-control part of his mind dissected why she was in such distress—with no bra on, there would be no restraining pressure, and it was no wonder both sides of her robe were soaking wet. The other part of his brain, the one closely linked to parts below his belt, had never seen anything more arousing in his whole life. This naked woman—well, naked under her robe—feeding his son with her breasts swollen to capacity, her hair all tousled from hours of making love, was enough to blow his manhood to smithereens.

Moving like a man in a trance, he went to the bathroom and ran a facecloth under warm water, then wrung it out

and went back to the kitchen. Still walking as if he'd un-
dergone a major head trauma, he handed it to her and turned
away.

"Murphy?" He probably wouldn't have responded, except her voice had a little tremor of doubt in it.

Keeping his eyes fixed on the top of her head, he answered. "Hmm?"

"Is something wrong?"

"No. Nothing's wrong."

There was a stiff silence, then she spoke again, her voice
so quiet he could hardly hear her. "I think there is."

He wanted to close his eyes, but he knew he'd simply
fall over if he did. Instead, he willed himself to answer.
"Honey, you don't want to know what's on my mind right
now."

"Yes, I do."

He tried to keep from responding, but his feet, and those
other parts of his body, had minds of their own. Going over
to her, he put one hand on the table and the other on the
back of her chair; he looked her square in the eye. "Are
you sure you really want to know?"

Looking worried and anxious, she nodded. Leaning down,
he brushed his lips against hers, turning that initial caress
into a hot, wet, searching kiss, his heart working like a bilge
pump as he moved his mouth hungrily against hers. She
made a strangled sound and grabbed his arm, her breathing
suddenly erratic. Murphy kept that kiss going until his ears
started to ring and his lungs totally malfunctioned—and until J.J. squawked.

Not sure his lungs were ever going to haul in enough air,
he closed his eyes and rested his forehead against hers for
a moment, vaguely aware that she was attending to their
son. Once he had enough oxygen in his system to stand up

without falling over, he pulled away. His hand again gripping the back of her chair, he looked down at her. "Now, that's what I had on my mind."

She looked as if her thoughts had been totally short-circuited. Closing her eyes, she took a deep, uneven breath, then glanced up at him, her expression still a little dazed. But a tiny smile appeared. "You've had that on your mind quite a bit lately, haven't you?"

He laughed and gave her nose a light tap. "Yeah. But I'm going to have to make a trip to the drugstore before I get it on my mind again."

There was a glint in her eyes as she glanced down at the nursing baby, a hint of suppressed laughter in her voice when she responded. "Well, with a load like that, maybe you should go now."

Murphy decided it was as if J.J. had set out on a mission to keep his parents together, and now that he had accomplished that in spades, he could junk the colic. Well, actually he didn't completely junk it. He still got fussy and had them jumping through hoops on occasions, but at least at night he would actually sleep between feedings. Which had both Murphy and Jordan absolutely giddy.

And Murphy recognized that with J.J. sleeping better at night, there was really no reason for him to stay at Jordan's. But since she never brought it up, neither did he. In fact, he had moved in even more. Without making any kind of an issue out of it, he started sleeping in the master bedroom as if he belonged there. It was nice, going to bed together, and it was even nicer to wake up in the night and have her right there beside him. It was almost like being married. Almost.

But it was more than the new closeness in their relationship that kept him there. It was the changes in Jordan, as well. There had been a big change since J.J. was fussing less and sleeping more. It was as if motherhood had eroded her former self, and for Murphy, it was as if he was getting to see the real Jordan Kennedy underneath. Funny, self-effacing, totally enchanted by her small son. And there were times when Murphy was caught so unawares, was so totally disarmed by this emerging person, that he felt as if he'd been caught in some kind of weird time warp. And every day he fell in love with her a little more.

Which was damned sobering. Because in spite of how much he wanted it otherwise, there was still that element of guardedness in her. Yes, she let him get as close to her as he wanted—but there were parts of herself that she still withheld, as if she was protecting herself. And unless he could somehow slip behind her wariness, he knew he was pretty much at a standstill.

But he tried not to think about it. He just kept hoping for a breakthrough—any kind of breakthrough. What he wanted more than anything was some demonstration of trust from her—something. Anything.

Well, at least if nothing else—thanks to Revenue Canada—they reestablished their client-accountant association. Now that he was over being ticked off at her, Murphy had to be honest with himself. It was true; one reason he hadn't moved to another accountant was out of spite. But the most important reason was that she was sharp, astute and she knew the tax act inside and out. So when his bookkeeper, who was due to leave on holidays that afternoon, phoned to tell him that Revenue Canada was questioning the corporate return, he pulled a bald-faced scam and told Jordan about it. And he did it because he knew exactly what she would do.

She had taken a six-month maternity leave from the firm, which meant that most of her clients had been temporarily shuffled to one of the other partners. But Murphy knew from odd comments that she was worried about losing some of her client base—she wouldn't talk about it, but he could tell she was concerned. So this way, he could let her know without coming right out and saying so that Munroe Construction had every intention of keeping her on.

They dropped J.J. off with Baba, who was standing on the street waiting for them when they drove up. His grandmother had dragged out a tiny crib that Murphy's grandfather had made when their first daughter was born, had it all polished up and set up in her living room, right by her favorite chair. Murphy had a hard time to keep from laughing. It was just so Baba.

After the family barbecue, Baba had taken it upon herself to be the family representative, and she started showing up at the condo, unexpected and unannounced. She'd just hop on a bus and arrive at the door, usually with some of her specialized goodies, and usually when Murphy was at the job site. Jordan was always so thrilled by her visits, and it was pretty obvious that she was totally taken by the older woman.

But what he really got a kick out of was watching his grandmother and Jordan together. They had gotten so tight that they started having these silent little exchanges—like when Jordan handed Baba two bottles for J.J., and Baba touched her own breast and gave Jordan a questioning look, and Jordan turned pink and nodded. It was all so—family. Murphy figured that after J.J., Baba was his next-best weapon.

The other thing that amused the hell out of him was Jordan's attitude about leaving their son for the first time. He had expected separation anxiety. Nope. Didn't happen. Instead, she had a self-satisfied look on her face when they drove away from Baba's—as if leaving J.J. with his great-grandmother was the best thing that had ever happened.

Then they hit the head office of Munroe Construction, which was located in an industrial strip mall on the southeast side of the city. And it took Jordan exactly twenty minutes to sort out a problem that would have taken him half a day to find, let alone fix. Getting the documentation meticulously organized, she used the computer in his office to write a rather brisk letter to Revenue Canada. With that prim-accountant look on her face, she referred to attached documents, item by item, meticulously pointing out *their* error. He loved it.

It was early afternoon by the time they left the office. And even though they were well into fall, heat radiated off the concrete parking lot and the sunlight was blindingly bright as it bounced off the windshield of Jordan's truck. The metal frame of the door was hot to the touch as he locked it behind him. Checking to make sure the door was secure, he glanced at her. "Do you mind if we stopped by my place first? I fixed one of Baba's kitchen chairs, and it's in my workshop. I should get it back to her."

Slipping on her sunglasses, Jordan shook her head. "No, I don't mind."

Murphy gave her a hard, assessing look. There had been a funny tone in her voice, and he wondered what it meant. Maybe it had to do with going to his place. Because in their previous life, she had been in his house exactly once, and that time she went as far as the kitchen. She'd been very skittish, as if she didn't feel safe there—or maybe, he realized now, it was that she felt as if she didn't belong. They were approaching the Explorer when she handed him the keys, avoiding eye contact. "Here, you may as well drive. You know the way from here."

He wasn't sure if it was about going to his place, or if it was about something else, but something was cooking with her. He'd sensed her withdrawal when they'd gone into his office to use his computer. At the time, he thought she was preoccupied with the problem. Now he wasn't so sure.

The street in front of his house was a narrow dead end, and the huge elm trees on either side of the road formed a leafy canopy overhead, their foliage breaking the heat. Murphy parked in the driveway and switched off the engine, leaving the keys in the ignition. "My workshop's in the back of the garage. Do you want to check out the backyard? You could pick yourself another bunch of flowers, if you want."

She gave him a quick glance, the expression in her eyes obscured by the sunglasses. Her voice was oddly uneven when she answered. "Yes. I'd like that."

Sensing some kind of distress in her, Murphy held her hand as they followed the old flagstone path around to the back, wondering what in hell was going on. When they reached the rear of the house, she didn't give the yard so much as a glance. She looked up at him. "Could I get something to drink?"

"Sure." He let go of her hand and rested his on the small of her back. "Come on in."

They entered through what used to be the old summer kitchen, part of which had been remodeled and turned into a laundry area. Murphy had always suspected the original Dutch Colonial design had been altered, and the summer kitchen was one of the reasons. The other was the interior layout. The house was basically divided in half from front to back, with the summer kitchen, kitchen, dining room and living room lined up in a row and taking up one half.

A central hall separated the two sides, with the large master bedroom at the street end, followed by a bath, another room that he suspected was designed as a nursery, then a large sunroom that he had turned into a home office.

He didn't use the second floor. The stairwell, which led upstairs, was located in the dining room. Because of the slope of the roof, the rooms upstairs also ran front to back, with two huge dormer bedrooms on either end, a huge windowless storage room on one side of the landing and a good-sized bathroom on the other. He hadn't done any restoration in the upstairs, partly because he wasn't sure what he was going to find under the three layers of very old linoleum. But also because he had no reason to.

All the blinds were drawn to keep out the heat, and the house was dim and surprisingly cool. He went to the sink and turned on the cold-water tap, aware that Jordan was inspecting the leaded-glass, six-pane cupboard doors, which had taken him the entire winter to restore. There were so many layers of paint on the frames that he'd had to use a gas mask when he stripped them, because he was certain there had to be lead-based paint in there somewhere. He waited for her to say something but she didn't. She just drifted off out of his line of sight.

Getting a tray of ice out of the fridge, he cracked it and dumped some into each glass, then filled them. When he turned around to hand her a glass, she was gone. Feeling oddly uneasy, he went looking for her. He found her in the living room, by the weird wall adjacent to the fireplace. That wall had always struck him as strange, as if it were one big frame. So he'd taken advantage of its location and had hung a collection of family photographs on the wall. Not studio portraits. But what his father called real pictures.

She was standing before that wall, her sunglasses shoved on top of her head and her arms clasped, a somber expression on her face. It hit him then—that her quiet mood had something to do with the pictures of him and his siblings that he had in his office, the one of the bunch of them in uniforms, lined up like a real baseball team for the annual game of slow-pitch against the company employees. Sobered by the realization, he went over to her, handing her the glass that already had condensation running down it.

She took it, rubbing her fingers up and down its wet surface. "These are great pictures," she said, her voice very quiet.

Suddenly wishing the water were something stronger, he took a long drink. Wiping his mouth, he stared at the grouping. "Yeah, they are."

She drank her water and studied the wall, her gaze going from picture to picture, her expression getting more and more strained. Her attention landed on one photo—one that was different—one of a Latin face. "There were pictures of her at your parents'—on the piano. Who is she?"

Holding his empty glass by the rim, Murphy folded his arms, a funny feeling unfolding in his middle. "That's Maria. She's sort of a foster sister, I guess. Mom and Dad have always supported international children's organizations. And Maria was one of their foster kids. Only she kinda turned into family."

Her movements stiff, Jordan set her glass on the magazine lying on an unused lamp table. Her voice was so tight, it didn't even sound like hers when she spoke. "I was a foster child."

Murphy closed his eyes, a kind of crazy relief ricocheting

through his chest and gut. Yes! he thought. Yes. Easing in a careful breath, he responded. "I kinda thought as much."

Her head came around, and she shot him a startled look. "Pardon?"

He reached in front of her and set his glass beside hers. Then leaning against the mantel on the fireplace, he rested his hand on his hip as he met her gaze dead-on. "I said I figured as much. You never mentioned family—in fact, you went out of your way to avoid it. It just seemed to add up."

Clasping her arms tighter, she looked away, her lips white. "Oh."

Watching her, his insides in knots, he kept his tone calm. "I keep hoping you're going to trust me enough to tell me about it."

She shot him a tight, caustic smile. "Well, Munroe. There's not much to tell. I was abandoned in a bus depot when I was about J.J.'s age. End of story."

She turned to leave, but he caught her arm. Ignoring her stiff resistance, he wrapped her up in a secure embrace, then forced her head against his neck. "Hey," he whispered softly, rocking her a little. "I'm on your side. And I understand why you don't want to talk about it, but I'm glad you told me."

She didn't say anything but remained stiff in his arms, and he held her even tighter. His chest was so thick, he felt as if it were full of wet concrete. He was standing on thin ice and he knew it. If he made one wrong move now, she'd be running for cover. He was pretty certain she had serious feelings for him, but he wouldn't want to swear to it. And he also knew, if it hadn't been for her strong sense of fair play and deep sense of honesty—and the fact that she wanted a family for J.J.—she never would have told him anything. But at least she had told him this.

Still rocking her, he pressed his cheek against her temple. His voice was very gruff when he spoke again. "That has nothing to do with your being a parent, Jordan. And just so you know—I think you're one hell of a mother, and I think J.J. was damned lucky to get you."

She let go a choked sob and went instantly slack in his embrace. Sliding her arms around his rib cage, she turned her face against him and hung on as if he'd just tossed her a lifeline. Resting his head against hers, he closed his eyes and swallowed hard, wishing he could just wrap her up enough to stop her from hurting.

They stood like that for a long time, until every speck of tension had left her body. Running her hand up his back, she took a deep breath and spoke. "So when are you going to give me a guided tour of this incredible house of yours?" She was doing the exact same thing his father did. He grinned and gave her a hard hug. "Well, first of all, let me show you my bedroom."

Her laugh was muffled but it was real. "I don't think so, hero. Not unless you've got a stash of those little foil packets somewhere."

"Nope. Don't have a stash." He pulled her head back and gave her a very heated kiss. "But maybe we can improvise," he murmured against her mouth.

They improvised so well that he was still light-headed and walking into walls two hours later, when he did give her a tour. But the really great thing about his sexual stupor was that Jordan thought it was all very funny, and all the shadows were gone from her eyes. Now if he could just maintain the status quo...

But he also recognized one hard, cold fact. With all of

her grim past experience, she had every reason not to trust anyone. Even him. Yeah, she'd been the one to walk out, all right. But without even realizing it, he'd betrayed her, too. Because he had let her go.

Chapter 9

The month of October was aces all the way. Munroe Construction was ahead of schedule, there hadn't been one single snag and they had enough work lined up to keep all the crews busy till spring. But as far as Murphy was concerned, what was happening at work was a sidebar.

What really mattered was his private life. By the end of the month, everything was coming up solid roses. It was as if J.J. hit twelve weeks, and he miraculously turned into a whole new kid. He started sleeping through the nights, and during the day he was a perfect, contented baby who smiled at everything and everybody.

And order had been restored at Jordan's. Not the former uptight, prissy kind of order—that had pretty much gone by the boards. But just an easy kind of order—a place where you could put your feet up and feel at home.

And that was the problem. It was getting to feel like home more and more. And it bothered the hell out of him that they were living together the way they were—caught in some kind of no-man's-land. Feeling like a home, but not really being his home. Feeling like a family, but not really being one. Feeling married to her, but not. It drove him crazy, but he didn't know how to change the situation without rocking the boat. Because if the truth be known, he didn't trust Ms. Jordan Kennedy all that much, either. If she took a walk once before, she could do it again. So to keep himself from going totally nuts, he tried not to think about it at all.

Murphy always tried to make it home for dinner. If J.J. was going to have a fussy period, it would be then, and he wanted to give Jordan a break from child care. And he also wanted to spend time with his son.

But tonight, there were no fussing squawks when he entered the apartment, just the tantalizing smell of dinner cooking. He toed off his work boots and set them in the closet, then began pulling his shirt out of the waistband of his jeans as he walked into the kitchen. It had been a hard day at work, and he was hot and sweaty and tired. And on top of that, the heavy traffic on the way home had made him irritable. But that tension started to uncoil the minute he laid eyes on her. She was seated at the kitchen table in a bright yellow loose-fitting dress with a long flowing skirt, her long legs wound around the legs of the chair, her head propped on her hand as she read the morning newspaper. She straightened when she saw him, her eyes lighting up. "Hi. I didn't hear you come in."

He didn't answer. That light in her eyes did things to his chest that made it impossible. Instead he went over to where she was sitting and leaned down to give her a kiss. Her mouth opened under his, and she wound her arms around his neck, her response sending a hot energy coursing through him. Satisfying himself with the taste of her, he caught one arm and tried to pull it away, his voice gruff when he spoke. "I'm going to get your pretty dress all dirty."

Clasping her arms tighter around his neck, she brushed her mouth across his bottom lip. "I don't care."

His pulse speeding up from the soft slowness of her mouth, he suddenly didn't care much, either. Emitting a low growl of approval, he caught her around the hips and lifted her up, locking her against him. She wrapped her legs around him as she continued to torment him with the lazy movements of her mouth, and he clasped her tighter, his breathing suddenly labored. Overcome with a heavy weakness, he turned with her and sat down in her chair, trying not to groan as she settled her weight on the thick, pulsing ridge under the fly of his jeans. It was as if she transfused him—and such powerful feelings flooded through him, filling him up and making his entire body pulse and throb.

His heart slamming against the walls of his chest and his breathing ragged, he finally drew away, abruptly pressing his face against the curve of her neck. She seemed to mold around him, as if she were melting into him, and he closed his eyes, forcing himself not to react. God, but she could ring his bells. Kissing the soft, warm skin of her neck, he roughly ran his hand up her back. "Ah, babe," he whispered gruffly. "You feel so damned good. But I'm filthy and I need a shower—I shouldn't even be touching you."

Grasping his head and lifting it, she covered his mouth in a kiss that spoke of every shade of carnal knowledge, sending a shock wave of need through him. Slowly, ever so slowly, she shifted against him, and Murphy inhaled sharply, his pulse running thicker. He locked his arms around her, unable to stop himself from thrusting up against her.

The skirt of her dress was wadded up, and desperate to feel her bare skin, he ran his hand up the outside of her thigh, his heart stalling out when he realized she had nothing on underneath. She ran her tongue along his bottom lip as she shifted her hips in the most provocative way. "I was waiting for you," she breathed unevenly.

Murphy nearly lost it right there, and he twisted his head away and locked his jaw, fresh perspiration breaking out on his forehead. But Jordan was having nothing of his restraint. She found his mouth again and, placing her feet on the floor, she raised herself up and fumbled with the snap on his jeans.

His breathing loud and jagged, he grasped her hand. "Let me get—"

"No," she murmured against his mouth. "You don't need to. I'm safe."

Murphy tried to think through the fevered haze in his mind. He had never gone without protection with her. Ever. And the thought of being totally naked inside her made his universe tilt at a dangerous angle. Putting his hands on her waist to lift her away, he felt her fingers touch the hard heat of him, and he groaned and involuntarily shifted his hips as she freed him. And right then, he couldn't have pulled back, no matter what. He grimaced and went rigid in an agony of pleasure as she slowly, so slowly impaled herself on him. The feel of her, tight and moist around him, sent him whirling into a senseless soaring darkness, and all he knew was that she surrounded him.

He wasn't sure afterward how come they hadn't broken the damned chair, and he wanted to laugh as he cradled her spent body against him. She was wound around him—arms, legs, body—with her face pressed against his. Feeling a little as though he had been pulled inside out, he hugged her tight, just feeling so damned good.

He ran one hand up the back of her neck, giving her another hard hug. "God. No wonder I like coming home."

She laughed against his neck, pinching his shoulder. "I do what I can to make you happy."

No, you don't, he thought, his expression turning sober. You still don't let me past your defenses.

Feeling like a heel for thinking that now, he forced himself to shut off those kinds of thoughts, and he turned his head and kissed her shoulder. "So. Do you have any more events planned for this evening?"

She chuckled and gave him a squeeze. "This isn't track and field, Munroe."

"Damn."

Relaxing her hold, she leaned back and looked at him, and the brightness in her eyes made his heart contract. She just looked so alive, so full of life. And so beautiful. He had wrecked her neat French braid, and there were wisps of hair against her face. With infinite tenderness, he carefully smoothed the loose tendrils back. God, but he did not want to lose this woman. Catching her head, he urged her down and gave her one more kiss, trying to tell her, without saying so aloud, how much he needed her in his life.

Wanting to avoid any more somber thoughts, Murphy made up his mind he was not going to climb on that blues train. Instead of thinking about the gray areas in their relationship, he was going to focus on the bright ones. Whoever had coined the phrase Live For Today must have had a woman like Jordan in his life.

They actually had a real sit-down dinner, with all the fixings and with the knife blades turned in and the dessert

spoon centered perfectly above the plate. Jordan had made
a beef Stroganoff that was head and shoulders above any
he'd ever eaten, and he told her so. She waved his accla-
mation off, but she had that pleased, self-satisfied look on
her face when he had his third helping.

When the baby woke up, they moved out onto the terrace
and sat in the warm autumn sunshine while she fed him,
catching up on each other's days. He gave J.J. his bath while
she indulged in a long soak in her bathroom, then with their
son napping on the Baba Blankie on the floor, they watched
a documentary on TV. It wasn't as if they did anything
special; it was just *family,* and Murphy stored up every minute.

The documentary finished at nine, and they both ended
up in the kitchen. Murphy commandeered what was left of
the dessert, and Jordan was making herself a cup of herbal
tea—which he knew she detested. Amusement tugging at
his mouth, he watched the distasteful expression around her
mouth as she poured boiling water over the tea bag she'd
dropped in the mug. The sacrifices nursing mothers made.

The phone rang, and giving the mug a disgusted look,
Jordan picked up the portable that was lying on the counter.
She pressed the connect button, shifting the mouthpiece
closer. "Hello."

An odd look crossed her face and her tone was suddenly
crisp. "Just a moment." Then she shoved the phone at Murphy. "It's for you."

He gave her a what's-your-problem? frown, then put the
phone to his ear. It was Taffy Valenti, the interior decorator
he used for show homes and for client consultations. She
was married to Marco's cousin—hence the name ending in
a vowel. Murphy had known her for a very long time.

"Hi, Taffy. What's up?"

"Just my damned blood pressure. God, sometimes I think all suppliers should be stuffed into a crate and dropped in the Florida Everglades."

Rocking back in his chair, Murphy grinned. "Yeah? You're such a hardhearted woman."

As the interior decorator explained her problem with a flooring supplier, Murphy happened to glance over toward the counter just as Jordan dumped the herbal tea down the drain. And she had a look on her face that he had never seen before. With her chin in the air, she headed toward the hallway, and Murphy let his chair rock forward, planting all four legs on the floor. What in hell was that about? She looked—miffed. A funny feeling started unfolding in his belly, and he shook his head. Nah, couldn't be. But a slow grin worked its way loose. Well, maybe.

He concluded his conversation with Taffy, set the phone on the table and headed toward the hallway. This was definitely worth checking out.

J.J. had been spending his nights in the crib the past week, and Jordan had him on the raised mattress; it was apparent she'd just finished putting dry diapers and a fresh pair of sleepers on him. Leaning his shoulder against the door frame, Murphy hooked his thumbs in the front pockets of his clean jeans and watched her. He tried to beat down the sudden flicker of hope, but it wasn't going to go down without a fight.

He knew that she knew he was there, but she didn't look at him. And from what he could see of her profile, she wasn't feeling exactly friendly.

He let her stew in her own juice for a moment, then spoke. "Do you want to know who that was?"

She gave J.J. his soother and slammed the safety rail into place. "No."

Hope flared a little higher, and his pulse picked up speed. "Are you *jealous,* Jordan?"

She shot him a snippy look, then looked away. "Of course not."

Murphy's heart suddenly started beating in double time. She was lying. Jordan Kennedy was lying. Wanting to grab her up and swing her around, Murphy kept his shoulder anchored to the door frame.

"Well, I just want you to know that there's no reason to be. She runs Valenti Decorating—you must have come across the name in my accounts."

Jordan still wouldn't look at him, but the tenseness in her shoulders eased, and her movements weren't quite so jerky as she very carefully and precisely folded the sleepers she had just taken off J.J.

Murphy watched her, waging a silent now/not-now battle with himself. For some reason, he felt as if he'd suddenly hit a fork in the road, and he had to make a decision. And he had to make it now.

He had known all along there would have to be some sort of confrontation. But he hadn't expected it to happen like this—he thought it would be something he'd work up to. Build a bridge a bit at a time. But maybe that was the problem. Maybe he had been putting it off too long. And maybe it was just bloody well time. Besides, he was certain Ms. Jordan had just got a poke from the green-eyed monster, and that gave him the kind of optimism he'd never experienced before.

Feeling as if he were stepping out into thin air, he said exactly what had been on his mind for weeks. "That's something you'll never have to worry about, darlin'. That

I'd ever mess around on you. I know you have your reasons for not trusting anyone, but I think it's time you put some trust in me.'' Knowing he was truly throwing himself into the deep end, he collected himself. ''You gotta know I love you, Jordan. And I want us to get married. I want us to make a home for J.J., and I want us to make some more babies down the road. I want it all.''

It was as if every single word were hanging in the sizzling silence between them. She didn't look at him, but just kept folding and refolding the sleepers.

Tension encased every single one of his muscles, and he waited, his heart jammed up so high in his chest he felt as if it were stuck in his larynx. With a crazy flutter growing in his middle, he took another deep breath and forged on. ''I've discovered something the past three months. I've discovered that I like sharing a home, I like having a family, but most of all, I like feeling married to you.''

Jordan turned, staring at him as if what he said were totally incomprehensible, her face absolutely ashen. It was obvious that she was shaken right down to her shoes, and Murphy understood that. He was feeling pretty damned shaken himself. It took every bit of control he had to stay where he was, knowing that he had, in fact, drawn a line in the sand. Holding her gaze, he spoke again. ''I know you've been running away from this face-off right from the beginning. I know that. But I also know we can build a good life together.'' His gaze deadly sober, he stared at her. ''Marry me, Jordan.''

He saw it happen. He saw her pull herself back inside, and a heavy dread started to spread through him.

As if tearing herself away from his gaze, Jordan turned to the change table and began folding diapers. He couldn't believe his eyes. He'd just asked her to marry him, and *she* started folding diapers? For the first time in months, he wanted to grab her and give her a shake.

Her expression fixed, as if this were just a routine conversation, she stacked one folded diaper on top of the pile. Then in the exact same tone she used when talking about debits and credits, she finally responded. "We already have a home for J.J. So I really don't see why we just can't continue on the way we are."

It was as if all the old anger flared up inside him, and his pulse went a little haywire. Furious at her for reverting back to her old defensive patterns, Murphy abruptly straightened, turning away from her, resisting the urge to put his fist through the wall. Trying to get a handle on the surge of bitterness, he made himself count to ten, then turned back to face her. Anger seething just below the surface, he called it as he saw it. "Well, Jordan. I don't want to continue on the way we are. I don't want to keep living in some kind of loosey-goosey limbo. I think it's about time we made a commitment. Is that so much to ask?"

Clearly upset, she started refolding the already folded diapers. "You're blowing things all out of proportion, Murphy."

It was as if she was *scolding* him, and Murphy truly saw red. And he lost his temper. "Okay, Kennedy," he snapped back. "If that's where you're coming from, how about if you explain my role here? Am I a live-in lover, or just a convenient nanny? Just how in hell do you see me?"

He could tell that that comment had hurt her, but she faced him, her head held high, her face even more ashen. "I don't know whatever made you think you're under some duty-bound obligation to marry me. And you'd better lower your voice or you're going to wake the baby."

Murphy stared at her. Wake the baby? The baby who was

now watching his mobile go around and around? Totally steamed over her snotty, accountant's tone, and even more ticked off over her bloody thickheadedness, he let her have it with both barrels. "I don't care if I wake the entire bloody city. This time we are going to settle this once and for all. I want to marry you because I love you, damn it. I want us to spend the rest of our lives together because I care about you, not because I'm under some rotten *obligation* to make an honest woman out of you."

Which was the absolute wrong thing to say. Her chin came up, and she defensively folded her arms in front of her. He had never seen her eyes ice over the way they did right then. "Well, that's just terrific, Munroe. Because I don't need you or anyone else to make an honest woman out of me. I can do that all by myself, thank you very much."

So furious that he was certain he was about to blow, Murphy ground his teeth together, trying to put a lid on his reaction. A tiny sliver of logic told him that she had very deliberately turned the tables on him, but he was so damned ticked off, he ignored that little voice of caution. His anger got the upper hand, and in no uncertain terms, he laid it on the line. "I'm sick and tired of tiptoeing around the real issue here. I love you, damn it, and if you don't believe that, there's not much point of me hanging around, marking time, hoping that you're eventually going to come around. I want a life, damn it!"

An awful expression crossed Jordan's face, and her eyes widened with alarm. It was as if she realized that she had pushed him too far, and it scared her. Coming over to him, she laid her hand on his arm, and it wasn't until then that he realized she was shaking.

She looked up at him, her face white, her eyes beseeching. "Do we have to make a decision right now? Can't we just give it a little more time?"

Realizing she was trying to mollify him, Murphy glared down at her, not really giving a damn at this point. Because this time, he had really had it. Crossing his arms in front of him, he cocked one hip and gave her a bitter smile. "Time ain't going to cut it, honey. If you haven't figured it out by now that I'm in it for the long haul, you're never going to figure it out."

He pulled away from her touch, then turned and stared out the nursery door, his fury turning into something cold and hard. It was as if the past three months had shriveled up to nothing, and he was left standing there, holding an empty bag. There was nowhere to go. The cold, hard feeling rose up, dragging with it all the old bitter feelings from before. Giving his anger a chance to set, he fixed his face into a stony expression and turned to face her. "If you don't trust me enough to believe me about something as basic as how I feel about you, then there's not much point in me sticking around." Feeling hardened from the inside out, he called the shot. "So it's your call, dinkums. But as far as I'm concerned, it's either all or nothing." Giving her another cutting smile, he turned to leave. "But if there ever is a next time, you're the one who's going to have to jump into the deep end. Because I'm sure in hell not making that dive again."

Without giving her another glance, he strode off down the hallway, more furious, more hardened and cold than he'd ever been in his whole life. She had done it to him a second time, and he had let her. But this time, he was going to be the one to walk. Because there was absolutely no reason to stay. There were some barriers that could be disassembled, and there were some that were permanent, and there was no getting around those. She had built those walls so deep, it was as if she'd constructed a damned fort around herself. And unless she opened the gate, there was no way in.

He left with the slam of the door. He needed to get away from her, and he needed to get the hell out of her apartment. Without any thought to where he was going, he stormed out of the building and got in his truck and drove.

And he drove and drove, his anger like a head of steam, pushing him on. He had no idea how much ground he covered, or how many country roads he'd been down, but it was well past midnight when he found himself parked outside his house without even making a conscious decision to go there—it was as if he switched to autopilot, letting his anger govern him.

It was a bad night. The first half he'd spent raging against her; the second half was where it got really ugly. Because that was when he faced the loss—the loss of a life together, the loss of her and the loss of daily contact with his son. At one point, when he was at the height of his anger, he flirted with the idea of punishing her by going after custody. But he was sickened by just how sleazy an idea it was—that he had even entertained that thought for a second. As furious as he was with her for not believing in a lifetime together, he could never, ever hurt her that way. It would kill her, and that kind of nastiness was not a level he wanted to sink to. She had given him a son out of choice; he would give him back to her the same way.

But what damned near ripped his heart out was knowing that his little boy was not going to be part of his everyday existence. No more morning bottles, no more baths at bedtime—and he would miss out on those little daily milestones, like the very first time that J.J. had pulled out his soother on his very own.

His hand resting on a support post, a bottle of beer in his free hand, Murphy stood on his front veranda and stared blindly into the night. His throat was so tight he couldn't swallow, and the fierce ache sitting squarely on his chest made it nearly impossible to breathe. God, he was going to miss J.J.—and he was going to miss her. Miss being with her. But there was no going back. He would just end up hating himself and hating her. But that sense of loss was so immense, he felt as if someone had reached inside him and ripped everything out.

Roughly gouging at his eyes, he forced himself to take several swallows from the bottle. Damn, but hindsight was twenty-twenty. He should have never confronted her; he should have let sleeping dogs lie, but he hadn't. No, he had to go charging in like some bloody bull in a china shop, smashing everything to smithereens. But now that it had all been dragged out in the open, there was no way they could ever pick up the pieces and put their old life back together again. There was no way he could pretend the blowup never happened. For him, there would be just too many cracks showing.

And maybe it was better this way—better for J.J. This way his kid wasn't old enough to realize what was going on. J.J. would grow up thinking he was just one of those kids who saw his old man on evenings and weekends.

The pain in Murphy's chest torqued up a notch, and he bent his head and gouged at his eyes again, the night closing in around him. He felt as if he had been buried alive in a deep, dark, empty hole.

By morning, Murphy was so damned numb, he couldn't feel anything at all. He hadn't slept, and he pretty much felt as if he'd been run over by an earth packer. It had started to drizzle about five in the morning and it was still drizzling at nine. With a mug of freshly brewed coffee in his hand, Murphy stood in the back doorway, his shoulder resting against the frame. The cloud cover was low and gunmetal gray, its denseness creating a certain hush, the steady *pitter-pat* of rain on the dried autumn leaves the only sound in the still morning. The backyard had that cleansed, wet look. The rain had soaked into the weathered cedar fence, and the trunks of the trees were darkened and shiny with moisture. And in the back garden, the fading blooms of the fall flowers drooped, sagging limply from the weight of the soft rain.

His eyes feeling as if they had gravel in them, Murphy took a sip of the coffee, feeling emotionally dead. He hoped the numbness lasted, because he had reached a cold, grim conclusion. There was no solution. He had kidded himself into believing that because he understood her, understood where she was coming from, he could change things. But there were some things he simply could not change. And there was no going back. Yeah, they would have to coexist because of J.J. And he would be forced to talk to her whenever it was necessary—like when he needed to make arrangements concerning his son. But that was as far as he was going to go. Even he was bright enough to realize that he wasn't breaking down walls; he was simply banging his head against one. And it was time for him to get the hell out.

Jordan had an appointment at nine-thirty that morning to take J.J. for a checkup at the well-baby clinic. And being the kind of concerned mother she was, Murphy knew she would keep that appointment. So he was going to take advantage of her absence to clear all of his stuff out of the apartment. He had to make it final. Because he wouldn't let it go unless he did. Draining his mug, he turned back to the house, his expression taut. It was time to get the show on the road.

It was a bad scene at the condo—a very bad scene. Every time he went into the nursery, or came in contact with anything that was related to his son, he pretty much lost it. He was finally able to accomplish his mission by resurrecting his anger, and he used that to fortify himself. If she didn't want him in her life, then by God, he was going to make sure not a single trace of him remained. He stripped the place of everything that was his, right down to his favorite brand of coffee in the pantry. But the hardest thing was closing that apartment door for the very last time, knowing he was leaving behind what mattered most.

He took his stuff home and unloaded everything in the garage. Then he went to the job site and took on every miserable job he could find that required heavy labor. Anything, so he couldn't think.

It was just before noon when Marco came out to where Murphy was working in the chilling fall rain, trying to dig out a survey stake that had been covered by a careless backhoe operator. He had been at it for forty-five minutes, and he was getting genuinely ticked off. Digging out wet clay was not his idea of good therapy. Sweat and rain were running down his neck, and the muscles through his shoulders burned.

Pausing by the second shovel that Murphy had jammed in the ground, Marco rested his hands on his hips and watched his brother-in-law, the rain rattling against his hard hat and slicker. He had an assessing look on his face as he continued to watch, saying nothing. Finally he spoke. "Jordan is on the phone in the shack. She wants to talk to you."

Stepping on the spade to force it into the clay, Murphy steeled his expression. "Tell her I'm not here."

Marco picked up a tail cutting of a two-by-four by his feet and tossed it on the waste pile behind him, then rested his hand on the handle of the second spade. "Do you want to tell me what's going on, Murph?"

"Nope."

"Look, pal. I don't know if you realized it or not, but you were in rough shape the last time things cratered between you two. And if that's what's going on now, it's going to be a hell of a lot worse this time."

Straightening, Murphy glared at his brother-in-law. He hadn't said jack-trap about what went on the last time. "You don't know what in hell you're talking about, *pal*."

Marco wiggled the spade handle and gave Murphy a lop-sided grin. "Give me a break, Munroe. Hey, I'm Italian— we're lovers not fighters, and we all have ESP when it comes to affairs of the heart. You might not have broadcast it around that something was cooking last year, but I knew. You had that goofy look on your face."

In spite of the big hole in his chest, Murphy found himself giving up a wry smile. Marco had a way of putting things. And he should have known he couldn't slide something like that past his foreman.

Marco's expression turned sober, and he fixed a level gaze on his brother-in-law. "And I could see you were go-ing through some sort of hell last winter. It was pretty ob-vious the affair had gone sour. So don't snow me, *pal*. So talk."

Murphy held the other man's gaze for a space, then looked away, his throat suddenly tight. "Not right now." Needing to tune out the heaviness climbing up his chest, he started digging again.

Marco hesitated, then spoke. "Fine. I'll go tell her you aren't here."

Fine, Murphy thought. You do that.

Murphy stayed on the job site until it was too dark to see, and he was halfway home when his sleepless night had caught up to him big time. And he felt almost sick.

He could hear his phone ringing as he mounted the steps to the front veranda, but he made no attempt to get to it. Instead, he took his time removing his muddy work boots and setting them aside. He didn't want to talk to anybody. Especially her. Not tonight.

By the time he straightened and unlocked the door, the ringing stopped, and he experienced a sudden knot of regret in his gut. Not even trying to analyze his reaction, he entered the darkened house, the onset of a headache causing shards of light behind his eyes. Turning on the old-fashioned globe light in the front entryway, he looped his damp jacket over the newel post of the railing that separated the entryway from the living room, then pulled his damp shirt loose from his muddy jeans. He was going to have a hot shower, take something for the damned headache and after that he was going to bed.

The shower was hot and long, the heat draining him of what little energy he had left. He went into his bedroom, a towel wrapped around his hips, and he was emptying the pockets of his dirty jeans when the phone rang again. He finished emptying his pockets, his jaw tight. Finally he released a long sigh. He was going to have to deal with her sometime—and it may as well be sooner than later. Murphy bent over and swept up the phone that was sitting on the floor by his bed. Straightening, he lifted the receiver, his expression grim. With deliberate intent, he answered it the same way he would on the job. "Murphy Munroe."

There was a tense silence, then Jordan spoke, and he could tell by her voice that she was not having an easy time of it, either. "It's Jordan," she said, her voice breaking. "I've been trying to get in touch with you all day."

He set the phone on the bedside table, then rested his hand on his hip and stared across the room, the headache moving right behind his eyes. He'd known she would be upset by his pack-and-move stunt, but her reaction was coming just a little too late. He answered, his tone short. "Yeah, I know."

There was a muffled sound, then she spoke, her voice very unsteady. "I didn't expect you to move out like that."

His face feeling as if it were carved out of boards, he responded, his tone blunt. "I don't know what you expected me to do, Jordan. You didn't really leave me any options. You made it pretty obvious that you couldn't care less. And you also made it clear you weren't in it for the long haul."

Her voice was quavering and thick when she finally responded. "I never thought of you as a nanny or a live-in, Murphy," she choked out. "I never meant for you to think that."

The initial flare of anger went flat, and he sighed and rubbed his eyes. "That was a cheap shot on my part. I'm sorry I said it."

"Aren't you coming back?"

He lifted his head, staring into space. He got a big, hollow feeling in his chest when he finally answered her. "No."

He heard her take some ragged breaths, as if she was crying, and he turned, wishing they didn't have to go through this. But they did. It was several seconds before she spoke again. "What are you going to do about J.J.?"

He exhaled wearily. "Well, I'm not going to try to take him away from you, if that's what you're getting at."

"No!" she responded, her voice breaking completely. "No! That's not what I meant." Her breathing was muffled as if she was wiping her nose, then she spoke again, her voice quavering so badly, he wasn't sure how she got the words out. "I meant—what I meant was that I—I don't want what happened between us…" There was another long pause, then she continued, "I don't want you to not see him because of me." Her tone changed, getting more urgent, more desperate. "He needs you in his life, Murphy."

Murphy felt as if a giant hand clamped around his chest, and he roughly rubbed his face, his eyes smarting. So it all came back to that—to abandonment—and most likely her own. Hell, with that kind of history, maybe they never even had a chance.

Suddenly tired to the bone, he dropped his hand. "I'm not going to abandon my son, Jordan," he chastised quietly. "I care a whole hell of a lot about him, and I intend on spending as much time with him as I possibly can. And I care about you, too. But that doesn't seem to count." He hesitated, then decided to say it all—because he knew a day would come that he'd regret not saying it when he had the chance. "In spite of everything, I want you to know you're the best thing that ever happened to me." Then without giving her a chance to respond, he reached over and dropped the receiver in the cradle, disconnecting from her, a huge gaping hole where his heart used to be.

Chapter 10

Murphy basically went underground the next few days. He unplugged every phone in the house and left his cell phone off, carrying a pager instead so Marco could get hold of him whenever he needed to. Since he wasn't fit to be around anyone, especially employees or prospective clients, he took on all the grunt work that was usually Marco's domain. Wanting a legitimate excuse to keep clear of absolutely everybody, he kicked the operator off the bulldozer and took over digging the basements for the next phase. Digging big gaping holes suited him just fine.

Jessica showed up at the job site one afternoon, looking very upset and wanting to know what was going on. Jess knew how to mind her own business, and she usually didn't push unless she thought it was important. This time she pushed. Maybe it was because there was a certain finality about saying it all out loud, or maybe she hit him on a day when his own defenses were down, but he finally unloaded the whole story. It should have made him feel better, but it didn't. It only made him feel worse.

He got to day six and finally faced the fact that he was going to have to get with a program. He'd licked his wounds long enough, and now he'd have to grit his teeth and make arrangements to see J.J. But every time he pictured his kid, he got this awful ache in his chest, and the thought of having to come face-to-face with Jordan was more than he could handle. He wasn't sure how he'd get around that, but he was going to have to, or he wouldn't get to see his kid at all.

Instead of wallowing in his own misery, he tried to stay focused on what needed to be done on the job. There were two basements that were roughed in and ready to pour. And the concrete contractor needed to be notified that they were ready.

Except Murphy couldn't notify him. The batteries on his cell phone were stone-cold dead. Swearing to himself, he strode across the uneven, chewed-up ground, thinking he was going to have to smarten up. He couldn't believe he had forgotten to charge up his cell phone—but he had. Which meant going all the way back to the construction shack to make a call. He needed to get a delivery time for the concrete. He needed this walk like he needed another hole in his head. What he really needed was a life.

Autumn had faded, and the trees were stripped of leaves, but it was an unseasonably warm day. Reaching the shack, he took off his hard hat and raked his hand through his damp hair, wishing he had brought something cold to drink. One of these days, he was going to have to pack his brain with him when he came to work.

Licking the dust off his dry lips, he yanked open the shack door and entered. He took two steps and stopped, not entirely sure he was actually seeing what he was seeing. Baba was sitting there in a warped metal chair, an empty car seat and the diaper bag at her feet, a small portable playpen beside her. But what really hauled him up short was that his son was in the playpen, sound asleep. He was so stunned to see his kid in his office, he just stood there, rooted to the spot.

Baba had been looking at the pictures in an industry magazine, and she closed it up. Giving him a calm look, she leaned over and placed the magazine on the battered desk. "I bring the baby to you," she said, as if this were something they had discussed.

His brain stuck in neutral, Murphy stared at her, then at J.J., who was out cold, not a soother in sight. She noticed him noticing the absence of the soother. She gave him a wise nod and a wily smile. "He is a big boy now."

One more milestone that he had missed, and Murphy experienced such a jolt of emotion, it was as if he'd just gotten nailed straight in the solar plexus by a giant fist. He wanted to grab that kid up and hug him in the worst way, but he didn't—he couldn't. Because he felt as if an elephant had suddenly sat on his chest. Instead, he turned away, the ache in his throat so fierce it made his jaws lock. It was so bad, he couldn't even swallow. He heard the scrape of the chair, then Baba patted him on the arm. "Come. Marco knows you take us home to your house. Then we talk."

Murphy wasn't sure how he made the trip from the site to his house without rear-ending somebody, because he kept checking his sleeping son, who was safely anchored in the car seat beside him.

Murphy was so filthy dirty, he didn't dare touch his kid. When they got to his place, Baba carried the baby while

Murphy packed everything inside. Still waging war against some very heavy-duty feelings, Murphy didn't argue when Baba shooed him off for a shower, knowing he had to get a grip before he talked to her.

When he came out, his hair still dripping water, Baba was sitting on the sofa, the playpen at her feet. She had put J.J. in it, and he'd gone back to sleep, only now he was sucking his thumb. So much for the missing soother.

His chest getting tight again, Murphy clamped his mouth shut in a hard line and began rolling back the cuffs of his clean work shirt, feeling as if he were standing on the side of a very steep hill.

Baba got up when she saw him. "Come. I make you something to eat."

His expression set in fixed lines, he followed her into the kitchen, not even trying to answer her.

There was a thick sandwich made out of homemade bread all ready and waiting on the kitchen table, with a bottle of cold beer standing beside it. There was also something white and lacy lying at the end of the table, something that looked as if it might be crocheting. "Sit," she commanded.

Murphy did as he was told, then took a long swallow from the bottle of beer, hoping that the simple act of swallowing would ease the cramp in his throat.

He set the bottle down, and Baba sat down kitty-corner from him, pushing the sandwich toward him. "Eat, and then we talk."

Maybe it was the gentleness in her tone, or her obvious concern, but whatever it was, it darned near took him down. Propping one elbow on the table, he shielded his eyes with his hand, trying like hell to keep everything together.

Baba reached over and rubbed his shoulder. "All right. I will talk." He heard her move the plate aside and pick up the crocheting, then she spoke. "She is a very, very unhappy person, Misha. She cries all the time." There was the sound of crochet thread being pulled from the ball, and then she spoke again. "But this is good."

She couldn't have stunned him more if she'd smacked him, and Murphy lifted his head and stared at her, every speck of that suffocating weight knocked right out of him.

Baba lifted her eyes and smiled at him, then continued on with her delicate handiwork, her fingers flying. "I surprise you, Misha. But it is true. She needs to know."

She pulled more thread out of the skein, then hooked her little finger around the thread. "I always knew I had married a good, good man, and he was my world. But I didn't know what a very good man he was, or how much I would miss him, until he was gone. And I was left with this big emptiness."

She looked up and met Murphy's gaze. "Then I knew how much I had lost. And she needs to know this, Misha. I know about her mama leaving her—such a terrible, terrible thing—how could a mother do that? What kind of person would leave a baby like that?" She shook her head and repositioned the piece of lace in her hand, then looked at him. "Do you remember when Cora was little and was afraid of the water? How she was so scared she couldn't put her face in? Do you remember?"

Both elbows on the table, Murphy rested his chin on his clasped hands, his gaze intent as he watched his grandmother. "Yeah, I remember."

Baba made a dismissive sound. "It was not the water that stopped her from swimming. It was her fear. And remember how you got her to put her face in? You held a cheap ring under the water—one with a big red stone you got out of a machine—and you told her she could have what was in your hand, but she had to put her face in the water and tell you what it was. You remember, Misha?''

Watching her, knowing this was leading up to something significant, he nodded. ''I remember.''

''And Cora had to decide. What was strongest—her fear, or her want of the surprise. Remember how excited she was after she put her face in the water—after she mastered her fear—and got the prize? This is what Jordan has to decide now—which is strongest. Her fear or her want for the prize.''

It was almost as if she had physically lifted a huge weight off his back. And he took his first deep breath in days.

She grinned at him, flashing her dimples. ''So I help her to figure it out. I bring the baby to you. Because she wants you to come for the baby.'' She started crocheting again. ''And I go to her, too, because she is alone and she is going to make herself sick. So I will be mother now.''

It was as if Baba's insight had shifted some gears, and he could finally get with a program. But before they agreed on a plan, Murphy had it out with his grandmother about her galloping all over the city on a damned bus. After some heavy-duty negotiating, they reached an agreement.

It was an agreement that made Marco's sister's husband's cousin's son damned happy. Murphy hired Roberto, who was starting his first year of university, and whose name clearly ended in a vowel, to drive Baba.

The plan worked. Sort of. Murphy wasn't sure how long they could keep it up. But at least twice a week after class, sometimes more, Roberto would pick up Baba and drive her to Jordan's, and Baba would bring J.J. back to Murphy's. And Murphy always had him one full day on the weekend, but he could never bring himself to keep his son overnight. He just couldn't do that to her.

When Jessica found out what was going on, she brought over the crib that Sarah had outgrown and helped him fix up the empty room down the hall for J.J. But if she had any advice, she kept it to herself. And if she had any opinions, she kept those to herself, as well.

Baba remained the middleman, and sometimes Murphy got the feeling that she was maybe playing both ends against the middle. Baba didn't keep anything to herself. She didn't interfere, but she *did* offer all kinds of unasked-for opinions. That Jordan was too thin. That she didn't think Jordan was eating right. That Jordan was worrying herself sick about going back to work. Which was too much information as far as he was concerned. Yeah, he got the gist of Baba's story about Cora and the ruby-red ring, but Cora had wanted that ring. He wasn't going to kid himself. The same couldn't be said for Jordan.

And he got to the point where he wished that Baba would just damned well stop with the opinions. He didn't want to hear anything about Jordan; he didn't want to see Jordan; he just wanted to somehow pick up the pieces and get on with his life.

But that was easier said than done. Because there would be nights where he would lie in bed remembering all the things he didn't want to remember. And night after night his own body would betray him, and he would be forced out into the night. But it didn't matter how far or how fast he ran; he couldn't outrun old ghosts.

But little by little, the big hole in his chest started to scab over, and he even had a couple of nights where he managed to do something productive, rather than feel sorry for himself. He told himself that he was on the road to recovery. Yeah. Right. Sure, he was.

One day marched into another. And the long autumn finally slid into winter. But even in spite of all the work that had piled up, Murphy wasn't all that sorry to see that first blanket of snow. Ever since he'd been a kid, there had been something about that first real show of winter that sct off a kind of expectation. It was almost as if winter were a brand-new beginning.

He stood in the open doorway that led onto the veranda, a mug of coffee in his hand, watching the white stuff filter through the naked branches. The cold, crisp air penetrated his heavy sweater, and he inhaled, liking the feel of the clean coldness in his lungs.

Fat, fluffy flakes continued to spiral through the halo of the streetlamp across the street, and the thickening dusting on the ground created the kind of hush that seemed to muffle an entire city. It was truly a beautiful night, and he remembered what it was like when they were all kids. There was something about that first snowfall that heralded adventure. Excitement. New challenges.

His phone rang, and he glanced at his watch as he turned to enter the house. Eight o'clock. Probably Mitch, wanting to kill some time.

He pushed the door shut and entered the living room, picking up the portable phone from the coffee table and pushing the connect button. "Hello."

It was clearly a cell-phone call with all kinds of weird background noises and voices, and Murphy thought he heard something that sounded like road noise. Finally a single voice separated itself from the rest. "Mr. Munroe?"

"Yes."

"My name's Jim Kaiser, and I'm a paramedic with Emergency Medical Services. Your wife is very anxious that I call you. She was just in an MVA—sorry, a motor vehicle accident—and she has suffered some injuries. Your son was with her, but he appears to be okay. We have them both on board and we're on our way to the trauma unit at the Foothills Hospital. She wants you to meet us there."

Murphy's insides knotted up into one cold, hard ball, and he stiffened, his voice sharp with alarm. "What happened to her? How bad is she? Is it serious?"

"No, sir. It doesn't appear so. She lost a bit of blood and has some contusions on her head and a possible concussion, but she appears to be fine. She put up a bit of a fight when we tried to start an IV. She was pretty insistent that we get in touch with you, so I figured it best if we did. But she's alert and stable. And your son is A-okay—he was properly restrained and he checks out fine."

The cold shock abruptly gave way to the shakes, and Murphy had to close his eyes and lock his knees.

"Sir? Are you there?"

Lifting his head and forcing away the awful feeling, Murphy glanced at the table by the door to make sure his truck keys and cell phone were there. "Yeah, I'm here."

"Um, sir, we don't normally make calls en route—we usually leave that up to the hospital staff to notify family. But, well, as I said, she put up a bit of a fight, and she's worried about what will happen to the little guy."

A weak smile appeared. "I got it, Mr. Kaiser. You never made this call."

"No, sir."

He checked his watch. "Tell her I'll be there in ten minutes. And Kaiser?"

"Yes, sir?"

"Thanks for breaking the rules."

"You're welcome, sir. Now, take care driving—with this snow, the roads are pretty treacherous. And there's no hurry. They're both doing just fine."

Concluding the call, Murphy tossed the phone on the sofa as he headed toward the door, snatching up his cell phone and keys on the way out, not even taking the time to grab a jacket. His heart slamming against his chest, he vaulted over the railing on the veranda on his way to the truck. If Jordan was being transported by ambulance to the trauma center, she was not fine. But he wasn't going to think about that. He was just going to get his butt over there as fast as he could and was not going to think about anything else. He didn't dare. He wasn't even sure he wanted to know how close he'd come to losing them both.

Murphy was never really sure how he got from point A to point B. But he got to the hospital, nevertheless. Not really giving a damn about parking regulations, he was prepared to leave his truck in the middle of the road, but fortunately there was a vacant space in emergency parking. An ambulance was in the bay, and his heart nearly went into full arrest when he saw someone carry a car seat inside.

He caught up to them as they were wheeling Jordan through to the ER. She was on a spine board, restraining straps across her chest and thighs and a cervical collar around her neck, a bright orange block keeping her head stabilized. Blue webbing was strapped across her forehead to further immobilize her, and there was blood everywhere. A dressing covered her left temple, and he could see particles of tempered glass in her blood-soaked hair. She had her eyes closed, and beneath the streaks of blood, she was frighteningly pale. Identifying himself to the EMS crew, he moved to the side opposite her IV, then fell in alongside the gurney. His attention riveted on her, he reached down and grasped her hand.

She opened her eyes and gazed up at him, a terrible distress in her eyes as she gripped his hand back. Her bottom lip swollen and split, she whispered his name, then tried to turn her head. "J.J.?"

The awful anxiety in his middle let go, and he was able to give her a reassuring smile. "It's okay, babe. They've got him, and they're just taking him into an examining area now. And he's fine. Everything is okay." She closed her eyes again, hanging on to his hand for dear life.

They rolled her into the space next to J.J., and a nurse looked up at him. Her tone was businesslike when she spoke. "You'll have to stand back, sir."

Jordan opened her eyes and tried to smile at him, but she got a glazed look and went even whiter. Her voice was barely above a whisper. "I'm going to be sick."

Knowing he had to give them room and feeling a little sick himself, Murphy turned away, watching them take J.J. out of the car seat in the adjacent area, his kid acting all cute as he gave them big smiles. Murphy closed his eyes, a sudden jolt of relief making him go weak, compounding the roil in his stomach. God, they were lucky, so lucky.

The paramedic, who had just finished rattling off the report and medical information to the doctors, came over. "Mr. Munroe?"

Murphy turned to face him.

He handed Jordan's handbag to Murphy. "This is your wife's. Figured you might want to hang on to it for now."

Murphy glanced down at the name tag, which identified the paramedic as Jim Kaiser. Murphy took the bag and extended his other hand, managing a wry smile. "I believe we didn't talk on the phone."

The paramedic grinned and took his hand, his eyes clear blue. He was maybe twenty-five years old and looked as if he should be out chasing girls instead of standing there in ER. Releasing Murphy's hand, he rested his hands on his hips and glanced back at his patient. "Well, there was no way she was going to let us touch her until I promised I'd call you. She was pretty worried about the little guy. I thought it was just better to put her mind at ease."

"I appreciate it." Aware that his hands were shaking, Murphy set Jordan's bag on an empty stretcher and shoved them in the back pockets of his jeans. "Can you tell me what happened?"

The paramedic looked back at Murphy. "Well, you might want to check out the accident report, but it looked like a Suburban ran a red light and T-boned her just behind the driver's door. It was lucky she was driving what she was, or the outcome might have been a whole lot worse." Jim Kaiser glanced at his partner, who was rolling up the straps attached to their stretcher, then he tipped his chin toward J.J. "I doubt if he'll even have a bruise on him."

He glanced back at Murphy, his gaze somber. "It makes it a whole lot easier for us when people take responsibility for their kids. Especially when they get good safety equipment like that car seat of yours, and make sure that it's installed properly. You'd be surprised how many we see that aren't." His partner flashed him a thumbs-up sign, and Jim Kaiser nodded, then gave Murphy a two-finger salute and turned to go. "You take care now."

Knowing he was incapable of speaking right then, Murphy nodded and returned the salute, his legs suddenly shaky all over again. Thank God he'd gotten the truck for her. Thank God.

A short time later, a woman from admitting came for

Murphy, asking him if he would go with her to sign some forms. Knowing they would need Jordan's Alberta Health Care card, Murphy took her handbag with him. There was a bottle inside, as well as two disposable diapers, and for the first time, he wondered where they'd been headed at that time of night.

J.J. was released into his care as soon as he returned to the trauma area, and he walked his son up and down the wide corridor, an anxious flutter in his belly. They had taken Jordan away for a CAT scan, and for some reason, that shook him up as much as the initial phone call had. Jordan had thrown up two more times before she'd been wheeled away, which pretty much assured that they'd keep her in overnight. It was going on nine-thirty now, and he had no intention of leaving her here alone. His parents were away, but he knew Mitch was at home. And J.J. was starting to fuss and rub at his eyes.

Knowing cell-phone use was forbidden in the hospital, he went out into the waiting room, fishing a quarter out of his pocket while juggling his son. Then clamping the receiver between his shoulder and ear, he dialed his brother, watching as J.J. tried to grab the phone.

Mitch answered and Murphy shifted the mouthpiece closer, and as briefly as possible, he told Mitch what had happened and where he was. Then he looked across the crowded waiting room. "I need you to do me a favor, bro. Could you give Baba a call? I'd like her to come get J.J., then maybe you could take her either to my place or Jordan's. Wherever she figures is best."

"I'll get right on it. You're sure Jordan's okay?"

His gaze sober, Murphy watched his son. "They've taken her for a CAT scan, so unless that turns up something, yeah, I think she's going to be okay."

Mitch responded, "Right. I'm on it. We should be there in about twenty minutes."

The hospital room was dark except for the muted night-light above Jordan's bed, and Murphy sat slouched in the chair between the window and bed, his feet propped on the safety rail, a cup of stale coffee in his hand. His attention was fixed on the sleeping woman.

They had her raised in a semireclining position, a clamp attached to one finger, the monitoring equipment blinking away on the other side of the bed. And she definitely looked as if she'd been in a wreck.

The CAT scan had turned up a hairline fracture in her left cheek and confirmed the paramedic's original diagnosis. It had taken twenty stitches to close the gash in her head. Although the air bag had restrained her, the force of the side impact had snapped her from side to side, slamming her head against the driver's-side window. She had a concussion, there was soft-tissue damage in her neck, her left shoulder had been jammed into the socket and was badly bruised, as was her right hip from the housing of the seat belt. The doctor, who was big and gruff and amiable, announced that she was "damned lucky" and that she was going to be "damned sore." And since she'd had quite a "conk" on the head, he wanted to keep her in overnight to be on the safe side.

Resting his elbows on the arms of the chair, Murphy cradled the foam cup in his hands. She was a mess. The jagged line of stitches ran along her hairline down to her ear, her face and bottom lip were swollen, and he could see the beginnings of what was going to be one hell of a black eye. Although the hospital staff had tried to clean her up, there was still dried blood crusted in her hair and on her hands, and there was a large, angry-looking scrape on one collar-bone. They had given her something for the pain right after they moved her to the ward, and she'd been out cold pretty much ever since. Murphy twisted his wrist and looked at his watch. They'd been waking her every couple of hours, which meant they were due in ten minutes.

Leaning back against the chair, he closed his eyes. Baba had elected to take J.J. to Jordan's, but she had wanted Murphy to take her over so he could show her where everything was. Mitch had stayed at the hospital, promising to call Murphy's cell-phone number if anything came up.

By the time Murphy got back, they had moved Jordan to the ward and she had gone to sleep, and Mitch had sacked out in an easy chair in the sunroom at the end of the hall. Murphy had told him to go home, but his brother had totally ignored him, giving Murphy his how-about-those-Cannons routine.

His legs started to go numb, and Murphy shifted, hooking one ankle across his knee. He continued to study her, a whole swarm of feelings filling up his chest.

When he had signed her in at admitting, he had made arrangements for her to be moved to a private room. Partly because he knew Jordan—and sharing a room with a stranger would have been a real strain on her—and partly because he knew they wouldn't kick him out if she was in a private room. In spite of how their affair had ended, there was no way he was leaving her alone tonight.

In the faint, muted light coming from the closed-in fixture above her bed, he could see that the past few weeks hadn't been easy on her, either. He could see for himself the things that Baba had told him about. She had obviously lost weight, and there were dark smudges under her eyes, as if she wasn't getting enough sleep. For the first time since he'd walked out on her, he experienced a stab of guilt. It had been a rotten thing to do, taking off like that. But after he'd laid everything on the table, there was no way he could have stayed. Not exactly a win-win situation.

A nurse entered and smiled at Murphy, then checked the monitoring equipment. She rested her fingers on Jordan's pulse point. "So how's our girl?"

"She's been pretty quiet."

The nurse nodded and leaned over her patient, gently shaking her uninjured shoulder. "Mrs. Munroe. Mrs. Munroe. You need to wake up and answer some questions for me."

Still slouched in the chair, Murphy watched her, a flicker of amusement tugging at the corner of his mouth. Here was a good example of a paper bureaucracy gone awry. Because he carried extended medical benefits on his policy for both Jordan and J.J., somehow his name had ended up on her file. He'd told them. But the red tape remained snarled. Although, he had to admit, the *Mrs. Munroe* hadn't bothered him as much as he thought it might. In fact it sounded damned fine.

The nurse shook Jordan's shoulder again, and Jordan stirred and wet her lips, her eyes remaining closed. "Mrs. Munroe, open your eyes, dear."

Jordan did as she was told, then let them drift shut again, just as she had during the past three checks. It was as if even the faint light was too much for her eyes.

The nurse rested her hand on Jordan's shoulder. "Do you know where you are?"

"I'm in the hospital."

"Do you know what day it is?" Murphy figured that was a bloody stupid question. He hadn't had a clunk on the head, and he wasn't even sure he knew what day it was.

Jordan kept her eyes closed through the rest of the interrogation, but she answered all the questions to the nurse's satisfaction. With brisk efficiency, the uniformed woman finished taking all of Jordan's vital signs, then straightened the blankets, checked the monitor one more time and left the room.

Murphy saw Jordan try to swallow, and he spoke, his tone very quiet. "Would you like a drink?"

Jordan's eyes flew open, and she shifted her head and stared at him, a stunned expression in her eyes. He was pretty sure she hadn't realized he was there; now he knew for sure. She never took her eyes off him as he went over to her night table and picked up the carafe, poured some ice water into a glass, then stuck in the flexible straw. Her eyes were wide and dark, and she followed his every move, her gaze fixed on his face. He was on her right side—her good side—but he was still careful not to jar her as he offered her a drink, adjusting the straw against the side of her mouth that wasn't swollen. "Here," he said, his voice husky. "You're going to have to try it off center. Your lip's pretty puffed up."

Closing her eyes, she drank most of the cold liquid, nearly emptying the glass. When she let the straw go, he took the glass away, setting it on the table. Then she looked at him, her gaze anxious. "Where's J.J.?"

He gave her a steady, level look. "He's fine, Jordan. Baba has him at your place. He was sound asleep when I left them." Knowing the nurse would probably smack him if she came back in, he eased down on the edge of the bed anyway, putting his right hand on the far side of Jordan's head. "So how are you doing? Do you need anything?"

She touched one hand to her breasts. She made an effort

to smile, but she didn't quite pull it off. Her speech was slurred from her swollen mouth. "I need J.J."

He reached down and picked up a small fabric carryall, setting it beside her. "I thought that might be a problem. So I brought the breast pump and whatever else I thought you might need."

She tried to sit up straighter, but she sank back and closed her eyes and swallowed hard, what little color she had disappearing. Hating the fact that he couldn't do one damned thing to help her, Murphy carefully smoothed a lock of hair behind her ear, then stood up. "I'll go get the nurse."

She opened her eyes, her expression etched with distress. "No."

He tried to reason with her. "You have a concussion, Jordan. You're going to need some help."

She looked up at him, her expression so wretched it broke his heart. "I can do it myself. If you could just raise the bed a bit."

Murphy clamped his mouth shut. He did not want to do this. He definitely did not want to do this. But leaving her alone wasn't even an option. There was no way on God's earth he could do that in the state she was in. Releasing an uneven sigh, he met her gaze. "Okay," he said, his tone husky. "We'll do it your way."

They had been through this before, and he knew what to do. Going to the sink, he grabbed two towels off the stack and tossed them in, and started running hot water. He closed the door, then went over to the bed. She was lying perfectly still with her eyes closed, and he winced. As if getting your face smashed up in an accident weren't bad enough. Now she had to contend with painfully full breasts. He could only imagine how she must be hurting. He pulled the curtain around the bed, figuring the least he could do was assure her some privacy. The controls for the bed were by her head, and he pressed the button to raise it, watching her face. "Tell me when," he said quietly.

"That's good," she whispered.

He reached behind her neck, and she managed to lean forward enough so he could undo the ties down the back of the hospital nightie, but she was clearly dizzy.

Murphy fixed the pillow under her head so it was more comfortable and stabilizing, then he went back to the sink and wrung out the towels, trying to make his mind go blank. He was not going to think about it; he was just going to do it.

When he rounded the curtain, Jordan was trying to get her arms out of the sleeves, and he could tell by the way her breath caught and how still she went that her left shoulder was extremely painful. He set the towels on the bedside table. "Here," he said, grasping the neckline. "Let's get the right arm out first. Then we can just slide it off the other."

He freed her good arm, then slid the nightie off her other arm, baring her to the waist. His heartbeat was erratic, and he locked his jaw together, trying not to think at all. Her breasts were heavily engorged, the skin stretched tight. An unexpected twist of humor surfaced. Having had some personal experience with heavily engorged and hard parts of the body, he had some idea of what she was going through. Folding one hot, wet towel in quarters, he gently laid it on her hardened breast, then repeated the process. She'd kept her eyes closed, but he saw tears gather along her lashes. "Thank you," she whispered.

He gently brushed back her stringy hair. "You're welcome."

The breast pump was electric, and Murphy unwound the

extension cord and plugged it into a plate at the back of the bed, then set everything up, including a container he'd packed.

With forced nonchalance, he sat in the chair and flipped through a magazine as she tended to herself, the quiet hum from the pump seeming abnormally loud. He was flipping through the magazine for the second time when the pump shut off, and he glanced up. A start of alarm shot through him. She was lying with her good arm over her eyes, and she was visibly trembling. Afraid she was going to pass out, he got up and went over to her, lowering the bed until she was back to the original semireclining angle. Setting the pump and the half-filled container aside, he sat down on the mattress, propping his arm on the other side of her. "What's the matter?" he commanded softly.

She swallowed hard, then murmured. "Nothing. I just got really dizzy looking down."

The damp towels were lying beside her. "Do you want me to warm the towels up?"

Her voice was barely audible. "No, thanks."

Shoving them aside, he gently slid the left sleeve up her arm, careful not to put any stress on her bruised shoulder. She still had her right arm over her eyes, so he drew the nightie up as far as it would go, then covered her with the sheet. He felt the towels. One towel was still warm. Turning, he tossed the cold one into the chair behind them. Then, using the tail of the warm one, he wiped her left hand and arm, carefully and thoroughly removing all traces of her blood. His expression solemn, he wiped between her fingers. There had been so much blood—so much of her blood.

When he finished his task, he tossed that towel on the chair with the other, his heart doing a yo-yo when he found her watching him, a kind of despair in her eyes that cut right through him. But it was a type of despair that he recognized—one that sprang from sorrow and regret.

Her battered mouth quivering, she reached up and touched his face with trembling fingers, her eyes filling up with tears. Then a ragged sob escaped her, and she covered her face with her hand. "Oh, God. I could have gotten him killed over some stupid errands. And I wrecked your brand-new truck—I should have checked the intersection."

A strange sensation sizzled through Murphy, almost as if he'd been injected with something that was hot and cold, but that feeling was immediately followed by a shot of genuine concern. Afraid to hold her for fear of hurting her, he slipped his hand under her head, his palm against her ear. "Hey," he chastised softly, drawing his thumb across her uninjured cheek. "That's not how it is, Jordan. J.J. is safe and sound because you were a good mom and made sure he was fastened in his car seat properly. And thank God you were driving the Explorer and not the BMW—the jerk that hit you was driving a big Suburban. It would have been a different story altogether if you guys had been in the coupe."

She wept with such intensity that Murphy knew it could only be making her condition worse, and it was killing him. Being very careful, he slid one arm beneath her shoulders. "Come on. Let's see if I can hold you without doing any more damage."

She came into his arms so fast, she nearly knocked him off the bed, and she hung on with a kind of desperation that damned near split his heart in two. He gently shifted her head, changing the angle. "Let's do it like that so it doesn't hurt your face, okay?" Closing his eyes and swallowing hard, he caught the back of her head, holding her with every ounce of care he had in him. Needing something for himself, he turned his head and kissed her uninjured temple. If he had doubts before, he knew it for a fact now. There was no way he would ever get over her. No damned way.

Trying to ease the commotion in his chest, he concentrated on his breathing. It only helped a little. Taking care not to hurt her, he smoothed down her hair, then he gave her a phantom hug and spoke, his voice very husky. "Look, darlin'. Some idiot ran a red light and plowed into you. That was bad luck. But the good luck was that you were far enough through the intersection that he hit behind you. And the second piece of good luck was that you guys were in a vehicle that could take a hit like that. And the third bit of good luck was that you had J.J. buckled up properly. That's all good luck. I got that truck to keep you and J.J. safe, and it did. So I'm happy."

Fairly sure her back hadn't sustained any injuries, he began slowly rubbing it, waiting for her to cry herself out. She had to have a wicked headache, and crying certainly wasn't going to make it any better. Man, he'd never felt quite so helpless as he did right then.

She almost stopped, then she sobbed against his shoulder, "I was so afraid you wouldn't come because of me."

Murphy's throat cramped up and he shut his eyes and tightened his hold, wishing he could simply absorb her. Wishing he could tell her that she had it all wrong—that he had come because of her.

Chapter 11

The physical and emotional trauma finally took Jordan down, and she fell asleep in Murphy's arms, her face ravaged by injury and tears. With nothing between them but a thin hospital gown, he was acutely aware of how thin she was, how fragile physically, and it was a long time before he could force himself to let go and settle her back in bed. And even after he'd drawn the covers up over her, he had stood looking down at her for a very long time.

Needing some air, Murphy took the elevator to the lobby and headed outside. It had quit snowing, and everything was covered in several inches, but the streetlights still had the pink aura of ice crystals around them. Hunching his shoulders against the cold and wishing he'd brought something a little warmer than a sweater, Murphy walked around the road that circled the parkade, his hands stuck in his pockets, his crystallized breath hanging in the air.

The funny feeling he had gotten in the room—when she

was holding herself so responsible—was, he realized now that he had time to think about it, a couple more critical pieces falling into place. And one of those critical pieces was that there were more than just abandonment issues here. To that little girl, who'd had so many medical problems, it must have seemed that there had to be something wrong with her—as if she were terribly flawed. Ten chances to one, she had always been made to think that she was the one at fault, the one who was such an inconvenience, the one who was so much trouble that no one wanted her, the one who must keep doing some wrong to be repeatedly taken from one foster home and dumped in another. It was as if she had been this tender seedling, never allowed to put down roots before she was ripped up and transplanted, again and again. That was the history lesson. But there was more to it than that.

Once he had it all figured out, it was as if someone had pulled his blinders off and he could see. And the pieces were clicking into place. Yeah, she knew she was pregnant when she pulled the pin, but the reason she didn't tell him right away was that she assumed total responsibility and blamed herself. He'd be willing to bet the farm on it. Yeah, he had been way off before, but this time he was damned sure he had it right.

It wasn't her wariness that was the problem—because she'd called him the minute the chips were down. And it wasn't her abandonment, either. What *was* the problem was a leftover belief from her childhood that when something went wrong, it was her fault. When he saw what he'd been missing all along, Murphy felt as if he had discovered the mother lode. Hell, maybe he wasn't ready to throw in the towel after all.

A shadow came up fast from the side, and he ducked and

whirled, ready to defend himself. Mitch grinned at him. "Do you want company, or is this a one-person road race?"

Suddenly aware that he was bloody cold, Murphy grinned back at his brother. His tone was irritable. "What in hell are we doing, running around out here in the middle of the night in the freezing cold?"

His brother at least had a jacket on, and he yanked up the collar. "I don't know. Looking for the age of enlightenment?"

Starting to shiver, Murphy chuckled. "Go home, you crazy bastard. Only fools are out walking at three in the morning."

Mitch raised his eyebrows. "Really? I thought it was only fools fall in love."

Murphy gave him such a powerful shove with his shoulder that Mitch went sliding into the curb. He saluted Murphy with one finger. "If that's the way you're going to be, you're on your own." Still grinning, Murphy watched his brother trot across the nearly empty parking lot to his vehicle, then he continued on his way back to the hospital.

He was shivering in earnest when he stepped into the glassed-in entryway. He paused to stamp his feet, noticing a deep pile of snow on a newspaper dispenser outside. Man, he bet something that soft and cold would feel good on Jordan's swollen lip right now. They had given her gel ice packs for her face, but nothing that was soft enough for her mashed mouth. He went back outside and formed it into a soft snowball, then reentered the hospital.

There was a nurse at the station, filling out charts when Murphy arrived on the unit. She looked up. "Oh. Mr. Munroe. We thought you'd gone home."

Making sure she didn't see what was in his hand, Murphy

swore under his breath. Great, now Jordan thought he'd gone home and left her.

Jordan's head was angled toward the window when he arrived at her door. Even though he couldn't see her whole face, he could see the worst of it, and she looked bloody awful. But what bothered him even more was the unsettling lack of energy he sensed in her—as if she didn't care about anything. Murphy had never seen her so listless. She turned her head as he entered, and the relief he saw in her eyes made his pulse falter. But he played out his game. He held his hand behind his back, the snow already starting to melt between his fingers. "I brought you something for your lip."

She looked a little dazed. "What?"

He sat down beside her and showed her what he had in his hand. She looked up at him, stunned and amazed, but what made him feel better than he had for quite some time was the honest-to-goodness shimmer of delight. "You brought me a snowball." As if it were the most special thing she had ever received, she took it from him. "I can't believe you brought me a snowball."

Locating a thin facecloth in her nightstand, he made a little ice packet, then handed it back to her. She closed her eyes and carefully pressed it against her mouth.

Murphy had to look away. The urge was so strong to exchange his mouth for the ice pack, he felt it right down to the soles of his feet. He clamped his mouth shut, disgusted with himself. Lord, he needed to give his head a shake—thinking things like that when she was just one big walking bruise.

Needing something to do to keep his mind from taking another left turn, he pushed the nightstand out of the way and pulled his chair right up tight to the bed. Then he sat down and stretched out, resting his arm beside her. It was as if she had locked on to him with some sort of radar. Without opening her eyes, Jordan switched hands and slipped her snow-cold palm under his, the pulse in her neck faltering when he closed his fingers around hers. Suddenly feeling as if he were nothing but one big exposed nerve end himself, Murphy closed his eyes, hoping like hell that Murphy's Law didn't kick in this time.

A huge plant basket encased in plastic arrived from Fairhaven Nurseries, Mitch's greenhouse, at six the next morning. It was supposedly from all the Munroe siblings—no doubt listed by name and rank, but Murphy knew who was really behind it, and he also knew that there was no way the greenhouse delivery van was making drops that early in the morning. The boss was out taking care of business himself.

Feeling a little as if he'd been in a car wreck, as well, Murphy was sitting in the chair when the arrangement arrived. The nurse set it on the crank-up table positioned at the foot of the bed, and Jordan opened her eyes. It gave Murphy a shot in the arm when she immediately checked to see if he was there. She was looking better—and worse. Thanks to the cold-pack treatments, the swelling had gone down in her mouth and face, and she had some color, even in the faint overhead light. But the bruising was beginning to turn dark, and he was right—she was going to have one hell of a black eye. Slouched in the chair with his arms folded across his chest, he was almost too tired to move, but he managed a half smile and gave her a little two-fingered wave when she looked at him.

The nurse stripped the plastic off. "Oh, my. This is gorgeous." Murphy had to admit it was pretty spectacular.

Plants spilled out, some flowering, some not, and in the middle of the arrangement was a white calla lily in full bloom. If he had been asked to pick a flower that most embodied Jordan, it would have been that long, slender, elegant bloom. The nurse handed the card to Jordan, then wadded up the plastic.

Murphy watched Jordan take the card out of the envelope and formulated a plan, which took some doing because he felt as if his head were full of sawdust. He needed a shave, he needed a shower and he needed at least four hours of sleep.

She read the card and laughed. Right out loud. He couldn't believe it. Sitting upright, he snatched the card from her hand. It was a cartoon drawing, with a jockey standing looking down at his dead horse, and thundering up the track behind him were six wild, snorting horses. And it read, "Just when you think things can't get any worse, they do."

He grinned and handed the card back to her. "Ain't that the truth."

Still smiling, she carefully eased up into a sitting position, clutching the half on, half off nightie against her. Wincing slightly, she stuck the card back in the arrangement, then touched a soft pink blossom. "This is really beautiful."

The nurse glanced at them. "It certainly is."

Murphy didn't say anything. The off side of her nightie had gotten twisted around, and he could see the very ugly bruise that was developing on her hip, where she had been rammed against the seat-belt housing. His stomach did a queasy roll, and he glanced down at the toes of his runners, realizing again just how close she'd come.

The nurse finished taking Jordan's vitals, then set about straightening the bed. "If you're feeling up to it, we can probably arrange for you to have a quick shower later. You'll have to be careful not to get those stitches wet, but we can rig up some kind of waterproof bandage.'' She smiled at Jordan as she straightened her pillow. ''I know what it's like. I was in a car accident a couple of years ago, and all I could think about was getting out of that bed and washing my hair.''

Jordan gave her a grateful smile. ''That would be wonderful.''

The nurse patted her pillow. ''Then I'll see what I can do. And I'll be right back to take you for a little walk.''

His hands loosely clasped across his chest, his legs stretched out in front of him, Murphy studied Jordan, considering what he was going to say and how he was going to say it. He'd done a lot of thinking during the night, and he'd come to some conclusions. One was that he truly believed he was on the money about her—that she assumed it was her fault whenever something went wrong. He'd also come to another conclusion; after this last piece of the puzzle, he wasn't quite ready to give up on her yet. Even as wiped out as he was, he was beginning to feel tense and antsy, as if he were about to walk across a long, tight wire and couldn't see his feet.

What he wanted to do was get up and pace, but he kept his butt planted in the chair. Holding his pose, he fixed his gaze on her. ''I'm beat, and it looks like they've got some stuff planned for you, so I think I'll head out. I'll stop by and check on Baba and the tadpole.''

She'd put her left arm in the other sleeve of her gown, and she continued to straighten the garment, her expression unreadable. ''Are you coming back?''

Still slouched in the chair, he watched her like a hawk as he put his battle plan in action. ''No.''

She didn't look at him, but he could see from her face that his response upset her. He got up and stretched his arms above his head and cracked his shoulders, then rested his hands on his hips. "They think you're going to be discharged today, so I left Mitch's numbers at the desk. He's going to come pick you up and take you home."

Bending over her, he braced his arms on either side of her head. And he remained like that until she finally looked at him. His expression was unsmiling when he spoke. "But before I go, there's a couple of things I want to say to you, darlin'." He reached up and tucked her hair behind her ear. "I've tried to quit caring about you, but I can't. I'm not made that way."

Her eyes were so wide, so still, it was like looking into a gray lake, and she was so taut, she was barely breathing. He gave her a lopsided smile, his gaze not wavering a fraction. "And if you ever need me, I'm going to be there for both you and J.J. But I'm not going to be a doormat, either. You're going to have to decide what it is you want."

Shifting his weight to one arm, he touched her nose, then ran his knuckles down her cheek, holding her gaze as if he'd hypnotized her. "Your getting pregnant was not your fault, Jordan. What happened in your childhood was not your fault. You're not some kind of bad-luck charm that wreaks havoc on other people's lives." Very gently, he touched the cut on her lip, his voice quiet when he continued. "You've had bad things happen to you. But you're a decent human being and you're one hell of a mom. And I think we could put together the same kind of life my parents have. It's all up to you, though."

Murphy leaned down and very gently brushed his mouth against hers, then lifted his head and met her gaze again. "You need to get Baba to tell you the story about the ruby-red ring. And then you're going to have to decide what you want, and what you're going to have to do to get it." He held her gaze, her expression dead serious. "Because the next move is yours, Jordan. I think you want what I want, but you're too damned scared to take a chance. But if you ever get your head together, if you ever decide to trust your feelings, you know where to find me. But just so you know—I'm not going to hang around forever, either. And I think you owe me an answer one way or the other. I want a life—I don't want to be living in limbo." He bent down and gave her another soft kiss, then straightened and stepped away, his gaze still serious. "It's all up to you."

Then he turned and walked out of the room, his heart pounding and an uproar breaking loose in his belly. He had just run the biggest bluff in his life. Now the question was, would she get back in the game—or toss in her hand?

It was a long walk out of the hospital, and for some reason, it was damned hard to go to Jordan's place afterward to check on Baba and J.J. He'd experienced a peculiar hollow feeling when he'd taken the two of them there the previous night. But it was worse today. Going through that door immediately turned the hollow feeling into deep-down reluctance, and once inside, every room seemed to close in on him. He tried not to think about it and just took care of business. He made arrangements for the truck to be towed to the auto-body shop, checked to make sure Baba was okay for groceries and fed his kid, then hung around until J.J. went down for his morning nap.

He was there two hours. It felt like a week. He had one cup of coffee with Baba. It felt like twenty. Fortunately for him, he found an old roll of antacid tablets under the seat of his truck when he left. He took two, then put the roll under an elastic band on his visor. He was damned sure he was going to be back living off those things again.

And he was right. Murphy discovered over the next two weeks that he was a lousy poker player. One minute he was sure she'd come around, then the next moment he'd be sure she wouldn't. And he went out of his way to avoid her, partly because of the game strategy, but more for his own sanity. Although he wasn't sure he had much of that left.

After the news of the accident made the rounds, his family formed a united front against him, some of them implying that his staying away after she'd been injured was unforgivable, and that he was acting like a jerk. Some didn't even bother to imply—they came right out and said so. Even Baba had switched sides and started doing a lot of *tsk-tsk*ing around him, passing on her opinions—opinions that Jordan wasn't taking very good care of herself, that she was looking worse since the accident, that it would make her feel better if he came to see her.

Murphy knew he couldn't afford to go see her. As far as he was concerned, this was like the ruby-red ring—if she wanted him in her life, she'd have to put her face in the water to get what she wanted. And if he wasn't that important to her, he was better off out of the picture altogether.

The only one who didn't express any opinions was Mitch. Mitch didn't say anything at all. Even though they hadn't talked about his situation, Murphy suspected that his big brother had pretty much put it all together. And he also suspected that his brother saw through Jordan. It was as if his brother understood what Murphy was all about—and maybe understood why Murphy had dug in the way he had. Yeah, Mitch was a man for all seasons.

But when the first of December had come and gone, and

she hadn't made a move, Murphy forced himself to face the facts; his big bluff had netted him zero. He realized he should have put a limit on how much time he was prepared to give her. But it probably wouldn't have made any difference. As far as he was concerned, her not making any decision was the ultimate verdict. She wasn't going to be responsible for the final cut—she was just going to let him go down carrying the ball.

If he was honest with himself, he had to admit he'd half expected that from her. But what really ticked him off and had him seeing red was that two weeks before Christmas, he found out through the family grapevine that his mother had invited her and J.J. to spend Christmas with the family. It was his young nephew who spilled the beans, when he'd spent a Saturday at the job site with his dad.

Murphy never said anything to the kid—he never said anything to anybody. It really didn't matter one way or another to him. In fact, it was just bloody well fine by him. He wasn't stupid. He'd realized in about two seconds flat that his sisters and mother had poked their noses in, trying to engineer a reconciliation. But it just wasn't going to happen. Because he wasn't going to be there. It was bad enough that Jordan didn't even have the guts to phone to tell him that it was definitely finished between them, but the fact that his family went behind his back really blistered his behind. For the first time, he understood Mitch's aversion to big family bashes. Especially when the women started circling the damned wagons.

But then came the final blow, when he was told by someone from the accounting firm that Jordan had been offered a position at the head office in Vancouver. That finished everything off—because if Jordan ran true to form, she'd take it. And she would take his son with her. That night he went out and got dead drunk, and he probably would have instigated a fight if Mitch hadn't shown up and hauled his ass out of there. After he sobered up, Murphy did exactly what he had done the last time around. He buried himself in work.

A chinook blew in the fifteenth of December, and the thermometer rose twenty-five degrees in less than an hour, the fabled chinook arch bisecting the sky in two.

The early-morning air was crisp and crystal clear, the shrill screams of Skil saws splintering the stillness, the *kerthunk, kerthunk* of compression guns adding percussion to the discordant sounds of construction. Meltwater gathered in the icy ruts in the unpaved road and wore narrow channels in the packed snow. It felt and smelled like spring, and it wasn't even the New Year yet. That was the beauty of Calgary winters. The warm chinook winds would blow in, breathing false spring into the air and breaking the tedious hold of winter.

It should have lifted Murphy's spirits but it didn't. They were back-ordered windows for two houses, and he had wanted to get them in before the weather turned cold again. But besides that annoyance, he was cranky and short-tempered, and had been for days. Deciding to give everyone a break, he climbed up on the rafters of a roughed-in bungalow and began sheathing the roof with sheets of plywood, working out his bad mood with a hammer. His jaw locked with determination, he made a decision. As soon as he finished off this roof, he was going to call his travel agent and see if she could book him a ticket to someplace—any place—for the holidays. Preferably someplace far away. Preferably someplace with no phones. Preferably someplace where it was hot and the beaches were private.

He turned to drag another sheet of plywood into place,

his gaze snagging on a midnight blue Explorer that was coming down the street. His immediate reaction—that crazy flutter in his chest—irritated him, and he clamped his mouth shut, giving himself a lecture. There were probably a thousand midnight-blue Explorers in the city. Except this one had tinted windows. And this one was stopping in front of the house he was working on.

Releasing an exasperated sigh, Murphy rested his hand on his hip and stared across the development, recalling her visit the previous spring—when he'd wanted to pitch a hammer into next year. He felt pretty much the same way now.

It was probably his own damned fault she was here. To avoid talking to her, he had reverted to his old arrangements with J.J. But he couldn't keep that up much longer, especially if she took the job in Vancouver, which meant he was going to have to talk to her and hammer out some kind of agreement. And he'd also have to start making his own pickups and deliveries, instead of using Baba as a go-between. Especially when the weather turned cold. And especially since it was pretty obvious the game was over.

He had broken one of his own rules and e-mailed her earlier in the week, saying he wanted to have his son for the entire weekend. To avoid seeing her, he'd asked her to drop J.J. off at his parents'. But she was here and J.J. wasn't, which meant he was going to have to go down there and see what in hell was going on. Who knew? Maybe she'd finally screwed up enough nerve to pull the plug; maybe she had decided to take the job in Vancouver, and maybe she'd come to tell him. That thought certainly didn't do a whole lot to improve his mood.

Thinking unpleasant thoughts, he lowered himself through the open rafters and strode into the kitchen, wishing he had something to kick. His face rigid, he began picking up scrap lumber and tossing the pieces out through the hole for the window, his temper rising. He was in no mood for this. No mood at all.

He heard her enter the shell of the garage, then climb the makeshift ladder onto the main level. Her footsteps echoed on the subflooring, and he heard her pause, as if checking the living room.

Turning to face the door, he leaned his shoulder against a stud, keeping his arms folded. He was going to erect some defenses of his own, and he was going to be as hard as nails.

She entered the kitchen, hesitating when she saw him, her eyes wide, her expression going very still. His determination to remain as hard as nails faltered when she stepped out of the shadows and he got a good look at her face.

He had seen her once from a distance right after the accident—when her face was still bruised and she hadn't gotten the stitches out yet. She didn't look so good then. She looked even worse now. She was wafer thin, the scar marring her perfect skin, and there was so much distress in her eyes, so much tension in her body, he was reminded of fine crystal vibrating at such a high frequency, it was about to shatter.

Murphy watched her, a hollow feeling settling in his gut, knowing this was definitely not going to be pleasant. Steeling himself, he stared at her, his tone sarcastic. "Are you just out sight-seeing, or did you get lost?"

She abruptly shoved her hands in her pockets, her movements stiff, her eyes going even darker. "Hello, Murphy."

"So," he said, his body language deliberately unfriendly, "did you come to tell me you're taking the job in Vancouver?"

He saw a reaction in her eyes, but before he could read

it she looked down at the floor, her expression shuttered as she began scraping the sawdust into a pile with the side of her boot. "I'm not taking the job in Vancouver."

"No?" he said, his tone uncivil. "I was under the impression it was a hell of a promotion for you—with big bucks attached."

Stilling, raking up sawdust, she answered. "It was."

So angry with her for bailing out on them, he had to force himself to put a lid on it. His tone was considerably less hostile and more controlled when he spoke again. "Well, if you're not here to tell me you're taking my kid to Vancouver, why are you here?"

She looked up at him, not a trace of animation in her pale face. She just stared at him for several seconds, then looked down again, flattening the pile of sawdust. "Actually, I brought you something."

A strange sensation began in Murphy's middle, and it spread like ripples through his whole body. He found it suddenly difficult to get his breath. His voice seemed thick in his ears when he spoke. "What?"

She didn't answer and she didn't lift her head, and Murphy got an adrenaline rush. Straightening, he never took his eyes off her, his movements unhurried as he crossed the room. He stopped in front of her. "What did you bring me, Jordan?"

For a second, he thought she was going to turn around and leave, but she didn't. But she didn't look at him, either. He waited, knowing the next move had to be hers. Finally she withdrew one hand from her pocket and uncupped it. She was holding a plastic capsule, like one from a bubblegum machine. He took it from her, his insides sinking away to nothing when he saw what was inside. A ruby-red ring.

Feeling as if he'd just had the wind knocked out of him,

his thoughts totally derailed, and he stared at the ring and then at her, a tiny flicker of hope flaring to life.

She drew a deep, unsteady breath, as if fortifying herself, then she raised her head and looked at him, her eyes dark and desolate, her expression waxen. And she was scared to death. "It's been really awful since you left." She swallowed hard and looked down, fussing with the pile of sawdust again. Her voice was shaking when she whispered, "And I was so scared. It was as if I was standing on this high, tiny platform and it was dark. And there was only one way off, but I was so paralyzed I couldn't even try to find it." Locking her arms tightly in front of her, she looked up at him, a terrible anguish in her eyes. "I love you, Murphy," she whispered, her eyes filling up with tears. "And J.J. and I both need you in our lives—every day."

His face feeling like stone, Murphy stared at her, hope warring with anger. It wasn't good enough. She had shot him down again. It took every ounce of discipline he had not to touch her. His tone was clipped when he spoke. "That's not good enough, Jordan."

Dashing away the tears slipping down her face, she looked away and swallowed hard, the desolation in her eyes making his chest hurt. "When I had the accident..." She quickly wiped her eyes again, then met his gaze, her heart in her eyes. "You were right when you said I blamed myself. And it took a long time for me to get past the fear. I've never had anybody. And it was hard for me to believe that someone like you could love me. I was so scared to believe that. But I do. And I know that you would never..." Her voice broke, and more tears slipped free. "That you would never leave me."

With an unbelievable feeling in his chest, Murphy grasped her by the arms, not sure he actually heard her right.

Her gaze unwavering, she tried to smile but tears got in the way. "I know you love me."

Overcome with such a surge of relief, he closed his eyes and gathered her up in a fierce embrace, a crazy lightness breaking loose. "Ah, God, Jordan. I do love you—so damned much. And I really thought I'd lost you."

She clung to him, hanging on for dear life, and he tucked his head against hers, his pulse suddenly running thick and heavy. It had been so long. So long.

A soft sob breaking from her, Jordan twisted her head, and Murphy's heartbeat went into superdrive when her mouth brushed against his. Widening his stance for balance, he grasped the back of her head, grinding his mouth against her as weeks of loneliness boiled up in him. It was as if all the barriers had come down and a fountain had sprung up, pouring emotion from one to the other and inciting a hunger that was raw and urgent. But they were confined—confined by location. Confined by clothes. Confined by a total lack of privacy.

His heart pounding and his breathing labored, he clutched her hips against him, his whole body so primed, he felt ready to explode. Tearing his mouth away, he tightened his hold, fighting for breath. "Where's J.J.?" he whispered hoarsely.

He could barely make out what she said. "At your mother's."

Clenching his jaw, he moved against her, a thick, heavy need pulsating through him. Grasping her head, he kissed her jaw. "Do you want to blow this joint?"

She shuddered and nodded, her breathing as ragged as his.

Murphy wasn't sure how he found the strength of will to let her go, and he sure in hell didn't know how he got them from there to his place without killing them both. All he knew was once he got them that far, he couldn't get her inside fast enough. And every item of clothing was an obstruction that drove his urgency higher. He was desperate to get inside her, and Jordan was so frantic that she was like lightning—like raw energy in his arms, and the instant he carried her down onto his bed, and naked flesh covered naked flesh, he was nearly beyond the point of no return.

But a tiny sliver of reality surfaced, and he tried to pull back, knowing he had nothing there to protect her. But Jordan wrapped her legs around him, drawing him in. "It's okay," she whispered frantically. "It's okay."

And the moment his throbbing flesh touched her moist heat, he totally lost it. And he entered her and the universe spun out of control, their driving need closing in around them. And the only thing in that universe was her.

It took Murphy a long time to surface afterward, the release so explosive, so intense that it stripped him of every shred of coherent thought—except one electrifying awareness. She was back, and this time, he was never going to let her go.

Still trembling from the mind-blowing catharsis, he buried his face against her neck, his breathing still uneven. Turning his face into her hair, he tightened his hold, inhaling the scent of her, the scent of their lovemaking. He kissed her neck, then brushed his mouth against her ear. "Are you going to marry me, Kennedy?"

She locked her arms around his neck, her voice breaking. "Yes."

Two seconds before, Murphy had been too damned spent to move, but a sudden high replaced that depleted feeling. Propping his weight on his elbows, he caught her head in his hands, making her look at him. His heartbeat accelerating all over again, he gazed down at her, his expression intent. "When?"

Her gaze clear and direct, she gave him a wobbly smile. "How about tomorrow?"

He grinned, then gave her a hard kiss, certain that he could fly if he was willing to let go of her. Releasing a satisfied sigh, he lifted his head and looked at her. "I don't think we could pull it off quite that quick."

There was a flicker of an old torment in her eyes, and she shifted her gaze, her touch like silk as she caressed his shoulder. "There won't be much to arrange."

Murphy got the picture, and he very gently tipped her face up so he could look directly into her eyes. "I want the whole damned world to know, Jordan." His face creased with a smile as he caressed her cheek with his thumb. "But how about if we turn my mother and sisters loose, tell 'em they've got five days and see what happens?"

A glint of amusement appeared in her eyes. "That sounds safe. I don't think even they could get out invitations to the whole world in five days."

He chuckled and gave her another soft kiss, then lifted his head, his expression altering as he combed her hair out on the pillow. Finally he looked at her, his gaze sober. "It really wasn't okay, was it? The timing?"

She held his gaze for an instant, then looked away and ran her finger along an old scar on his shoulder.

"Jordan?"

A pink flush crept up her face, and she released a sigh. "No." But then she looked up at him, a touch of anxiety in her eyes as she immediately added, "But it wouldn't be so bad, would it?"

He continued to finger her hair, loving the feel of it against his callused hands. He smiled down at her. "No, it wouldn't be so bad at all," he answered, his voice husky. His expression sobered as he traced the outline of her ear. "Except it would be so hard on you, two pregnancies that close together."

She grinned, giving him a little poke in the ribs. "Don't you think you're counting your chickens a little early, Munroe?"

"It's not chickens I'm worried about."

Still smiling, she lifted her head and kissed his jaw. "Well, then. How do you feel about that other old saying—you may as well be hung for a sheep as a lamb?"

Laughing, he rolled with her, pulling her securely on top of him as he settled flat on his back. "So you're going to be my wife?"

Looking down at him, she smiled that soft smile of hers, an expression on her face that touched his heart. "I'm going to be your wife."

"And are you going to have all my babies?"

The smile deepened. "I'm going to have all your babies."

His expression altered, his heart contracting with a lifetime of love. "And are you going to love me forever?"

She met his gaze with a steadiness that made his whole world swim. "I'm going to love you forever."

Overcome by the certainty in her response, he pulled her down and wrapped her in a fierce embrace. "This time we're going to make it, darlin'," he whispered gruffly. "We really are."

And this time he knew they would—together.

Epilogue

The hotel banquet room was first-class all the way—long, white tapers and Christmas arrangements on all the damask-draped tables, a huge Christmas tree in the corner decked out in tiny white twinkling lights and silver bows. Yeah, it was first-class all right.

The band was playing, the dance floor was jammed, and the noise level had risen ten decibels in the past ten minutes. Murphy leaned back against the no-host bar, watching the action. It was the annual Christmas party he and Mitch threw for their respective staffs, and the place was hopping. Both crews acted as if it were the New Year's bash, and streamers were flying and horns were blowing, and everybody was having a damned good time.

His gaze lit on a woman weaving her way through the draped tables, a bottle of champagne in one hand, a pair of red shoes in the other. She had on a very sexy red dress that showed off her long, long legs and a figure that didn't need one iota of imagination. Her blond hair was slipping free of an elegant French fold, and wisps of hair framed her face and curled along the back of her neck. Murphy grinned, watching her progress. This was hardly the prissy accountant that had once knocked his socks off. Nope. This was his slightly tipsy wife of one year, and she still knocked his socks off.

Their anniversary was the following day, and their second son had been born nine months to the hour of his conception. He and his big brother, J.J., were at home with Baba, a stockpile of breast milk in the fridge. The stockpile was because Mom and Dad were spending the night in a luxurious suite upstairs. And because Mom, who hadn't had a drink in nearly two years, had decided to fall off the wagon tonight. And fall she had.

Murphy's grin deepened as she stopped at the buffet table, helping herself to some hors d'oeuvres, swaying to the music. She had changed so much since he first met her, he sometimes found it hard to believe she was the same woman. And every day, he fell in love with her a little more.

It had taken her a while, after they were married, for her to open up and tell him about her miserable, lonely childhood. And it had taken her a while to drop all her defenses and discover who she really was. But it was as if her taking his name had started her on the road to a whole new identity, one that was totally hers, one that hadn't been assigned to her by some caseworker. And it had helped, having his psychologist sister take her under her wing—and it had helped that Jessica and Jordan had developed such a solid friendship. But the biggest support for Jordan was having a real family for the first time in her life, and she simply blossomed.

And she had absolutely thrived on making a home. Not

wanting to expose J.J. to the dust from more renovations, they had lived in her condo until Murphy got the upstairs floors stripped down and everything painted. Then they moved back in.

The first thing they did was redesign the work space in the sunroom so she had her own work area since she planned on doing most of her work from home. And the second thing they did was remodel the unused half of the summer kitchen into a large bedroom and a bath for Baba. Baba insisted on staying with the boys whenever Jordan had to go in to the office and Murphy couldn't be there, so they wanted her to have a space of her own whenever she stayed over.

But the construction was pretty much the extent of his contributions. Yeah, he'd done a whole lot of head-nodding and voicing of approval when she got on a roll, but mostly he just went along for the ride, getting a whole lot of satisfaction out of watching her get excited. As far as decorating and colors went, he didn't really give a damn. But watching her take ownership, turn a house into their home, watching the sparkle of enthusiasm appear in his wife's eyes—now, that mattered a whole lot.

Finishing off a mouthful of some treat or another, Jordan licked her fingers, still swaying to the music, a dreamy look on her face. Weaving just a little, she picked up the champagne bottle and started toward him, and he could see she was also humming to the music. He grinned to himself. His little darlin' was going to be just a tad bit hung over in the morning.

She crossed the space between the tables to the bar, moving in that loose-hipped sway of a runway model, the luscious red of the dress matching the luscious red of her lips.

Giving him a very lazy smile, she came up to him and

draped her arms around his neck, her shoes in one hand, the bottle in the other. She licked a tiny blob of whipped cream off her bottom lip, her voice husky. "Hi, big boy. You haven't danced with me yet."

Looping his arms loosely around her hips, he met her gaze, trying to keep a straight face. "No, I haven't."

Dropping her shoes, she started straightening his hair. "Mitch danced with me. And Marco danced with me. And your dad danced with me."

Fighting to hold back a grin, he nodded solemnly. "Yes, they did."

She moved against him, still swaying to the music, and Murphy felt his temperature shoot up five degrees. She trailed her finger slowly along his neck. "So why haven't you danced with me?"

Bracing his weight against the bar, he pulled her closer. "Because," he said, dipping his head to brush his mouth back and forth against hers, "if I dance with you, I'm going to have to spend the rest of the night sitting at the table with a tablecloth over my lap."

She leaned back and looked up at him, a siren's smile appearing, a dangerous gleam in her eyes. "We could go upstairs." She ran her finger down his tie. "We could go upstairs and make another baby."

He got such a surge of blood in his system, she nearly gave him a heart attack. He stared down at her, amusement finally surfacing. "I don't think so, Jordan."

She slanted a smoky look up at him, giving him that slow smile again, so blatant that he was sure his toes were beginning to curl. "We could go upstairs, get naked and try out that beautiful big hot tub."

He gave her an unwavering look, wanting to laugh and

strangle her at the same time. "I'm not getting naked with you."

"Then dance with me."

Deciding she deserved some of her own back, Murphy caught her against him, then walked her backward to the closet behind the curtains where they stored extra beer. Shoving the door shut behind him, he lowered his head, her breath moist against his mouth. "You wanna play games, princess? I'll play games." He gave her a kiss that was meant to shut her up, but it backfired totally, and he was suddenly in over his head. Feeling as if he were trying to breathe under water, he plastered her against him, working his mouth hungrily against hers, her no-holds-barred response making him shudder. She could get him going with a single look, but right now she was doing more than revving his engines. She wanted to fly.

Hauling in oxygen, he tried to ease off, but she moved against him, whispering in his ear. "You might want to check under the dress."

Knowing he was inches from going under, he ran his hand up her thigh, taking the fabric with him, the satiny lining sending a current through him. Her filmy hosiery stopped at her thigh, and then there was nothing. Absolutely nothing. His heart stopped altogether. He jerked away and looked down at her, certain he was going to simply quit breathing altogether.

She gave him another lazy smile. "I just hate panty lines, don't you?" He didn't think he was capable of it, but he gave a huff of stunned laughter, and she moved against him, tracing her long, painted nail along his neck. "And you might want to check your left jacket pocket."

Laughing, his whole body one big pulse point, wanting

to finish what she'd started like he needed his next breath, he looked down at her. "You set me up."

She unzipped his fly, giving him a caress that just about put him through the roof. "I did."

Knowing he was going down for the count, he reached behind her and pushed the lock on the door, his heart going into high gear when she caressed him again. "You're one bad act, Mrs. Munroe," he said, his knees wanting to buckle.

She looked up at him, sassy, sexy and full of sauce. "But you love me anyway."

And he knew she believed it. Lifting her up against him, he covered her mouth, putting everything he felt for her in that kiss. It was Christmas, all right, and the magic was there. Because she knew that he loved her—that was the best gift she could ever give him.

The very best gift of all.

*   *   *   *   *

INTIMATE MOMENTS®

Silhouette®

invites you to Go West, dear reader, to

Cameron, Utah

for the conclusion of Margaret Watson's
exhilarating miniseries.

September 1999
The Marriage Protection Program...IM #951

Janie Murphy knew she was Deputy Ben Jackson's
only hope for gaining custody of orphaned Rafael. But
Janie thought Ben would understand her refusal when
he learned about her past. Instead, he proposed an
irresistible trade—her hand for his protection. And
suddenly Janie's heart faced the greatest risk of all....

Available at your favorite retail outlet.

And if you want to uncover more of this
small town's secrets, don't miss...

The Fugitive Bride (Intimate Moments #920) April 1999
Cowboy with a Badge (Intimate Moments #904) January 1999
For the Children (Intimate Moments #886) October 1998
Rodeo Man (Intimate Moments #873) August 1998

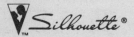

Silhouette®

SIMUTAH3

If you enjoyed what you just read,
then we've got an offer you can't resist!

Take 2 bestselling love stories FREE!
Plus get a FREE surprise gift!

THE FORTUNES OF TEXAS™

This BRAND-NEW program includes 12 incredible stories about a wealthy Texas family rocked by scandal and embedded in mystery.

It is based on the tremendously successful *Fortune's Children* continuity.

Membership in this family has its privileges…and its price.

But what a fortune can't buy, a true-bred Texas love is sure to bring!

This exciting program will start in September 1999!

Available at your favorite retail outlet.

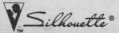

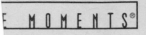

MOMENTS®

and

DOREEN ROBERTS

invite you to the wonderful world of

RODEO MEN

A secret father, a passionate protector,
a make-believe groom—these cowboys
are husbands waiting to happen....

HOME IS WHERE THE COWBOY IS
IM #909, February 1999

A FOREVER KIND OF COWBOY
IM #927, May 1999

THE MAVERICK'S BRIDE
IM #945, August 1999

Don't miss a single one!

Available at your favorite retail outlet.